FIVE STORIES

W.P. KINSELLA

Five Stories

with illustrations by CAREL MOISEIWITSCH

TANKS

1.2

ISBN 0-919758-21-5

WILLIAM HOFFER / TANKS
60 Powell Street
Vancouver, British Columbia V6A 1E7 Canada
(604) 683-3022

For my friend Lee Harwood
who suggested the title **Homer,**
which I rejected.

Frank Pierce, Iowa

Just as gymnasts have a repertory of moves, and basketball players have set offences and defences, so writers have a number of conventional or experimental choices when it comes to telling a story. This tale will be what is called a boxed story, a time-honored form. In case you're curious, Joseph Conrad's **Heart of Darkness** is a classic example of a boxed story.

Such a story is introduced, as I am doing now, by one narrator. Then a second narrator takes over and tells a story within a story. The first narrator then usually returns for some brief closing comments.

The second narrator in this case is my friend Marylyle Baron. For several years prior to her death she imparted to me what I call The Oral History of Johnson County, Iowa. After Marylyle's death in her 90th year I took custody of her daughter Melissa (Missy), a victim of Down's Syndrome. Missy lives with me now in my huge frame house with the wrought-iron widow's walk, in the nearby town of Onamata. Missy is beyond middle age and has far outlived her life expectancy. She is a delightful companion, sweet and guileless as a child, always cheerful, a perfect listener.

This story was told to me in the kitchen of Marylyle's farmhouse a mile outside Onamata. Her kitchen always smelled of cinnamon and coffee. She sat across the table from me, her white hair pulled tightly in a bun. We drank coffee, while across the room Missy stroked her orange cat which was curled into a circular pillow-shape in her lap.

"In 1901 there was a U.S. Post Office in the store at Frank Pierce, Iowa," Marylyle begins. "Zundel's General Store it was known as. There wasn't much else, a dirt street, a blacksmith shop with a heavy sliding door, a barber shop scarcely the size of a granary, though it had a high false front and a piece of peeled timber painted in circular red-white-and-blue stripes and attached to the front of the building just to the right of the door. There were five or six houses, frame or log or a combination of the two, and a one-room school, actually a granary on skids with sod banked about the sides and a window cut into the south side by Jim James, one of two handymen in the town.

"And of course there was the church, the only building in Frank Pierce that had seen paint, other than the false front of the barber shop. St. Zacharias was only about 20x20 and drew its congregation from the farm families, some of whom traveled over five miles by horse and wagon to come to Sunday services.

"When that same group of farm families persuaded the Bishop in Des Moines to send them a priest they promised a rectory, but somehow it never got built, and Father Camino, a slim, dark-eyed young priest from New Mexico, was boarded with one of the town families for a while, until he decided that if a heater were provided he could live adequately if not comfortably in the back six feet of the church. The area behind the altar was cordoned off with blankets: a heater, a generous supply of wood, a couple of chairs, a bed and bedding, and a bookcase were donated. The priest still took his meals with a town family but was able to spend the remainder of his time in private away from worldly distractions.

"The story I want to tell you happened on a Sunday morning in August. It was approaching noon. The service at St. Zacharias had been in progress for nearly an hour. A searing sun burned down from a cloudless sky, the humidity was high, the air like hot flannel. The sun's rays reflected from the yellow dust of the main street with such force that particles seemed to rise in tiny formations like gnats and move lazily over the earth. There was a hint of a breeze but not enough to effect comfort, only to make the heat more noticeable.

"A dozen wagons were parked on the shady side of St. Zacharias, harness bells tinkled, wagons creaked and groaned as horses grazed on the long grass next to the white wall.

"Across the street from the church was the baseball diamond. A ragged, chickenwire backstop and one tiny bleacher made of six sun-faded planks was all that distinguished it from vacant land. The field might have been a pasture; it needed cutting badly. The infield was covered in two-inch-high weeds, the outfield grass was bent and cow-licked. There had been rain and no baseball game in Frank Pierce for over two weeks.

"The only people visible in the sunstruck, silent town were two men at the bleacher, one sitting on the third plank up, the other standing on the ground in front of him. The sitting man, Ezra Dean, was the village jack-of-all-trades, and was supposed to have the baseball field mowed, manicured and ready for a one o'clock game. But his team of horses was still grazing in his back yard a block away, his mower was still parked, grass growing high against the spokes of the wheels. In fact Ezra had not even honed the blue cutting discs as he would have if he had planned to do the job.

"The standing man was James John James, caretaker of the school, the church (though he was an agnostic and lapsed protestant), the barber shop, and the general store. Some might have considered him and Ezra rivals, but such was not the case, each had clearly defined duties. For instance, Jim James did not build cabinets, or dig wells, or do farm work of any kind. Ezra was always available as a temporary hired hand, and was also a veterinarian of sorts, always willing to practise common sense and folk medicine on a sick animal.

" 'I expected to find you riding your mower,' Jim James said to Ezra, 'maybe even hurrying the horses along so as to create a breeze for comfort.'

"Ezra was a stocky man dressed in heavy work clothes. Railroad suspenders tracked over the shoulders of a collarless ivory-colored shirt. This morning he was barefoot. His hair was dark brown though his mustache was long and brick-colored. He looked at Jim James. With Ezra sitting three rows up and Jim standing, their eyes were virtually level.

" 'It won't be necessary to mow today.'

" 'The game's been canceled?'

" 'It will be. Not canceled. It just won't happen.'

" 'The sky's clear,' said Jim James. 'What do you know that I don't?'

"James John James ran a hand through his bushy, sand-colored hair. He too was dressed in work clothes; his boots were handmade of black leather.

" 'The world's about to end,' said Ezra without emotion.

" 'Oh, Ezra, don't tell me one of them pain-pushin' travelin' preachers has got to you.' Jim James shook his head. 'If you'll let me, I'll hitch up your team and mow the baseball field. The players will be mad as wet hens.'

" 'No need.'

" 'Care to explain yourself?'

"From the direction of the outfield, the burble of a meadowlark rose sweet as fresh water. Father Camino's voice droned from the church, harness bells jingled faintly.

" 'I had a dream—' and here Ezra Dean faltered, expecting Jim James to laugh, but he didn't. If there was one thing Jim James knew it was that Ezra's word was as reliable as sunrise and sunset. If Ezra said the baseball field would be mowed by Sunday noon then only death or catastrophe would stop him.

" 'And?' said Jim James.

"Beyond the outfield was the corn, the tall stalks shimmering like green ocean beneath the fierce sun. The crop ripening, filling the humid air with the sweet smell of life.

" 'I was visited in my dream by a boy of about ten. He just emerged from the cornfield, right over there, in that spot where the stalks are parted. He was dressed in a suit and tie, a little gentleman. He stared at me with brown eyes filled to overflowing with the most terrible sadness. The voice that spoke to me may have been his voice, but it came from all around me, not just from the boy's mouth.'

" 'We all have strange dreams,' said Jim James. 'You're not alone.'

"A quarter mile deep in the cornfield the railroad passed, invisible at that time of year, though both men knew the sun would be

glinting shrilly off the silver tracks. The railroad had not considered Frank Pierce, Iowa, important enough for even a whistle stop. Once a day windowpanes rattled, dishes vibrated, dogs barked, as the train grumbled across the plains. Today the distant odor of creosote was the only indication that the railroad existed.

" 'I am alone,' said Ezra. 'No one else knows what I know. The church is in session. The world goes on unaware...'

"Across the street, a gray hen ruffled her feathers in the yellow dust beside the front porch of a house, clucking occasionally to herself.

" 'The world is ending then?'

" 'Not the world,' said Ezra Dean. 'No. It is just us who have been called. Frank Pierce, Iowa.'

" 'Not even all of Johnson County?'

" 'Frank Pierce, Iowa,' Ezra reiterated.

" 'If I didn't know you for a truthful man, I'd call you a liar,' said Jim James. 'If I didn't know you as a temperate man, I'd call you a drunk.' He strode a few steps toward home plate, scraped the yellowish dust with his foot. A cloud rose, settled almost instantly on his trousers and boots.

" 'I'm tellin' you only what I know as truth,' said Ezra, examining the toenails on his left foot, painstakingly, as if there might be a message printed on them. 'Our world, this town, will die at noon.'

"James John James pulled on a brown shoelace just below his beltline and extracted a silver pocketwatch. Holding it in the palm of his right hand he studied it, watching the button-sized circle at the bottom of the watchface where a second-hand jerked like an insect leg.

" 'We'll know soon,' he said. 'What I don't understand is why you think your dream more important than anyone else's? And why, if only Frank Pierce is to cease to exist, don't you run? And why, if you believe your dream is truth, you, who profess to believe in higher powers, stay away from church, and not even put on your shoes to meet your maker?'

" 'Because I **know** my dream was truth,' said Ezra, speaking with more dignity than he was used to. He had never felt so important. There was no way he could find the words to tell Jim James why he would not run, could not run. 'I'm not at all sure that what will happen to us has anything to do with **them**,' he went on, pointing toward St. Zacharias. 'If you count you will find not one soul is absent from Frank Pierce today; if you count the wagons by the church you will see that every parishioner of St. Zacharias is in his pew this morning. I doubt if I, or even an unbeliever like you, could run, though you should feel free to try. If, of course, you believe me. All I know, Jim, is the child of my dreams said to me, 'Ezra, tomorrow, when the sun is highest in the noontime sky, you will be set free.'

" 'Was the dream before or after midnight? Perhaps the end spoken of is not due until tomorrow. I think we should cut the grass, just in case.'

" 'I don't blame you for making light of the idea.' Ezra went on. 'But let me tell you the real reason I didn't run. I think it's going to be fun. That little boy, that sad, serious, little boy, said there won't be any pain or misery involved in the passing. We will simply become invisible to all but our own eyes. We will become weightless and no sound will issue from our lips.'

"Jim James again backed up a few steps; he leaned against the edge of the backstop. He produced a pouch of tobacco and papers from a trousers pocket and proceeded to roll a cigaret.

" 'Alright,' said Jim James. 'Suppose it is as you say. We make no more sounds, no one outside of Frank Pierce sees us for ought to see. What then?' He struck a blue-headed wooden match on the backstop and cupped his hands around the cigaret, though there was only a hint of a breeze.

" 'Perhaps we drift with the wind, as flower seeds are carried to new beginnings. Who is to say what wonder we will discover when we become aware of what lies invisible about us. Perhaps the air is full of shades. Perhaps there are layers and layers of history living right here, dimension piled upon dimension — the past like curtains hung in rows — like the gauzy greenness of the Northern Lights. What do you think of that?'

" 'I think the baseball players are gonna be after your hide when church lets out and the grass ain't mowed,' said Jim James, exhaling smoke.

" 'Come on, Jim. How many years have we played ball here on this diamond?'

" 'Before I came to Frank Pierce — twenty years I suppose.'

" 'Each one of those games is out there like a sweet, shy ghost, waiting to be seen again,' said Ezra.

" 'I don't think I like the gist of your idea. You scare me, Ezra. I don't like what I'm hearin' at all.'

" 'How many times do you reckon this has happened before, Jim? How many times does a town or a county, or a section of a city just disappear off the face of the earth, leaving only the land behind, soft and natural and renewed — something man doesn't have sense enough to do himself. Frank Pierce, Iowa, is going to be wiped from memories, easy as cleaning a slate with a damp cloth.'

" 'I think I'll mosey up the road, or maybe cut across the field to the railroad tracks...' but Jim James remained immobile, leaning on the unpainted backstop.

"From the church the small pump organ fired notes into the still noontime air — they seemed to have life. Ezra thought the notes flying from the windows and open door cast flitting shadows on the earth, he thought he saw the notes rise through the roof like heat, then evaporate like steam into the pale sky.

" 'Think of it, Jim. We'll be free of the weight that binds us to the earth — we'll soar with the wind like the leaves of the autumn, we'll soar like music. Instead of being the baseball players we'll be the ball, the bat, the bases. Adventure like we've never known — I rode with Teddy Roosevelt in....what was the year? — it will be even greater than that.'

"Jim James had seized the wire of the backstop with one hand. Though the wire was cutting into his fingers he seemed intent only on holding onto something tangible.

" 'I think I know now why I've been entrusted with this secret,' said Ezra Dean, suddenly rising, stepping down from the bleachers and walking toward his friend. 'I am not afraid, yet I know there will be many who won't understand, who will need comfort.'

"Ezra Dean opened his arms toward the high, clear, noontime sky.

" 'I wish only to drift by earth, and then only from Frank Pierce to places from which my legs can safely return me,' said Jim James, drawing deeply on his cigaret.

" 'I'll help you to adjust, my friend,' said Ezra. 'What is about to happen to us will not be death.' Here Ezra clamped a hand firmly on Jim's shoulder. 'But if you are so afraid, there is still time. Run, my friend. Run through the corn like a fielder chasing the ultimate fly ball. Run like your life depends on it.'

" 'I can't,' said Jim James. 'I can't,' and he gripped the mesh of the backstop more fiercely.

" 'I know,' said Ezra. 'Look!' and he pointed across the baseball diamond to where, emerging from the rows of tall, fertile corn, was the boy, a well dressed young man of about ten, with hair parted in the middle and brushed into place. As the two men stood side by side on the baseball field the boy advanced slowly, solemnly, toward them.

" 'Feel the total silence that falls about us now,' whispered Ezra, for the organ had become silent, Father Camino's voice stilled. The silence became more pronounced, the buzz of a distant bee, the twitter of birds, the tremble of harness bells, the groan of horseflesh, all ceased.

" 'It's our imagination,' said Jim James; his whisper sounded like a shout. 'The voices from the church stop only for silent prayer.' He made no effort to remove his friend's hand from his shoulder. 'The silence is always here in the heat. A breeze, I felt a breeze on my face. How do you explain...'

"The words died on the lips of James John James. He talked on, though no sound issued from his mouth. He gestured with his free hand. He looked with alarm at his shoulder where Ezra's hand still rested. Jim James could not feel that hand. He reached out to touch Ezra, but his hand passed through empty space.

"The boy, dark-eyed and solemn, was near to the pitcher's mound now, walking steadily, mechanically, when, suddenly he did a back-flip, a graceful, ballet-like movement. Landing on his feet, his expression changed to a smile so angelic, so full of release, that both men found themselves smiling. Ezra took a step or two toward the child.

"Though he knew that sound had ceased, Jim James thought he heard the bright, energetic chatter of baseball players, the crack of hickory on horsehide, the murmur of spectators. He thought he could detect player-shapes at or near each position, but faint and fleeting, like a passing reflection on a window.

"The boy was laughing now, tossing a ball in his pudgy hands. The searing heat still reigned. That angel's breath of a breeze moved the bleachers, the backstop, the church, the people who were emerging from the church, staring around trying to understand — moved them all gently as dust demons move over polished hardwood.

"Ezra Dean flapped his arms, rose a few feet in the air, drifted easy as a leaf floating down from a tree. He turned a cartwheel, landed beside the smiling child, who flipped the ball to him underhanded. Ezra caught it, dipped toward second base as if tagging a sliding runner.

"Ezra waved at James John James, who still clung to the backstop, though his hands were empty. Ezra's mouth formed words, though no sound issued forth: 'Look at me, Jim. Look at me; I fly with the wind like the leaves of the autumn.' "

Marylyle's story ends with the town of Frank Pierce, Iowa, disappearing like Brigadoon into the haze of a sultry summer noon, on an August Sunday in 1901. All that was left was the tall, ripening corn; the only sounds came from outside the immediate area of the town: a few bird chirps, the drone of a bee, the eerie rustling of the green corn.

Such events were accepted in the early days of Johnson County, a time when the presence of magic was taken for granted. Marylyle's favorite expression was, "Things are out of kilter in Johnson County." And, indeed, up to and including the present day, they are.

What Marylyle didn't include, perhaps didn't know, though I'm more inclined to think she forgot, or for some reason didn't think it was important to the story, was to make some comment on the name of the town. Surely she knew that Frank Pierce, Iowa, was named for Franklin Pierce, fourteenth President of the United States, 1852–1856.

Why would a hamlet in Eastern Iowa be named for an unmemorable former President, some forty years after his term of office had expired? Some of the early settlers must have known the story of how immediately after his election in 1852 — he would not be inaugurated until March of 1853 — Frank Pierce set out for Kansas on a peacemaking mission, trying to win over the strong secessionist element in the Sunflower State. On his way there, somewhere in Iowa — old newspapers establish only that it was in a desolate area of rolling plains and cornfields some miles east of Des Moines — there was a train wreck. It was probably sabotage, though no clear conclusions were ever reached. President Pierce survived, unhurt, but to his horror, his only living child, an eleven-year-old son, was crushed to death in front of his eyes. Even by inauguration day President Pierce was still in a state of emotional collapse.

As you see the boxed story is now complete. Where did Marylyle Baron hear the story of the disappearance of Frank Pierce, Iowa? I did not ask her sources for fear of drying up the supply. There **was** a Frank Pierce, Iowa. If you consult the list of Abandoned Post Offices, in the archives of the University of Iowa Library in Iowa City, you find that Frank Pierce Post Office came into being in 1895, and was **abandoned** in 1901. Some post offices were absorbed by larger ones, some simply discontinued because of shifts in population. On the line beneath **Reasons for Abandonment,** beside the name Frank Pierce, is the single word, "Unknown."

BEST WISHES
SAM & RENATE

Oh, Marley

" 'Oh, Marley, you dumb bitch,' he said to me, 'I'm gonna kill you,' and then he took out the knife."

Marley, across the tiny table from me, takes a sip of her coffee. She lights a cigaret, flicks the paper match into an amber-colored ashtray. She is explaining to me why we can't make love, ever.

"He called his knife an Arkansas toothpick, though somebody else told me a real Arkansas toothpick has a long, thin blade — a stiletto, that's it. I knew he carried it; I mean you don't live with somebody for three months and not know he carries a knife in his boot.

"Tod looked real graceful when he drew it out, even though he was out of his head, drunk, and blissed to the gills on every kind of drug you can buy on the street. He had a three or four inch slit up the back cuff of his jeans so he could whip those pants away from his boot and draw the knife all in one motion. He showed me more than once how he could do it, when he wasn't stoned or drunk. In fact he showed me the first night I ever brought him home with me, after I'd met him in a bar called Hanrahan's: him sittin' and grinnin' all lopsided on the little loveseat I had in my apartment — one I'd made real pretty yellow slipcovers for, yellow with big crimson squiggles. It was kind of scary, but kind of a thrill too, to have a boyfriend who carried a knife."

Marley is new to Vancouver, new to this house, moved in the first of the month to a room across the hall from me. A table, a two-burner black gas stove with white porcelain handles on the jets, a tiny half-fridge the size of a TV, a single bed, a wardrobe; I know what's there without ever being in her room, for all the rooms in this old house are the same. Marley is a big girl-woman. She's nineteen. Woman or girl? The first time I saw her she was wearing a baby-girl-pink coat, white stockings, white shoes. I thought perhaps she was a nurse.

I first spoke to her at the mail boxes in the front hall. She was wearing faded jeans, a long-sleeved man's workshirt of blue and black plaid. I'd guess Marley weighs close to 300 pounds. I like big women. Some guys do. I don't think about it, though I have a friend who wants to apply Freudian interpretations to everything anyone does. "Back to the womb," he says when I talk about my fondness for big women. Then he rambles on about Jocasta Complexes. I point out that he's gay and I don't try to analyze him.

"Since you're new here maybe I could show you around downtown," I said to Marley in that dark, varnish-smelling front hall. "We could go to a movie, maybe out for a drink afterward. I get pretty lonely up there in my room trying to write all the time."

I had read her name on the tag on her mailbox, lettered on a strip of coffee-colored plastic tape, something the landlady made up each time she got a check from a new tenant. **M. Sconiers,** it read.

"I guess that would be okay," she said about my request for a date. "I'm Marley, short for Marlene. Everybody calls me Marley." Then she said, "You're sure you don't know me?"

"No, I don't know you," I said, puzzled. I decided to treat her statement as a joke. "You must come from the East," I said. "Here in Vancouver we don't let radio or TV waves or even newspapers come in from the East. We have our own world here. It's a great place to start over, or hide out."

Marley just stared at me in the dim hallway. I thought there was genuine fright in her eyes. She had a wide, pale face with a few yellowish freckles on her cheeks and across the bridge of her nose.

"I'll knock on your door at seven. Hey, don't change clothes. I don't like dresses, okay?" My Freudian friend would get a few miles out of that.

"I didn't want to think he was serious," Marley says, drawing on her cigaret. "But I knew he was. His eyes were a faded blue with tiny chips of bright blue trapped in there like sunlight. I mean he didn't have nothin' to be mad about. I never messed around on him, and I cooked. Used to cut recipes out of **Family Circle;** I'd cook him things that was healthful. Of course they didn't always turn out. He was mad because he knew we had a half-bottle of Southern Comfort in the cupboard, but it was gone when he staggered in to look for it.

" 'I gave it to Monique,' I told him. 'She was goin' to a party and both her and her old man was broke, so I loaned it to them.' Monique was a good chick; she'd of paid me back.

" 'You're holdin' out on me, you bitch,' he said, and he slapped me, openhanded. 'You dumb bitch, I need a fucking drink.' And he slapped me again on the same side of the face. After the first slap I'd sat down on that pretty little love seat.

"It was just like the time when he owed money to somebody and he wanted to turn me out, you know, make me turn tricks to pay off his debt. 'I'm no whore,' I told him. 'You can slap me all day and I still won't turn no tricks for you.' That time he gave up. Later on Tod said how sorry he was for how my eye looked and all. He got some money someplace and bought me a whole carton of Baskin-Robbins. Then we got it on, and wasn't it good.

"Another time he brought this friend home with him, Derek was his name. Tod made sure I had four or five drinks, and we smoked a little weed. Then Tod started comin' on real strong, you know he unbuttoned my blouse and started playing with my tits, and this with

Derek sitting right on the other side of me. I said, 'Hey, we got company,' and Tod just said, 'Oh, Marley, you just be a good girl now and we'll make you feel better than you ever felt before.' I hardly even realized it but they each had a nipple in their mouth, and the top of their heads was touching. Derek was cute in a kind of dangerous-looking way; he had a full head of black, black hair, all shiny and sleek, like Elvis used to look.

"I shouldn't be tellin' you this, should I? It's just that I been here in Vancouver for over a month and you're the first person even noticed I'm alive. I'm a talker, no question. 'When Marley starts talkin' it's like turning on the bathwater full blast and havin' the tap stick on you,' was what Tod used to say.'You need to run her down with a semitrailer to get her to shut up.'

"The only other person I've talked to since I've been in Vancouver is my doctor. I had to fill out this little card the first time I went to his office, even though I'd been referred to him by my doctor in Hamilton. Hell, he's a psychiatrist. You might as well know. I'm not one to keep secrets. Everything out in the open. That's just my way. They asked me to state on that card what my problem was. You know what I wrote down? **Acute Loneliness.** And it just about blew the nurse's mind. She looked at me like I was a real freak or something. I mean that **is** my problem. They claim if you know your problem you're halfway to a solution. Isn't that true?"

"I'm sure it is," I said, barely getting the words out before Marley plunged on again.

"That's why we can't get it on." She smiled at me. Her eyes were a soft, hazel color.

"Because you're lonely, or because you're seeing a psychiatrist? I don't understand."

As I had suggested, we had gone to a movie, a Woody Allen twin bill; one of the movies starred the girl who played Mary Hartman, Mary Hartman. "I like Woody Allen," Marley said, "his characters don't fit in either."

We held hands at the movie; Marley let me kiss her once, but that was it, **let me.** Afterward I brought her to this ice-cream-parlor-cafe, a brightly lit place. We each ordered a strangely named dish with lots of whipped cream, chopped almonds, and chocolate sauce. It may have been called a Tar Baby or a Tarred Roof.

I had suggested to Marley that I'd like to spend the night with her. I can tell by the way she looks at me now that she wants to. After the movie we walked for a while, arms around waists, past the closed downtown shops, thighs rubbing, giggling like children at the window displays, at our reflections in the neon-pocked windows.

"I can't spend the night with you because of Tod. Because of what he did."

"I don't care about Tod. He's in your past. Remember you came to

Vancouver to start over."

"I can't let you see me," she says, a tear oozing out of an eye and sitting like a dewdrop on her pink and white cheek. Marley's hair is a lemon color, the shade 70-year-old women dye their hair. One of the first things she did, it may even have been in the hall of the rooming house, was to assure me it was her natural color. "Nobody has this color on their own. It embarrasses me," she said.

"He used the knife," she goes on, wiping the tear away, drawing in smoke, trying not to cry. "Tod used the knife on me. But the worst part is I lived. It would have been so simple if he'd killed me."

"Oh, Marley," I said, reaching across the glass-topped table to take her dimpled hand. "Tell me only what you want to tell me. People don't have enough time to be curious about the past. I'll tell you a story about me if you like..."

"Not now. I've got to tell you about what he did to me. If I tell you you'll know why I can't show you," and she looked at me miserably. I hadn't realized she was wearing mascara, but the lashes of the eye that had cried left a dozen black dots on her cheek, so neat and well space they might have been an unusual beauty mark.

" 'Oh, Marley, you dumb bitch,' he said, pulling the Arkansas toothpick out of his boot; then he stabbed me on the right side just below my rib cage. Actually it chipped the rib, the doctors told me at the hospital. I didn't feel anything, a twinge, not what I'd imagined being stabbed would be like.

"I was still sittin' on that cute little loveseat, the one I'd covered in yellow. I couldn't believe it. I stared down; I was wearin' a white tee-shirt and jeans. I was barefoot. I remember thinking, Tod don't like me plonking around the apartment in my bare feet, he's told me so a few times, that it gets on his nerves. Maybe if I'd been wearin' shoes, or my boots, these same ones I got on tonight, maybe he wouldn't have stabbed me."

Marley is wearing a pair of soft suede boots, the right one is badly worn. I've noticed her weight turns it almost on its side each time she takes a step. The waitress brings more coffee. Marley takes a new cigaret from the open pack on the table. I take the book of matches from her hand and light it for her. She smiles.

"I looked down," and she looks down now at the black-on-blue flannel shirt she is wearing, as if expecting a rose of blood to appear on the front of it. "There was a big, tomato-sized splotch of blood and it was growing — all I could think of was wine. And I remembered reading in **Family Circle** about how to take out wine stains. Was it cold water? Salt and water? Vinegar? I thought all those things in the couple of seconds before Tod stabbed me again. He was dancing around like a madman, holding the knife like he was swordfighting or something, sticking me with it again and again.

"He hit my arms, both of them, and blood just leapt out and splattered on the yellow loveseat cover. He hit my chest. It wasn't like you'd think; the pain wasn't awful. Just a twinge each time, like a growing pain, or a minor cramp. Then one thrust hit my belt, and the next one went in just above it, and the next and the next. He drove the thing into both my thighs, and both my breasts. All I could think of was I was being murdered, and it didn't feel near as bad as I would of expected."

"Marley, are you telling me this because you want me to understand you, or because you want me to dislike you enough to walk away?"

"I'm telling you why we can't ever be anything but friends. I like you, but I can't ever be," and she paused helplessly, not able to find the right word, **"that way** with anybody ever again, no matter how much I want to."

"Shouldn't I have something to say about that?"

"You don't know the whole story."

"What I know, Marley, is that people don't hate you because something awful has happened to you, or even because you've failed. People hate you for being a success. They can forgive almost anything but success."

"I'll never have to worry about that. But maybe what you say is true because what happened to me was an odd kind of success. I became a celebrity, or curiosity would be a better word." She paused for a moment. "About the twentieth time Tod stabbed me I started to feel faint. I guess I'd been screaming all the time, but I don't remember that. They say Tod was yelling too. I just started to feel dizzy and like I was sinking down into a big, fluffy feather comforter. I remember thinking, if this is dying, it ain't scary at all.

"Somebody called the cops. They got there pretty quick. I guess 'cause both of us was screamin' bloody murder." She paused. "That could be a joke, couldn't it? Anyway, they ran up the stairs and kicked in the door to our rooms. They say Tod was standing over me, stabbing me the way someone real frustrated pounds a pillow. The cops drew their guns and told him to stop, but he didn't even slow down so they blew him away. Each cop put a bullet in him. He never stopped swinging the knife; as he was falling dead he stabbed me in the leg, just below the knee.

"They radioed for an ambulance. They say I was spurting blood in dozens of places, like a punctured garden hose.

"The ambulance men hauled me out of the house, me layin' on my back big as a whale on the stretcher. Nothin' might have come of it, I mean publicity and pictures and stuff, if this free-lance photographer hadn't been listening to police calls. By the time they hauled me out he was there, his flashbulb popping a mile a minute all the way from the front door of the house to the ambulance.

"That photographer not only sold the picture, he sold a story to **National Enquirer,** and the next week just as I'm startin' to feel a little better, there I am on the front page, all ugly and bloody as a side of beef, under the headline: **Woman stabbed 73 times suffers no serious injury!"**

There is such a fine line between pathos and humor that I have to bite the inside of my mouth, firmly, to keep from laughing. I have always had the ability to mentally step back from a situation and see it as it really is. On one hand Marley is pathetic: big, and stupid, and pathetic. But on the other hand there is a terrible innocence and vulnerability about her. I do not laugh.

"It was so terrible to see that story. It would have been better if Tod had killed me. The picture was taken from the most unpleasant angle, from below as I was being lifted into the ambulance. I looked like I was made of innertubes. The strain of my weight showed on the faces of the attendants.

"And the story wasn't even serious. It laughed at me. 'Emergency room doctors stated that 57 of the wounds could have been potentially fatal to an ordinary-sized person.' It went on to say that because I weighed over 300 pounds, the knife couldn't get in deep enough to hit any of my vital organs. There were copies of that **National Enquirer** at the nurses' station and in the waiting rooms at the hospital. People from all over the hospital came to look at me. Local TV came. A girl from the TV station phoned me and was real sympathetic, said I'd get a chance to tell my side of the story. And I did. I guess she didn't have anything to do with the editing though. The story came out as a series of shots of this whale in a white gown, with first the TV reporter talking and then my tinny little voice in the background. The **National Enquirer** even ran a follow-up story; it called me The Heinz Lady, you know, because of the 57 wounds that might have killed me.

"It was as if I wasn't a person at all. Everyone smirked behind their hands. I was a freak on display and I wasn't even getting paid for it like a freak in a circus would.

"I've got 73 scars on my body. I can't stand to look at myself, so I know nobody else can. Sometimes when I look down at myself, it looks like there's pink worms all over my body, wriggling and wriggling, and I want to run away screaming. But it's something I can't ever run away from. I'm sealed up inside this skin. The one person I want to get away from most I can't."

"Let me tell you a story, Marley," I say. I push my cup to one side, and reaching across the table take both of her hands in both of mine. "Let me tell you a story, because that's what I do. I sit up there in my room — I have a view of the schoolyard across the way where girls in green-and-white jumpers play grass hockey on soft spring afternoons. I tell stories that no one else reads, except editors, who send them back to me. I pretend, Marley. I pretend so hard that I dig my nails into the palms of my hands until I draw blood. I don't even know I'm doing it until it's done.

"I came here to start over too. I've had five years of pretending that it was the right thing to do. Do you think you're the only one with bad memories? Marley, I have a little girl growing up a thousand miles from here. I have a past too. I haven't always lived in a lonely room in a crumbling rooming house. I have scars too. But mine are on the inside, and I'm responsible for most of my own wounds. It seems to me it would be easier if I could blame my scars on somebody else..."

I talk on for another ten minutes, but with little success. I tell Marley some of the details of how I quit a job as an up-and-coming executive in order to write, and how my wife quit me when I quit the job.

"She's remarried now, to a salesmanager for a pharmaceutical company, and my daughter is being raised with all the advantages my wife feels she's entitled to. She'll be a debutante when she turns eighteen."

I've made my pitch, and Marley seems to have turned it aside. Conversation runs down.

"I guess it's time to go," I say.

"I guess it is," says Marley.

The old-fashioned ice cream parlor-sandwich shop where we are having coffee also has a bakery counter, but it is closed this late at night. On the way out we pass a refrigerated case where eclairs, cream-puffs, jelly donuts, and turnovers sit on wax paper-covered trays waiting for morning. A variety of cakes, some large as trailer tires, doubled and tripled by mirrors, reflect enticingly, their cool, iced surfaces spangled with brilliant yellow and pink rosettes.

As we leave we stop by the display case to admire the repetition of cakes, some with Vs cut from them, revealing their inner composition.

"Don't they look good," says Marley.

"I'll get you one if you like."

"Oh, but they're closed," says Marley, pointing to the dark and deserted counter.

"Everything is for sale if the price is right and the buyer persistent enough," I say.

An old Greek sits at the family table at the back of the shop, nodding over an empty coffee and a full ashtray.

"Hey!" I call, tapping a coin on the top of the glass counter.

"Closed," the old man calls, barely raising his head.

"We want to buy a cake."

"That one!" I say to Marley, pointing. On the bottom shelf at the back is a round, chocolate-iced cake, with a circle of white rosettes, like whitewashed stones around its circumference. Inside the circle, written in white script on the brown background, is the message: **'Best Wishes, Sam and Renata.'**

"Why that one?" says Marley.

I clink the coin on the counter again. The old man glares toward us, reluctantly stands up and makes his way across the room.

"Marley, let's pretend," I say. "Let's start over completely. Sam and Renata didn't pick up their cake. So let's take their place. Let's make believe."

"You're crazy," says Marley, but she is smiling as she says it.

"We want that one," I say to the proprietor.

"You the people?"

"Yeah. Renata's plane was delayed," I say.

"Since noon yesterday? I give up on you. Ordered by phone, not even no deposit."

"I've been at the airport, waiting," I say. "I sent my cousin Luigi. My dumb cousin. You must have a dumb cousin," I say to the old man. "He's still out looking for this place. I loaned him my car. We had to take a taxi in from the airport."

"Sam," Marley says, hugging my arm. "I met Luigi once, he's not that dumb. He's not that dumb," she says to the proprietor, but slowly and hesitantly as if speaking in a new language for the first time.

The old man laughs. "I got a brother like that; three times we set him up in business, three times kaput," and he spreads his hands in a gesture showing the emptiness of his brother.

He boxes the cake. I have just enough money to pay for it.

"Good luck," he says, and waves as we leave the shop.

It has rained recently. The night is cool and fragrant, the streets blue and deserted.

"So where has Renata been?" Marley asks, again speaking with hesitation.

"You came West for the first time," I say. "Our fathers arranged the meeting. We both come from solid, old immigrant families. 'You been a bachelor too long, Sammy,' my father said to me.'I talked on the phone to my old friend Guido in Hamilton last night; he's gonna send his daughter out for a visit. Her name's Renata; you gotta meet her at the airport.' He sounded just like the Godfather when he said it." Marley laughs and snuggles her face against my shoulder. "I didn't want to at first. I mean I don't like my old man messing in my personal life. And I met Guido once when I was a kid. I mean, forgive me, he's your papa and all, but he looked like a gorilla. That's what I was expecting, a little, wizened up gorilla girl. I met the plane out of respect for my papa."

"You're right about how Daddy looks. But he's goodhearted. I was scared to death too. I figured the poor guy who was supposed to meet me would sneak off into the crowd when he saw how big I was. I was afraid he'd know about me...you know..."

"Renata's all over that," I said. "You didn't have to worry. Everything's worked out. If Papa had only told me you were a big girl they couldn't have kept me away from the airport with soldiers. See, maybe we'll hit it off good and maybe we won't, but you're attractive to me, and that's important..." I go to say more; I'm inclined to babble when I'm in a difficult situation.

"Shhhh, Sam," Marley says, "let's just walk for a while."

We make our way slowly toward home, through the dark, lilac-scented streets of East Vancouver. We each have an arm around the other's waist. Marley carries the cake snug in its cardboard box, holding it by its knotted green string.

"Pretend hard, Marley. Pretend hard."

She snuggles her head against my shoulder again. We come to a stop beneath a tall, drooping lilac. Marley raises her face to be kissed. Beside us, where a tine of yellow streetlight touches a lilac coil, Tod's knife lurks, glittering, sinister, waiting for one of us to make a mistake.

Diehard

I remember good old Herky saying many a time, "The only way to kill an old catcher is to cut off his head and then hide it." We'd always laugh even if it was the hundredth time over the years that Herky had said it and I had heard him say it. We'd laugh, me and Herky and whoever else was around the big table at Bronko's Polish Falcon Bar. Bronko's ain't the Hyatt-Regency, if you know what I mean. But then Superior, Wisconsin ain't San Francisco, and me and Herky and the boys at Bronko's Polish Falcon ain't lawyer and stockbroker types, so it all evens out.

Herky grew up right here in East Superior, not a dozen blocks from Bronko's. He was German. Arnold Waldemar Herkheiser was his full handle. The house where he grew up still stands, a sad, old two storey place, covered in imitation brick the gray sooty color of a melting snowbank.

When we came home in the fall from our first year in Triple A baseball Herky married Stella Piska, who lived next door to St. Wenceslaus Church there on Fourth Street. The year Herky hit the Bigs for the first time him and Stella bought the old Wasylinski place, right after the old folks had to go into a nursing home. I helped Stella and Herky clean the junk out of that little house: tons and tons of Polish newspapers, **Life** magazines, **Collier's, Saturday Evening Posts** by the hundreds. The whole second bedroom was stacked right to the ceiling and the basement was stuffed full, some magazines stacked so close to the furnace it was a wonder the place hadn't burned down years before.

Stella still lives there. Their kids are married now; the girl lives in Seattle, the boy in Minneapolis. I've always been half in love with Stella, and, what with my Margie bein' gone goin' on four years now, I figure after a decent period of time I'll propose to Stella. I figure we can have a pleasant old age together. But that's the future. What we got here is a problem in the present: what to do with Herky's ashes.

The service was at St. Wenceslaus' yesterday. There'd been a viewing time down at Borowski's Funeral Home on Tuesday night. They laid Herky out real nice. He looked good, his silver hair combed up in a big pompadour the way he liked, that broken beak of his about a half inch to starboard, the way it had been since he slid into Sherm Lollar's knee at third base in, what would it have been, the '44 season?

And his hands, those big mitts of his were resting on his belly; at one time or another he must have broke every knuckle he owned. The first time I cried for Herky was when I looked at those great, scarred hands, the right thumbnail split down the middle, ridged like the peak of a roof. I knew I was crying for me as much as for Herky. I'd lost a friend I'd known all my 62 years.

Stella had laid out Herky's catching gear on the bottom half of the coffin. Pretty cruddy stuff compared to what catchers have today, the thin shin guards, the small mask, the old cowhide mitt the size of a plate with the round indentation in the middle. It added a nice touch. The Red Sox remembered and sent their Midwest scout to the funeral — a classy organization. Walt Dropo and Mel Parnell, teammates of ours on the Red Sox, came; and Swede Tenholm drove down from Hibbing, Minnesota, where he manages a mine there in the Iron Range.

"Geez, Hector, he looks better than you do," the other old ballplayers said to me, after viewing the body. "All you'd have to do is lie down and we could have a double funeral," said Swede.

They kidded me some more about my playing days. I'd been a good field, no hit infielder for four seasons with the Red Sox. I put in five more years in the minors; in those days you could play your way up and down in the minor leagues. Now, if you're not a true major league prospect, you're driving a truck by the time you're twenty-five.

We went back to Stella's after the service. Neighbors brought tons of food and the place was crowded. The living room seemed so small; nobody sat in Herky's chair, that square box of a chair covered in maroon velvet with a raised-leaf pattern, ferns in concentric swirls. Both arms of the chair were worn bald from Herky hanging first one leg and then the other over the sides. There were food stains, grease, and beer can rings on the arms and seat cushion of that chair. Stella furnished the rest of the room at least three times over the years but Herky's chair dated back to when they got married, 1943. He was 20, Stella was 18. The wedding picture hangs in the dining room, right above the silver chest on the buffet. I swear we were never that young: me and Herky fresh-faced, our hair brushcut and watered; Herky's brother in his Marine uniform; Stella not as good looking as she is now, all sharp angles and frizzy hair, made almost ugly by the wartime women's fashions.

The children and grandchildren said their goodbyes. The son and his family would take the sister to Minneapolis for a day before she flew home to Seattle. The neighbors trickled away one family at a time, with much hugging and reassuring. Stella and I were left alone.

We sat at the kitchen table drinking coffee laced with Irish whiskey, Old Tennis Shoes, as Herky called it. Herky's ashes sat across the room on the kitchen counter, amid cake boxes, and plates of sandwiches draped in wax paper. Borowski the undertaker had said,

"Why don't you drop over next week and pick up the ashes," but Stella insisted she wanted them that day. Borowski delivered them himself, early that evening.

We had several drinks mainly in silence; the kind of silence lifelong friends share with comfort. Finally, it was Stella who looked over to where the blue, long-necked urn sat like a heron among rocks.

"What should I do?" she asked.

"Some women keep their husband's ashes on the mantelpiece, or in their bedroom." Stella shook her head. "The attic? The basement? The garage?" At each suggestion Stella continued to shake her head gently.

"I don't have any desire to keep them. They're not Herky. I've got my memories here inside me." She patted her dress just below her breasts. Stella's yellow hair is graying now, her face is thinner, her eyes sharper. But she's still a beautiful woman. "I think it's sad to keep something like that," she went on. "It's the kind of thing dreary old movie has beens do to seek sympathy."

"I could scatter them the next time I go for a walk," I said. "Herky and I must have walked the tracks and the trestle out by the flour mill a thousand miles or more. That was his favorite place in the world, walking across the trestle looking down at the fields of marsh grass, especially if the moon was out and glinted off the tracks and the water in among the grass."

"It's an idea," said Stella,"but I'd like something special, someplace special."

Though we both played for the Boston Red Sox, once our playing days were over we were never more than interested fans. We followed the standings in the newspapers and watched The Game of the Week on Saturday, but we didn't have the money to travel to Boston, in fact neither of us was ever back there again. We went down to Milwaukee once in a while, but we mainly watched minor league baseball until 1960 when the Minnesota Twins came into being.

On Saturdays and Sundays we could jump in the car right after breakfast and get to Met Stadium in time for batting practice. The four of us, hundreds and hundreds of trips down Interstate 35 to the Twin Cities. The Met was a lot like Fenway Park, a solid, friendly stadium with natural grass and open spaces. We even bought season tickets one year, but it proved too much for us, getting home at 2:00 AM and having to get up to go to work, then drive back to Minneapolis the next night, sometimes not arriving until the second or third inning. But what a season it was. That magical year when Minnesota won their only pennant.

The Season. The Season was what we called that year. We went to the World Series, and it was more exciting than playing in one. Both Herky and I were with the Red Sox in 1946 when we lost to the Cardinals and Harry Brecheen in seven games. Herky caught two of those games and I got to pinch hit twice, 0–2, and play three innings as a

substitute second baseman. But if any one of us mentioned The Season, we all knew it was 1965, the year the Twins went to the World Series.

They were 102–60, first by seven games over the Whitesox. Sam Mele was manager. And they had Don Mincher, Harmon Killebrew, Tony Oliva, Frank Quilici, Zoilo Versalles. Earl Battey was the catcher. Jimmy Hall hit like crazy; he never had another good season.

And the pitchers: Mudcat Grant, Jim Kaat, Jim Perry, and Camilo Pascual, who at 9–3 (.750) had the best winning percentage of his 18-year career.

Oh, we loved those Twins. Sometimes after a game we'd go down to the clubhouse and Herky would talk catching with Earl Battey.

Then there was the series. Los Angeles had such pitching. Tony Oliva, the American League batting champion, hit only .192, poor Earl Battey was at .120, Don Mincher .130. Only Killebrew and Versalles were able to hit. But the Twins took them to seven games anyway. Jim Kaat against Sandy Koufax.

The seventh game! Two lousy runs!

"Two runs," Herky would cry, and he'd actually have tears in his eyes. "Two runs away from the World Championship."

We were disappointed but not bitter. It was just that Koufax was so good. Herky would shake his head and marvel at the speed of his fastball, the fade of the curve.

"What a joy it would be to be rooting for him instead of against him," Herky said.

"Stella," I said, after maybe the fourth Irish coffee, "I just thought of something. You know Herky and me never talked about him dying. I wish we could have. If we could have talked about death we could have really said goodbye...." As I said that I thought of Herky, pale as his white hospital shirt, too weak to raise his head from the pillow.

"I know," said Stella, "we didn't talk about it either."

"One thing I remember, Stell, was a night at the Met in Minneapolis; it was one of those perfect baseball nights; the air was soft and warm, there wasn't a hint of a breeze. When we looked up past the blaze of floodlights, the stars winked silver and gold, like bits of tinsel floating in ink. The Twins were winning; all was right with the world. Herky leaned over and said to me, "You know, Hec, if there's anything after this life, the first words I want to hear when I wake up are 'Play Ball!' That's the closest we ever came to having a talk about **life**."

"We lived it, Hec," said Stella. "We didn't have to talk about it."

"What I was thinkin', Stell, was maybe the stadium, you know, the Met. Maybe all across the outfield. I'm sure that would make Herky feel good."

"But they're gonna tear the Met down in a couple of years. Soon as the new stadium is ready."

Stella was right. They were just nicely getting started on the new stadium. They'd play both football and baseball there. It was going to be enclosed. There'd been a lot of controversy, letters to the editor and such, a lot of people hated the idea of an enclosed stadium. But Herky had been philosophical about it.

"I've caught games in snow storms in April and May. I've seen a whole week of games rained out at the Met. I've seen football games played in a blizzard, the field frozen hard as concrete. We need both kinds of stadium, not that it will ever happen. When the weather's warm, and sweet and perfect, play at the Met, but move inside when the weather's terrible.

"You know what's gonna happen, Hec? In a few years, like 30 or 40, all the stadiums will have retractable roofs. It will be the best of both worlds — green grass, blue skies, but a nice clear dome to keep the rain and wind out."

"What about the new stadium?" I said to Stella. "How about getting Herky a seat behind home plate in the new stadium?"

"I think you've hit on a good one," Stella said, and she reached across the kitchen table and squeezed my hand.

We talked for another hour about the idea. The liquor and our emotional exhaustion after the funeral combined to produce a crazy euphoria, a giddiness, like the four of us used to get sometimes on the long drive home from Minneapolis after a big Twins win. We'd be singing, joking, happy as children. But there were only the two of us now.

"Secrets are so much fun," laughed Stella.

I slept on the sofa, fully clothed.

"You know what my daughter had the nerve to suggest?" Stella had said the night before, just before she went to bed. "You know, Mama, now that Daddy's gone, it isn't proper for Hector to stay over, even in the spare room. What will people think?" 'Let them think any damn thing they want,' I said to her. 'I guess Hector's stayed here a few times over the years, so him and your dad could get up at 3:00 AM to go duck hunting. I stayed at Hector's many a night when poor Margie was dying. If anybody thinks anything about it they can go straight to hell.' "

The letdown the next morning was so solid we could feel it. The sky was low and waxy. Our hangovers had a life of their own. Stella fixed me a big breakfast: fried eggs, toast, bacon, coffee. But all either of us was able to manage was the coffee.

Though we didn't talk about it, we were both wondering if we were doing the right thing. I stopped at my place to change clothes, and I thought of suggesting we rethink our idea. But I could see Stella sitting grimly on the front seat of my car; I took two aspirin and a deep breath and pointed the car toward the interstate and the long drive to the Twin Cities.

We didn't have much to say on the 150 miles to Minneapolis. Stella sat over by the door; the urn with Herky's ashes sat between us.

It was a reverse of the situation when he was alive; Stella always sat in the middle; whoever owned the car drove, while the other one sat by the window.

I had a difficult time finding a parking spot near to where they were building the new stadium, the Metrodome. Talk was they were gonna name it for that little yap Humphrey. If the Democrats had had a real candidate in 1968 Nixon never would have got elected. I glanced over at Stella. She looked drawn and tired; her face was the same pale color as her hair.

The paved streets were breaking up and were covered in dirt tracked out of the construction site by trucks. It had rained overnight and the streets were slick. We'd both dressed sensibly, me in my green workpants, boots and a mackinaw, Stella in jeans and a car-coat. We walked on past the yellow-lettered sign that said: **Hardhats Must Be Worn Beyond This Point.**

Cement trucks rumbled by, groaning like dinosaurs. A crane passed back and forth overhead, slabs of concrete dangling from its beak. Finally we heard a voice above the melee shouting, "Hey! Hey!" From a wooden construction shack a beefy man emerged; he was wearing a red-and-black checkered jacket, steel-toed boots and a scarred and dented silver hardhat. Stella and I waited for him to catch up to us.

Stella, waving the longnecked urn in her left hand, had to yell to be heard. My head ached and the construction noises were like someone whittling little pieces off the back of my head with a jackknife.

"I suppose there's nothin' wrong with it," the man said. Then he smiled, a loose-lipped, lopsided smile. "This does give a whole new meaning to a guy saying, 'I'd die for a front row seat at all the Twins games.' No offence."

"None taken," I said. "He was a real diehard fan of the Twins. There's nothin' Herky would have liked better than season tickets behind home plate, with nothing foolish like workin' for a living to interrupt his enjoyment of baseball."

"A hell of an idea," the foreman said. "I'm more of a Vikings fan myself. But, by God, if I die before this place is finished I'll have my old lady plant me on the fifty yard line."

"Where is home plate gonna be?" asked Stella.

The man stopped and stared around him; he looked puzzled for a moment as if trying to get his bearings.

"Come on back to the shack and we'll look at the blueprints to make sure," he said.

At the shack he fitted us each with a bulky yellow hardhat with **Visitor** stenciled across the crown.

He held the blueprints up to the light, making them look like ghostly writing on a midnight blue background.

"See, the press box goes here," he said, marking a section with a dirty thumbnail, "so the plate would be here," and he pointed out another squiggle on the blueprint.

The three of us picked our way across the muddy site. Bulging cement trucks pregnant with concrete grumbled past us. Stella cradled the indigo-colored urn in the crook of her left arm.

"The first row of seats will be right along here," the foreman said.

The odors of freshly sawn wood, of wet cement, of old fires, filled the air. The cloudcover lightened a bit and though we still couldn't see the sun, the intensity of light quickened dramatically.

"First row, Hector, what do you think?" said Stella. "An aisle seat. Herky can put his feet on the screen, chug a beer, spill mustard down the front of his shirt while he tries to eat a hot dog, keep score, and tell the catcher how to call the game."

"Looks good to me," I said.

The concrete forms were held together by aluminum-colored industrial staples. The foreman caught the attention of a cement truck driver heading for a spot fifty yards away. He walked out, and as the truck laboriously backed up, a safety instrument bleating annoyingly at every turn of a wheel, he directed it to a standstill next to us. He yanked the spout down and positioned it for pouring.

"You got to put it down if you want us to cover it up," the foreman said.

"Oh, my," said Stella.

The close sky, the raw, chilling air, the confusion about us all took their toll on our resolve.

"There was no place Herky loved more than a ballpark," I said. "Even after they close this one in he'll still have a choice view of Twins games, until long after either of us will care about it anymore."

Stella smiled a wan smile, and leaning over stared into the dark recesses of the concrete form.

"If you want this will be our secret," I said. "Tell the kids you did something more conventional."

"Our secret," said Stella, and squeezed my hand.

The foreman banged on the back of the truck, and a slide of concrete rushed into the void. He steered the spout down a six-foot-length of form, banged on the truck again and the flow stopped.

"Now," he said.

I put my arm around Stella's waist; we each gripped the blue-glazed urn. Together we lowered it as deep into the form as our arms would allow. Stella closed her eyes and grimaced as we released it. The urn dropped less than two feet before it met the wet cement.

"Thanks," we said.

The foreman nodded, signaled the truck again, and a second rush of cement was released into the form, filling it to the brim.

"Play Ball," I said softly, as Stella and I picked our way back toward the construction shack and the street.

A Hundred Dollars Worth Of Roses

My mother, before she married Paul Ermineskin, was Suzie Buffalo. Her family all moved away from the reserve long before I was born. My grandparents have been dead a long time too. I guess Ma mentioned once or twice that we got an Uncle Wilf, but it don't sink in very deep.

I'm sitting in the sun in front of our cabin when this strange dude come hoofin' it up the hill. He's maybe fifty, healthy-looking and muscular; he's packing an expensive saddle, and a black suitcase covered in a layer of red and yellow stickers. That suitcase got the names of more cities on it than most maps.

"Which is Suzie Ermineskin's place?" he ask me, squint one eye against the sunshine.

"You found it. But she's off to Wetaskiwin for the day. I'm her son, Silas."

"Silas, eh? You named after the guy in the Bible who spent a lot of time in jail?"

"No. My mom had a brother, died as a baby. They thought they'd give his name another chance."

"I knew him," the stranger say. "Only lived for ten days. Me and Max Buffalo built the coffin. Big Etta lived for the whole ten days at our cabin; tried every trick she knew to save that baby. Say, is Etta still around?"

"Sure is," I say, and point up the hill where Etta's cabin sit back in the poplars.

"I'm sort of your uncle," he say, set down the saddle and stick out a thick-fingered hand for me to shake. "My folks died when I was a baby; Max Buffalo and his wife, your grandparents, raised me as one of their own. Wilf Cuthand is how your mom would know me, though I've never been a guy to keep with one name for long," and he smile a big, open smile, show a lot of happy lines around his eyes and mouth.

Before Ma gets home Wilf Cuthand has made a friend out of me. He is really interested to hear I write books, and when I go and get one he look it over real careful.

"By god," he say, "you know this is one thing I ain't done that I should have. I'm going to have to write a book about my life."

I can see that he means what he says. Then he tell me a story about something that happened to him at the Cheyenne Rodeo twenty years or so ago. A gambler want him to throw the calf roping event, an event Wilf is the heavy favorite to win; that gambler offer more cash than first prize money for Wilf to lose, 'cause he got a bet on somebody else to win.

"I took his cash, then I went out and won the event anyway," Wilf says. "That guy was so mad I thought he was gonna kill me right behind the chutes. 'Let's go in the tack room and talk,' I said to him. He agree, grinning kind of sly 'cause he's dying to get me alone. Soon as we're inside that storeroom he pull a blue gun from inside his coat. 'I'm gonna shoot your knees off, cowboy,' he says to me. 'You're gonna be sorry for the rest of your life that you double crossed me.'

"Just as he's aiming the gun at me about fifteen cowboys stand up from behind the packing boxes. 'They're all unarmed,' I told him. 'But the way we figure it, you got at most six bullets in your gun. Killing cowboys is like shooting tumbleweeds — so there'll be about a dozen of us left when you're out of bullets. You must have seen a car stripped down slow and smooth by experts. That's how we're gonna take you apart unless you start running in the direction of Phoenix and promise never to attend another rodeo in your life.'

"We meant what we said about him travelin' on foot. We'd boxed his car in. You know nobody ever claimed it. At least not while the rodeo was in Cheyenne. And no one ever heard of that gambler again."

Wilf laugh a deep, hearty laugh as he finish up the story.

I'm kind of surprised that when Ma gets home she ain't near as excited to see Wilf as I would have expected.

"Oh, it's you," is what she said after she come in the cabin door and seen Wilf sitting across the kitchen table from me, a mug of coffee in his hand.

"I know it's only been thirty years, but I thought you might at least be surprised," said Wilf. "Boy, talk about your stoic Indian."

Ma get a smile around the edges of her face.

"I always knew you'd turn up. Why should I be surprised?" she say. But when Wilf Cuthand stand up from the table, tip his beat-up kitchen chair over backward and hug Ma to him, picking her right off her feet and swinging her around, she don't put up a struggle; she even laugh. Something I realize Ma ain't done a lot in her life. But all that evening Ma keep a wary eye on Wilf like she afraid he going to steal something from us.

"I was down in Newfoundland a couple of years ago," he say at the supper table. "I was supposed to be on that Ocean Ranger, you know, the oil rig that sunk. I lost a lot of good friends. I had some time off and I went to the mainland, met this girl in Halifax. Somehow I was a day late reporting back for work. Hey, I phoned up this flower shop and I sent that girl a hundred dollars worth of roses."

"Did you marry her?" ask Delores, my littlest sister.

"No. I didn't even plan to see her again. I just wanted her to know I appreciated her saving my life."

"Hmmmmfff," say Ma, get up from the table, take her plate to the kitchen counter.

I bet there's hardly a place Wilf Cuthand ain't been at one time or another.

"I'm curious," he says, cutting into a slice of saskatoon pie. "There ain't nothin' worse than a person who ain't curious. You know what a cat's like when you place him in a strange house; he explores everything real careful. I been that way with the world. I've been like a cat exploring all the strange rooms of the world."

And he tell us a story about how he was a paratrooper during the Korean War, and how he float down behind enemy lines on a cold, clear winter night.

"I'm gonna see the world," say Delores. "I'm gonna do Indian Dances all over the world."

"She's real good," I say. "Dances in a group called The Duck Lake Massacre."

"You've got the right idea," says Wilf. "You dance for me one of these days. I might be able to show you a trick or two. I was a pretty fair thunder dancer when I was young. And Delores, you plan now to have your own dancing troupe when you're grown up: The Delores Ermineskin Dancers. You can do it if you set your mind to it."

By the time I've known him for a few days I've decided Wilf really has had enough experiences to write a book. He is as full of stories as I am, except his are truer than mine. He claim to have fought oil well fires with Red Adair, the most famous oil well firefighter in the world. He tell of once walking right into the center of a fire, all dressed up in an asbestos suit. Nobody who hadn't been there could describe it so believably. He knows too, how to pilot a helicopter. He been to Africa and drove a jeep alongside a herd of ten thousand wildebeests and zebras.

"Weren't you scared?" Connie Bigcharles ask him one afternoon at the pool hall. "How did you know where to start?" Connie is Frank's girlfriend and she ain't one to admit being afraid.

"You have to keep asking yourself questions," Wilf say. "Is it better to stay where I am or better to go to strange places?"

"You must have always chose the strange place," says Connie.

"Connie, what do you want to do more than anything else in the world?"

"I want to be an actress and see myself on the TV. I want to wear pretty clothes like actresses do."

"Why can't you do that?"

"I don't know how."

"Do you know where there's a TV station?"

"Yes. There are two or three in Edmonton. More in Calgary."

"Why don't you go to one of them and ask for a job?"

"Oh, I'd be too shy. They wouldn't have any work for me. I'm an Indian. I'd be too scared."

"Scared! Let's have a little ceremony. Everybody speak the word

GRAND FORKS
RODEO
ALL ROUND
COW BOY M60

scared into their hand, then we toss it on the floor and stomp on it." Wilf do just that. Delores follow him quick, and in a minute so do Connie and Frank, Rufus and Winnie Bear, even me. "How do you think I got a job with Red Adair?" Wilf go on. "How do you think I got into the movies and TV? I walked right up, scared as I was, pretended I knew what I was doing, and **asked** for work."

"You did?"

"Sure. When I felt my knees shaking I just thought, Hey, I got rid of that word scared. It don't exist no more. 'What experience have you had?' Mr. Adair said to me. 'I was a firefighter for seven years in Bismarck, North Dakota,' I said. 'It's a tradition among the Sioux, just as the Mohawks are steelworkers, the Sioux are firefighters.' Red Adair squinted at me and half smiled. I don't know whether he believed me or admired my ability as a liar. 'You got yourself a job,' he said. 'Thank you, Mr. Adair,' I said. 'My name's Joe Dynamite.' "

The conversation continued back at our cabin at suppertime.

"That was all there was to it? You just walked up and asked for every job you ever got?" said Connie.

"Well, I got turned down ten times for every job I landed. But you got to have stamina too, and thick skin. Every time somebody said something mean to me I just pretended to grow another layer of skin so next time it wouldn't hurt so much. By now I got almost fifty layers of skin. Nothin' affects me anymore. Hell, there ain't anything mysterious about what I've got to say. You can do whatever you set your mind on doing," and he shift Delores from one knee to another where he been bouncing her like she riding a bucking horse.

"You believe I could be an actress like the girls I see on TV?" says Connie.

"If you want it bad enough. Most people are all talk and wishes. Listen, there's an old Navajo saying 'If you want something and you don't know how to get it, then you don't want it bad enough.' We've all got to dream, and we got to have heroes or we ain't anything at all. Dreaming of heroes is what life is all about. Anyone can be like their heroes if they really set their mind to it."

"J.R. Ewing is my hero," says Frank. "Could I be like him? Rich and mean with beautiful women standing in line to shine my Mercedes."

"No, you couldn't," says Wilf.

"But you said...."

"You could be rich if you set your mind to it. Seems to me you already got more women than your fair share. But you couldn't be mean. You've got a soft center, just like my girl Delores here," and he tickle her ribs to make her giggle. "Almost everybody here got a soft center — Silas, Winnie Bear, Rufus — seem like Suzie is the only one got a flint arrowhead where her heart ought to be." We all stare over at Ma, who been doing dishes in the blue enamel dishpan. Ma bang a couple of plates together, real hard, and keep on with her work.

* * *

"Tell us another story," Delores say to Wilf at supper a couple of days later. "I like your stories better than Silas'," she go on with that painful honesty little kids have.

"Let me tell you a little bit about my movie days," Wilf say. "By the way I agree with Delores," and he wink at me. "Silas, you're okay as a storyteller, but you better hope I never decide to go into competition with you. You guys must have seen me in the movies or on TV, without even knowing me. Back in the fifties when there were lots of westerns on TV why I was in about two shows a week. Every time they wanted an Indian I'd be there. I'd wrap a blanket around myself and be eighty years old, or I'd whip off my jeans and shirt and run across the set in only a loincloth. I'd wear braids, or long hair with a head band and lots of eagle feathers. My name would appear way at the bottom of the credits:

Sixth Indian: Thomas Many Guns

"I made a good living doing that. I liked TV 'cause you only had to do things once, or twice at the most. Some of the shows we did were live. In movies you had to do a scene maybe forty times, until it didn't feel natural anymore. At the end of one movie we were making, I was supposed to walk off into the sunset with people waving goodbye to me. I walked down the path and turned left about twenty-five times, but the director kept having me repeat the scene. 'I want you to turn right next time,' he told me. I could see having to do twenty-five takes turning right. I walked down the path and turned left again. 'You were supposed to turn the other way,' the director hollered. 'I'm an Indian and it's Sunday,' I called back. 'Indians can't turn right on Sunday.' The director thought that over for a minute, then said, 'Okay, let's print it.' "

We all laugh and pound our thighs at that story.

"Seems like Suzie's the only one here don't like me," Wilf says.

Ma been sitting back in the darkness by the cookstove. Seem to me she got her babushka tied tighter around her head these days.

"If you're such a big wheel," she say harshly, "how come you got nothin' to show for it? For fifty-some years all you got to show is the clothes on your back and a bagful of stories sounds more like Silas' lies than truth to me."

Wilf stay silent for a minute. It the first time I seen him taken back by anything since he got here.

"Suzie, you know what I've got to show for fifty-five years? I'm happy. I don't know how many people in the world can say that. My guess is not very many. You know how tough we had things when we were kids — well I didn't let that bother me. I just said to myself, I'm not going to wait around to see what life will bring me; I'm gonna go out and meet life. I done it. And I'm not sorry. Most people my age have lived one year fifty-five times. I've lived fifty-five separate years, and I'm gonna live every one that's left to me the same way. And I'm trying to teach your kids and their friends to follow my example. I don't apologize for it."

"Hmmmfff," go Ma, from her dark corner, but I'm not sure if the sound is scornful or if she's sniffing back tears.

A few days later, Wilf, who living in with Dolphus Fryingpan, because Dolphus have an extra bed in his cabin, show us an example of not taking no for an answer.

"You and me are goin' to the dance Saturday night at Blue Quills Hall," he tell Ma.

"I'm not," says Ma.

"I'm taking you," Wilf say. "Whether you get dressed up or not is up to you. I'll be by to get you at eight o'clock. You know, Silas," he say to me, "when your mom was young she was the best polka dancer in a hundred miles. An old man name of Conrad Raven used to fiddle and we used to dance until we pounded dust out of the floorboards of the community hall."

I've never thought of Ma as ever being young, though it reasonable that she was. She's never even had a boyfriend in all the years since Pa left us. I guess children don't like to think of their parents as being real people.

I am surprised as anything at the way Ma look that night. She chucked her head scarf, and her hair, that I only ever seen untied when she washed it, is combed out and fanned over the shoulders of a white blouse she borrow from Sadie.

That is something else that surprise me: Ma being able to wear Sadie's clothes. I've always thought of Ma as big, huge even. I know she only stand to my shoulder, but parents always seem big to kids.

Ma's blue-black hair got a few silver threads in it. I mean, I just never knew she was pretty. She wear a bright green skirt and green shoes she got from Connie Bigcharles. Ma usually wear a shapeless, colorless dress and brown stockings.

Wilf wear a pearl-colored western shirt and a silver buckle the size of a small book that engraved Grand Forks Rodeo, All Round Cowboy, 1960. He polished that buckle until it shine like chrome on a new car.

"You're twice as pretty as the woman I took to the Academy Awards Dinner back in '62. I was in a picture that was nominated that year. I paid a guy a thousand bucks for his tickets, figured it was something everybody should do once in their life."

It is the first time I ever seen Ma do more than one dance with anybody. She never get to sit down from one end of the evening to the other. When there is a Virgina Reel, me and Sadie get in the same group and I dance with Ma for the first time in my life, even if it is just joining elbows and swinging in a circle.

Wilf and Ma stomped up a storm all that night at Blue Quills, and Ma is just as good a dancer as he said. Ma was really shy at first and

Wilf about had to carry her on to the floor for the first waltz of the evening.

It is also the first night since I can remember that Ma gets in later than me. Day is pushing pink light in the windows when Ma come in. I hear Wilf say something about breakfast, but Ma shush him and send him on his way. I know Dolphus Fryingpan is off on the rodeo circuit, so it ain't too hard to figure where Ma and Wilf been for the past four hours or so.

"It's about time Suzie got herself a man," Mad Etta said that evening at Blue Quills, from where she sat high up on her tree-trunk chair, alongside the Coke machine.

And over the next couple of weeks it does look like Suzie Ermineskin has got herself a man. Her and Wilf spend almost every night together, though she never bring him to her bed. It seem funny, but I've brought Sadie home for years and years, but Ma don't feel right to bring her boyfriend home. They even go to Edmonton for a weekend where they stay at the Chateau Lacombe Hotel, go to the movies and to fancy restaurants for steak and Chinese food.

"It's like old times," say Wilf at Hobbema Pool Hall one afternoon. "Except in the old days, when your Ma and me was young, we didn't have two pennies to rub together. Though we were raised in the same house Suzie and me weren't related. Way back in those days I liked her a whole lot. I wanted her to go with me when I hit the road. I asked her to go with me." I guess Wilf can see my eyes get wide. "She was the prettiest and smartest girl on the reserve. I was afraid for both of us if we stayed, her more than me..." and his voice trail off.

The pool hall is completely silent. We is all standing like we was in a photograph, waiting for him to go on.

"She turned me down. It was simple as that. I even offered to get married if she'd come with me. Only time in my life I ever proposed to a woman. She was afraid of what was out there. I was afraid too, but the difference was I couldn't wait to find out what it was I was afraid of."

Wilf has by now got us all dreaming. Rufus admit he always wanted to be a bartender.

"Well, you can be," say Wilf. "A mixologist is what it's called. All it takes is a little nerve. You look up **Bartending Schools** in the Yellow Pages, call and find out how much it costs. Save your money. Enroll. Nothing's stopping you but yourself. After you graduate you go to hotels and big restaurants and sell yourself. Don't go whispering 'I'm an Indian,' or trying to pretend you're not. Say 'I'm the first Indian bartender in Alberta. Let me make you a drink called a Chicken Dancer...' "

"But I wouldn't...," say Rufus.

"You'd make it up. Play it by ear. Take a chance."

Wilf do the same thing to each of us. I'm thinking of trying to get an agent to really sell my books to big publishers and to the movies and TV. And Frank admit he want to own an auto wrecking and second hand business. Wilf got good answers to all our questions and objections.

"But we're Indians," somebody say.

This is the only time since he been here Wilf lose his patience.

"You can be a success and still be an Indian," he say real sharp. "Don't any of you ever use being an Indian as an excuse for failure. People are people wherever you go. Indian, Black, White, Yellow, doesn't make a damn bit of difference what color you are outside. It's what you've got inside that counts. The failures all excuse themselves by saying 'I'm just a poor Indian, what do you expect,' a whiner's a whiner, a loser's a loser, white or Indian," and he look around fierce at us, his eyes flashing.

"What do you figure's gonna happen with Ma and Wilf?" I ask Mad Etta.

Etta look at me for a long time. I feel like her old eyes are drilling holes in my chest.

"You know," she says.

"I do?"

"If I thought you were dumb I wouldn't of made you my assistant."

"What do I know?"

Etta smile deep in her face. "That Wilf is like the first soft weather of March; weather that turn the snowbanks soft as putty, put the smell of life in the air, set us to dreaming of summer."

"But what you're describing is called a false spring."

"Good," says Etta. "I told you you knew."

A few nights later Ma come home about midnight. Everyone else is in bed; the rooms in our cabin been made by hanging blankets on clothesline cord. Sadie is snuggled down deep in the quilts beside me. Ma make herself coffee and sit at the table a long time. I doze off, but wake as the cabin door close. I recognize Wilf's boots on the kitchen floor. Wilf has been carrying his suitcase. I can hear the metal edges clack as he sit it down on the linoleum.

"What do you want now?" says Ma. Her voice is tired.

"I came to say goodbye. And I come to apologize if I made you unhappy. I know you don't like what I been selling to the young people. Are you sorry I came back, Suzie?"

"No. I guess not," Ma say after a long pause.

"Are you afraid of me?"

After an even longer pause Ma says "No. I'm afraid of me."

"I know. If I don't leave now I might never leave. I'm too old to put down roots. Yours are too deep in the ground to be pulled up...."

I've never really thought of what Ma has missed out on. She's been like a windbreak for us kids. She's done whatever she could to help us, mainly she just kept us together, when over half the families on the reserve fell apart. She never let white social workers get their hooks into our family.

"What if...what if I was to come back in a few years, when Delores is on her own and you're as free as you were thirty-five years ago? Think you might travel a little with me?"

"I don't know," says Ma.

"It'll be something for both of us to dream about. Something to keep us going. Even if it don't work out it's better to wake up than not to dream at all. All the time I been here I been telling the young folks to find someone to look up to. Dreaming of heroes ain't such a bad occupation.

"Suzie, you don't think I know what you've done here. But I do. You chose a harder life than me, and you stuck it out in a way I might not have been able to. You've lived your life for your kids. I've lived my life mostly for me. The wisest thing you ever did was turn me down all those years ago. I think maybe you saved my life."

"You gonna send me a hundred dollars worth of roses?" say Ma, and her voice is younger than I think I ever heard it. It is a girl's husky voice, no older than Connie's or Sadie's.

"Would you like that?"

"I don't know." But Ma's voice catches as she says it. There is a long silence and it would be my guess that they are holding onto each other.

"Keep lookin' out the window there, Suzie. Keep lookin' down the hill to the highway. One day a panel truck from Boxmiller Flower Shop in Wetaskiwin will come driving slow up the hill. Painted on the side of that panel truck is a picture of a guy with a funny helmet on his head and wings on his heels. The driver will have a hundred dollars worth of roses for you."

"No," says Ma, and I can tell she is crying. "There's other things we need. Delores...."

"They'll be for Suzie Ermineskin and nobody else. You've spent all your life giving. There won't be any card. You just think of this old man with wings on his feet...."

I hear Wilf walk across the floor, stop and pick up his suitcase and saddle, then head out the door.

Ma pull up a chair and sit at the kitchen table. She blow out the lamp. I can see tines of moonlight strung across the floor. I cuddle down in my bed. It gonna be nice, seeing Ma staring down the road, dreaming.

Homer

One of my first memories is of **Uncle** Homer Hardy, though he sure wasn't my uncle, he being about as white as I'm Indian. Still I remember him being at our cabin, sitting sideways at the oilcloth covered kitchen table, his chewed-up-looking brown hat on his knee, him banging his coffee mug on the table to make a point, never once noticing the black coffee slopping over the top.

Homer was short, with fierce brown eyes buried in gray whiskers. A few strands of gray hair hung down the back of his neck, but he was mostly bald; his head was freckled, and what could be seen of his face was sun and windburned to the color of red willow.

"Homer's a prospector," my pa would say to us kids after Homer had left. I didn't understand about mining or gold, and it was a lot of years before I come to know what it was Homer did.

Usually he came by to try and get something from us, which, looking back, was not a smart idea, for there wasn't many people as poor as us.

"Paul," Homer would say to my dad, "I just need a grubstake. A few pounds of flour, some coffee, sugar if you can spare it. I'll shoot me rabbits for meat," and he'd nod toward the window, where, outside, his tall, buckskin horse munched grass, a 22-rifle in a leather scabbard just behind the saddle.

"I know where there's gold," Homer would say, and his eyes would blaze. "Back on the Nordegg River. Sittin' right there for the taking. You grubstake me, Paul, and we'll go ridin' into Wetaskiwin in a Cadillac automobile, lightin' our cigars with left over ten dollar bills," and Homer would smile, showing that his teeth was mostly missing, and his gums was the dark pink of ink erasers.

Pa would give Homer a few supplies. Ma would grumble, but she admit to me in recent years that she didn't mind too much. "It was like buying a ticket on the lottery nowadays. You know you ain't gonna win, but it give you somethin' to live for until next week or next month."

Homer would pack the groceries up in a canvas sack, and he'd smile and jig around just like a kid been given a new toy. He'd dig in the pockets of his overalls and come out with a few hard-dimpled raspberry drops, or some triangular Vicks Cough Drops. They was used-looking and covered in lint and specks of tobacco dust, but boy, I remember how my mouth water while I'm seeing him search his pockets.

We wouldn't see Homer again for three or maybe six months. And when we did nothing would have changed. He wouldn't be rich, and if anybody asked, he'd just grin kind of sheepish and say, "That one didn't pan out like I figured. But I **know** where there's gold now. Right there for the takin'...."

It was strange but no one I know ever felt cheated by Uncle Homer. He would sweep in and out of the reserve, kind of like a one-man carnival — what he promised always being 100% more than he delivered.

One of the reasons everybody liked Homer Hardy was because he was a storyteller. In his saddlebag, in the front of a floppy black Bible, he carried a picture of his parents. In the middle-distance, in front of a sod house, a huge, barrel-chested, bald-headed man stood in knee-deep prairie grass, a slight, long-skirted woman with knitted eyebrows beside him.

"That's my papa, long before I was born. He walked to Utah with the Mormons. My mama was his fourth wife, a shirt-tail cousin of Brigham Young. Papa could play the fiddle and was the best jig-dancer in the Plains States. Why one time in Wyoming, Buffalo Bill heard about my papa and sent for him to come to his camp outside of Cheyenne somewheres. And papa went, played the fiddle and jig-danced like the devil himself. Buffalo Bill gave him a gold coin — a month's wages, my papa said it was.

"Another time papa was out herdin' sheep in Oregon, or maybe Utah, he was never too plentiful with details. He took his rifle out of the scabbard, dropped it accidental like, and it hit a rock and discharged. Shot him right here in the chest," and Homer'd grab the left side of his chest, while us kids, and my folks too, sat watching him, our mouths hanging open.

"Bullet went through his lung, and through to his back where he could feel the point of it pushing against his skin. Well, sir, he lay down in his little line-cabin and figured he was a goner. He took a pencil and wrote on his soft, brown cowboy hat, 'I shot myself accidental,' so's his wife, the one before my mama, wouldn't think he committed suicide.

"He lay there for over a week until a rancher happened by and found him. Nearest doctor was over forty miles away and they rode papa there in a buckboard. There weren't no roads, just went cross-country over the open range. He should of been dead six times but he wasn't. Doctor looked him over and said, 'This bullet's got to come out. You reckon you can stand it without anaesthetic?' "

Homer was like his daddy when it come to wives. He had at least four, maybe more.

"I never been ashamed of the fact that women find me attractive," he'd say, and smile, his eyes glinting like maybe some of the gold he spent his life lookin' for was in there.

Even Mad Etta like Homer Hardy. I was at her place one day maybe ten years ago when Homer Hardy turn up, driving an old, square-fendered truck, what used to be some color once, but was now just a sun-faded metallic.

"Etta," he say after she's fed him a meal and give him a cigaret. "Etta, if I just had enough money for a tire for my truck I could get that load of ore to Edmonton to the assay office, and none of us would ever have to work again."

Etta she heard every hardluck story ever been told, and they roll off her broad back like a duck shed water. But next day Fred Crier down at Hobbema Texaco Garage put a new tire on Homer's truck, and I hear tell Etta, she rode down in the truck box, sitting on top of the ore, just so's she could pay for the tire. Also, Homer stayed overnight at Etta's cabin and some say she had a certain contented look about her, perched up there like a queen on that hill of chipped rock.

Homer's women was part of his stories. He never laugh at any of them, always at himself.

"First one should of knowed better," he say one time, "she worked right in the assay office in Edmonton; she got to see the results from my samples. Her name was Bernice, a maiden lady, as we called them in the old days, and she was quite a bit older'n me. Come to think of it, all my wives have been a good bit older'n me," and he grin from behind his scratchy gray whiskers, what circle his face like a big vegetable brush.

People have been known to say that Homer married his wives for their money. Each one of them **had** money, at least when they married Homer Hardy. But Homer spent it on old trucks, and supplies, and mining equipment, pumps and generators, and lawyer fees for filing claims. Homer never deny that he gone through a lot of other people's money in his life.

"I could have settled in with any one of my wives and never worked again. I could have sat in Bernice's rooms there in the Kensington Apartments in Edmonton, but I'd of felt just like a gopher never come out of his hole, and besides, one of the reasons she married me was because I was dangerous. Women like to take risks, but they need somebody to push them along a little. Her eyes used to shine when I'd tell her about the gold we was going to wallow in. I'm real sorry I disappointed her. When her money was gone — she'd inherited a trunkful from her daddy who was one of the first managers of the Bank of Commerce in Edmonton — why she didn't have no choice but to throw me out. We stayed friends though. I was always welcome at her home, and she'd sometimes toss me a dollar or two to file a new claim. I hitchhiked all the way up from Montana when I heard she passed away. Was a day late for the funeral. But I went out there to Pleasantview Cemetery and stood by the flower-banked grave and said my goodbye. I think it was a good idea I was a day late. Her relatives would have been mortified. They never could figure what

she saw in a bandy-legged prospector who only changes his underwear twice a year."

Homer he had stories about his other wives too, though he never did have a bad word to say about any of them.

Maybe five years ago he married for a fifth time, this time to an Indian lady, Martha Powderface. Martha was a widow lady, at least as old as Homer. Her family was wanting to put her in the Sundance Retirement Home in Wetaskiwin, but she married Homer and went with him to dig gold up on the Pembina River, and live in a tent on the riverbank.

"You know, Silas," Homer said to me the next year, "it's too bad Martha doesn't have money. Oh, now I don't mean that as a criticism, I just mean that if, fifty years ago, I'd had a woman **with money** who'd go out to the camp with me, I'da been successful. I'da made the earth give up the gold it keeps hiding from me. Martha's a good woman, Silas."

Uncle Homer was a musician of sorts himself; he could play the spoons. Spoon players, like prospectors, are few and far between these days. In fact, when I think about it, I don't know a single person able to take two teaspoons, and by holding them in one hand in some mysterious way, clack the undersides together to make music. A good spoon player can sound pretty close to a banjo, and a harmonica and spoon player can sound like a whole Western Band.

Homer would no sooner be in the door of our cabin than we'd be beggin' him to play and sing for us. And I can remember seeing my sister run for the spoon drawer, where all the knives and forks and other cutlery was kept, when we heard the wheels of Homer's wagon creaking up the hill from Hobbema.

"Sing about the fly," we'd yell, and Homer Hardy would smile from under his chewed-up hat, clack the spoons and sing:

> The early fly's the one to swat,
> He comes before the weather's hot,
> And sits around and files his legs,
> And lays about 10,000 eggs.
>
> And every egg will hatch a fly,
> To drive us crazy by and by,
> Yet every fly that skips our swatters,
> Will have 10,000,000 sons and daughters,
> And countless first and second cousins,
> And aunts and uncles scores and dozens.

That song went on for about twenty minutes, or at least it seemed like it to us kids — there was verses and verses, and we'd laugh and giggle, and Illianna would sit on Homer's knee, and pretend she was looking for insects in his beard, and finding them. And my brother

Thomas, who was the baby then, lay on the floor in blue rompers, grinning from his toothless little mouth.

Other songs were about people his father grew up with; the names and places didn't mean anything to us, but the tune was always snappy:

When I was working on the ditch,
Near Shell, for Isaac Jones,
I got acquainted with a boy,
Who runs the gramophone,
He was a charming little lad,
And his mama called him Sweet,
But I had no idea that,
His waterloo he'd meet,
His waterloo he'd meet.

There was about fifty verses to that song too. And sometimes we'd all join in, even my pa, who was never very sociable, and like me had a voice flat as a prairie.

One time I was telling Old Miss Waits, my teacher from the Reserve School, about Homer, and what a wonderful storyteller he was.

"He claims he never been to school," I said. "Taught himself to read by having a friend print the alphabet, then matching up letters with those he found in the Bible."

"I suppose that's **possible**," said Miss Waits. "You know, Silas, one negative aspect of education is that it destroys the natural storyteller in us, for education makes us aware of our own insignificance. Our own life story, unless it is particularly bizarre or magical, becomes uninteresting beside what we have learned. The uneducated person, however, is still at the center of his limited universe, and not only considers his life experience worth repeating, but will do so without invitation."

At the time I just stared at Miss Waits and tried to remember how she strung together them big words. But now that I've had a few years to think about it, I agree with her. When I was a kid nobody on the reserve had TV and only a few had radios. We make our own jokes. I remember the time Collins One-Wound was sitting on his corral fence smoking a cigaret, just gazing at the cattle and mud, when one of his kids, might have been David, or maybe even my girl, Sadie, though I doubt it was Sadie 'cause she always been real shy, sneaked up behind Collins walking soft as if they wearing moss moccasins, and go "Boo!" real loud.

Collins, whose mind I guess be a thousand miles away, fall forward like he been shot, and when he stand up he is covered in corral muck from head to foot. That story go around the reserve for days, and everybody who hear it laugh and laugh, slap their hands on their thighs, have to wipe tears out of their eyes. Even today, must be fifteen years later, Collins One-Wound is still called "Muddy" by some people.

Since television and movies and cars with stereo players come along, falling in the mud in a corral ain't near as funny as it used to be.

Homer Hardy thinks his life has been interesting and he tell about it every chance he get, and because **he** thinks it is interesting, it **is**.

One time Homer he took me with him on a mining trip. He had a piece of tattered paper in his saddlebag he claim to show the location of the Lost Lemon Mine, a story everybody in the West know about.

"Back almost a hundred years ago two miners named Lemon and Blackjack went into the mountains down near the Montana border, and they struck gold," is the way Homer Hardy told the story. "The biggest strike you could imagine," and Homer would ball up his fists to show how big the nuggets was that Lemon and Blackjack found.

"At their camp Lemon went crazy and he killed his partner, and he rode away with just a few nuggets. He was raving when he reached civilization, though his pockets was full of gold to back up his story. But try as he might, he never could lead folks back to the spot where him and Blackjack found the gold. Men is still lookin' for that lode." Homer paused as dramatically as if he was an actor on stage. "But I know the **real** story," he go on. "Two young Indians was hiding in the bush and watched the murder. They rode off and told their chief what they'd seen. One was named Crow Mountain, and the other took the name Kills Him Alone, because of what he'd seen, and nobody ever spoke his former name again. The old chief, Red Ears, was a wise man; he looked into the future and seen thousands of us pale faces ruining his hunting and tearing down his mountains piece by piece, so he swore the two braves to silence for the rest of their days. Then he had them ride out and move the campsite, Blackjack's body, and generally change the terrain so no one would ever be able to find that gold mine.

"But I'm gonna find it. And you're gonna help me, Silas. I got this here map from Red Ears' grandson; had to trade my truck and a case of whiskey for it, but it's the real thing. What are you gonna do with your million dollars, Silas?"

There is something about the word **gold** that makes the blood run faster, and makes your eyes kind of glaze over with hope. I don't know when I ever been so excited as in the days we making the trip from Hobbema to the Montana mountains. Where we going was off in the bush beyond a coal mining town called Blairmore. I remember looking at the mountain and feeling all tingly, seeing the trees angling up the ridge in single file, hitched together by shadows like a packtrain.

But once we got there it was sure different — it rained, and the sun, when it did shine, was hot; the air was alive with mosquitos and black flies, and it ain't no fun to eat half-raw fish over a sickly fire. That land was a lot tougher than we was. After two weeks we limped home — and ever since I been content to buy a lottery ticket when I get the urge to be wealthy. But it didn't faze Homer one bit, he just rest up until his rheumatism is better and his insect bites healed and off he go again.

Two years ago about now Homer had his accident. Him and Martha Powderface was prospecting a little river somewhere in the Rocky Mountain House country, when Homer slip as he scrambling over river rocks and break his leg, not just in one, but in two places.

"I'd a been a goner if it wasn't for Martha," he tell us afterward. "She rigged up a travois out of saplings and tent canvas, and she drug me over fifteen miles of rough country to where we'd parked the truck. And you know what? Martha had never drove in her life. But she's a quick learner," and he smiled across the little studio apartment in the Sundance Retirement Home, where they was living now, to where Martha was cooking oatmeal on the tiny white stove.

"Lucky that truck could be driven in Cree," Homer go on, and he laugh, showing where his teeth used to be, and Martha smile too, from under the flowered babushka she's taken to wearing over her white hair lately.

Homer is pretty well tied to his chair in front of the 12" TV. Between his broke leg and his rheumatism he need two crutches just to move the five steps to the bathroom. But his troubles don't stop him from dreaming.

"The streets of Edmonton are paved with gold. That ain't no lie. They gravelled them with rock right out of the North Saskatchewan River, and you could see the glint of gold in the first pavement of Jasper Avenue, and Whyte Avenue. One time I took my jackknife and dug a nugget the size of the moon on my thumbnail out of Whyte Avenue right at the corner of 104 Street."

One of Martha's sons, Eagle Powderface, listen to enough of Homer's stories that he get fired up to try his hand at prospecting. But his enthusiasm run dry, just like mine, when he actually have to live in the rain, wind, and cold of the mountains for weeks at a stretch. Besides that he never find any gold.

I guess prospecting is a little like storytelling, it ain't as much fun since life got easier and information more plentiful.

About two weeks ago I heard Uncle Homer was in the hospital. But before I could even get up to see him he was back at Sundance Retirement.

"Doctors just opened him up, took a look, and sewed him closed again," says Mad Etta. "I went over and took a gander at him, but there ain't no cure for old age."

The next night, though there is a wicked blizzard blowing, me and Sadie stop by Homer and Martha's place. Mad Etta travel with us, wrapped in a buffalo coat and covered in a tarp, she covered in about an inch of snow by the time we get from the reserve to Wetaskiwin.

Homer has sure failed bad since I seen him last. He is propped up on pillows in the convertible sofa-bed, look shorter than I ever remember, his toes poking the bedclothes only halfway down the sheet, his whiskers ermine-white now, and his scalp pale, freckles like wheat grains scattered on his skull.

But he's still tellin' stories. Even has one I haven't heard.

"When I was just a boy in Wyoming, only twelve about, soon as the trees started budding papa sent me and my brother up into the hills with our ponies, a packhorse drooping with grub, and about 500 head of stock. Ben, he was a year older'n me; we rode herd on them cattle until round-up time. Never saw another soul all summer. There was a small buckaroo cabin, not much more than a log shelter, but someplace for us to put our bedrolls down out of the rain.

"The spring I was sixteen, when we came to that cabin, it was one terrible scene. Sometime in the winter a wild mustang had pushed the door open in order to take shelter. Wind probably blew the door closed behind him. He'd died maybe a month before. Ain't no words to describe the smell. And you ever tried to get a dead, falling-apart horse out of a tiny cabin door? 'He must of had to kneel down to get in,' is what my brother said.

"Well, we lassooed his legs and tried to pull him out piece by piece, but we wasn't too successful, and as luck would have it it rained a lot and we sure needed some shelter. Worst job of my life gettin' that carcass out of there. And the smell of death stayed with that cabin all summer. We finally covered the floor with cow chips," and when he see Sadie wrinkle up her nose at that idea, he go on, "You never figured cow chips would smell sweet, would you? Well they did. And they soaked up the odor of death." He pause for a few seconds. "I reckon Martha may have to do the same with this place in a week or two," and he kind of wink across the crowded room at Martha Powderface.

Homer rest for a while, but the wind that was blowing snow hard against the small window by his head, wake him again. He must have been dreaming about someplace else, because he have a surprised look on his tired face.

"It's out there, Silas," he say. "Eagle, it's out there right now, even in the winter, in the snow. Little flecks of sunshine trapped in rock, lighting up the night. With gold in your poke you'll never be cold. All you need to get is a blowtorch. It's there. And I know right where it is."

Homer lay his head back on the pillow. Martha Powderface pull the cover up under his chin.

HIGHWAY OF HEROES

HIGHWAY OF HEROES

TRUE PATRIOT LOVE

PETE FISHER

DUNDURN
TORONTO

Editor: Allison Hirst
Military Adviser: Captain Wayne Johnston, CD
Design: Jennifer Scott
Printer: Friesens

Unless otherwise credited, photos are by the author and courtesy of Sun Media Corporation.

Library and Archives Canada Cataloguing in Publication

Fisher, Pete
Highway of Heroes : true patriot love / written by Pete Fisher.

Includes bibliographical references.
Issued also in electronic formats.
ISBN 978-1-55488-971-6

1. Highway of Heroes (Ont.). 2. Afghan War, 2001- --Repatriation of war dead--Canada. I. Title.

UB395.C3F57 2011 355.1'60971 C2011-901866-7

1 2 3 4 5 15 14 13 12 11

We acknowledge the support of the **Canada Council for the Arts** and the **Ontario Arts Council** for our publishing program. We also acknowledge the financial support of the **Government of Canada** through the **Canada Book Fund** and **Livres Canada Books**, and the **Government of Ontario** through the **Ontario Book Publishing Tax Credit** and the **Ontario Media Development Corporation**.

Care has been taken to trace the ownership of copyright material used in this book. The author and the publisher welcome any information enabling them to rectify any references or credits in subsequent editions.

J. Kirk Howard, President

Printed and bound in Canada.
www.dundurn.com

Page 1 image: The Highway of Heroes. February 3, 2009.

Dundurn
3 Church Street, Suite 500
Toronto, Ontario, Canada
M5E 1M2

Gazelle Book Services Limited
White Cross Mills
High Town, Lancaster, England
LA1 4XS

Dundurn
2250 Military Road
Tonawanda, NY
U.S.A. 14150

For all the heroes

Members of the Port Hope Fire Department stand atop their fire truck as the procession for Master Corporal Scott Vernelli, Corporal Tyler Crooks, Trooper Jack Bouthillier, and Trooper Corey Hayes passes, March 23, 2009.

CONTENTS

FOREWORD

This book represents an extraordinary tribute to every one of our fallen heroes and their families. The men and women of the Canadian Forces choose to serve to protect their country. Tragically, some have made the ultimate sacrifice. The Highway of Heroes is a tribute to the sons and daughters of Canada.

Young and old have lined the highways of this country to demonstrate their appreciation for the Canadian Forces and the sacrifices of our men and women. This remarkable outpouring of respect and affection makes a difference. It demonstrates that Canadians keep the sacrifices of our men and women in their hearts and minds, and serves as a source of inspiration for our nation. But more importantly, it means so much to the grieving families. While they must endure the loss of a loved one, they receive some solace in seeing the nation turn out to share in their grief. These gestures of support lift their spirits and inspire a nation.

The stories and images contained in these pages are great examples of this inspiration. Peter Fisher has achieved a remarkable tribute to the spontaneous expression of gratitude for our fallen heroes by Canadians from across the country.

On behalf of the men and women in uniform, I would like to thank all Canadians for this tribute to the memory of our fallen and for your outstanding and continued support.

W.J. NATYNCZYK, GENERAL
Chief of the Defence Staff

Courtesy of Canadian Forces.

Chief of the Defence Staff, General W.J. Natynczyk.

ACKNOWLEDGEMENTS

I hope this book will give readers a sense of what a journey along the Highway of Heroes is like, a journey that no one wants to take, and that I and thousands of others hope each time will be the last.

As I was writing, it became obvious who I needed to thank first: the families of the fallen and the heroes that keep us safe every day. If it wasn't for their heroism, not only since 2002, but for decades before that, Canada wouldn't be the country it is — as I see it, the greatest country in the world.

I also want to acknowledge the outpouring of support from all those who stand on top of the bridges and beside the highways. I know that the families of the fallen are grateful and I thank you. What you do is so important.

This is a journey I've been on since 2002, and I couldn't have done it without the support of a great many people. If I forget to thank anyone, I hope you will forgive me. As I researched this book, everyone I spoke to was more than gracious and willing to share their stories.

I want to thank Beth Bruder, Allison Hirst, Jennifer Gallinger, and the staff at Dundurn Press. They have been amazing, and I am grateful that they have given me the chance to share my photos and to put my thoughts into words. I would also like to thank the Ontario Arts Council for their generous support through the Ontario Writers' Reserve program.

I love the community of Cobourg and Port Hope and Northumberland County. As in any community, the people have differing views, but they are down-to-earth, and I'm grateful to have grown up there and to now have the opportunity to raise my children there.

To the editorial department at Northumberland Publishers in Cobourg, although we have a small staff, you are the best and I love you all. I've always said that, being a photojournalist, one gets to see the best and worst in people; it's a different experience every day. But since 2002, through the tears and the sorrow, I've witnessed the best of this country come together along this stretch of highway.

I think often of the first conversation I had years ago with my former managing editor, Mandy Martin, about the fallen soldiers coming home, and how the story of the special way that it was being commemorated needed to be covered. I'm grateful to Mandy that her door was always open.

A special thank you to my managing editor, Sharie Lynn Fleming, and reporter Jeff Gard, who gave me the flexibility and "space" I needed to be able to complete this book. They were always there to listen, and their words of encouragement were deeply appreciated.

Thanks also to Joe Warmington, who is not only a good friend, but a columnist for the people. I've never known someone who puts more heart and soul into his work, and it shows. Sometimes I think we are more like brothers. Joe has always said it doesn't matter whether you work for a small paper or one of the biggest in Canada, it's about being accountable. He's taught me a lot over the years, and I'm very grateful.

To my friends, Paul, Steve, and Dennis, you've always been there for me, in good times and bad, and I know that we could write a book about our lifetime together and the stories we've shared — but maybe we shouldn't. You're the best friends I could ever ask for.

To Arnie, Larry, and Wayne, just a few of the people who've shaped the *Highway of Heroes* into what it is. Thank you for all your help with the book. To Caroline and Hector, who were a tremendous help during my quest to right a wrong and were key to getting the message out to the people. To Darlene, Wendy, Peter, Tara, and Fred, thank you for giving me your time and your thoughts; please know, you're never alone.

To my wonderful family: I'm so grateful to my parents, who have supported me in more ways than one throughout my life. I know I should always say this more, but I love you. All my good qualities I have inherited from you. You mean the world to me. To my sister, Barb, who has been a wealth of support during hard times; whenever I've needed you, you've been there. I couldn't have asked for a better sister and I'm lucky to have you.

And finally, to the two people who mean the world to me, who've kept me grounded, who are the lights in my life, and my shining stars — my two children, Corby and Natalie. I love you both more than anything. During the hard times, walking in the door and seeing your smiling faces helped so much. This book is not only for the heroes and their families, but also for you.

PROLOGUE ❦ A SOLDIER'S LETTER HOME

This morning, the most sobering event in my life took place as we said goodbye to Petty Officer Blake on the tarmac of Kandahar Air Field. I did not know him. He arrived here just about a week before I did, as part of the same rotation (Roto 9).

While we came here prepared to face tragedy, it does not subtract from the sheer sobering reality you face as you stand here holding your salute with a thousand brothers-in-arms as one of our fallen begins his final journey home.

I had a sinking feeling in my stomach the other night as I realized first that the Internet was not working, then my cell phone. I went to the trailer filled with small booths, each containing a phone, provided for us to call home. No dial tone. Comms lockdown! We lost someone, I realized. (This, as we all know, is done until the next-of-kin are notified). As I walked back to my tent I overheard a civilian contractor complaining to his friend that he couldn't get online to book his vacation which he plans to take in September. They don't know.

In the morning, the maple leaf over Old Canada House flew at half mast. Later in the day (being called upon to assist with the Viewing and Ramp Ceremony), I stood in the mortuary adjacent to the runway where the bodies of Canadian, American, and British sons and daughters are lovingly prepared to begin their journey home. In a place where one can seemingly never escape the dust and putrid odour which hangs in the air, this room is cold and sterile. I never want to come here again.

A small anteroom off the side contains a large table where the flags to cover the transfer cases are meticulously pressed and prepared. Off to the side hang several flags which have been rejected due to small imperfections. "See here?" Sergeant Mullen points to where a small portion of red dye has run over into the white part of the flag (only noticeable upon close inspection). "Would you want that for your child? No one would," she answers herself. "You can take one if you like, we have to burn them and I don't like to burn a Canadian flag if I don't have to." I decline.

The Military Police then arrived to break the seal on the refrigerator so we could move his body to the Afghan War Memorial for the Viewing. Nestled in the Task Force

Kandahar compound, the memorial is a beautiful, peaceful place. Matching white marble walls rise from a base of black marble, which is also used to cap the walls. On these are mounted black marble plaques, each etched with the face of a fallen soldier along with his name and unit. The memorial is shaded by several large drooping trees which resemble willows and add to the serenity of the place. Workers finished polishing the memorial just moments before we placed the flag-draped transfer case on it, next to a photograph of PO 2nd Class Blake and his General Campaign Star. I decided not to stay for the Viewing — it is a time for those who knew him to grieve together.

I emerged from my tent at 0500 hours this morning into a thick soup of what can best be described as viscous fog mixed with dust. It is something you may have difficulty imagining. There was a dust storm last night (as we frequently experience) which then mixed with a thick fog. It seemed that the moisture particles bound to the dust particles and kept them afloat. At the end of the ceremony our berets, eyebrows, eyelashes, hair etc. were "frosted" with dust. If one didn't know better, they would think to see it that we [were] all frozen in place.

This cloud insulated the ramp ceremony, making it almost surreal. No outside sound penetrated. From where I stood at the side of the LAV III from which PO Blake's body was carried, only the open tail of the Hercules could be seen on the other side of the formed body of Canadian, American, British, Australian, and Slovakian troops — the body of the aircraft vanishing into the cloud. It was quite an insular ceremony. As the boots of a thousand soldiers marched on, I felt privileged to be a part of this national — and international — tribute to a fallen Canadian hero. Yes, there was a swell of emotion as we held the salute to our fallen brother as he made his way feet-first onto the aircraft — departing the way he had arrived. I thought of the caution I had received from Master Corporal Lee before going out onto the tarmac: "Whatever you start to feel out there, lock it away. We can't afford to get emotional here; there will be plenty of time for that when we get home."

As I type this now I can feel the cold steel of the transfer case, the weight of the handle pressing into my palm. We have more to carry now: the torch of PO Craig Blake. We cannot stop to feel the emotion fully yet because his work here needs to carry on through us who remain. God rest his soul; and may we never forget.

Sincerely, [Corporal] Joseph [Curry]

CFB Trenton personnel salute as the hearse carrying Private Tyler William Todd leaves the base for the journey along the highway, April 14, 2010.

Crowds line two bridges in Durham Region during the author's ride-along in the procession for Master Corporal Scott Vernelli, Corporal Tyler Crooks, Trooper Jack Bouthillier, and Trooper Corey Hayes, March 23, 2009.

INTRODUCTION 

They are three words that mean so much to so many: the Highway of Heroes is more than just a highway; it's a representation of our brave soldiers and of the people who support them.

As a photojournalist for more than two decades, the journey I've taken since 2002 has been one of the most heart-wrenching, yet at the same time one of the most fulfilling of my life. It has been a journey of extreme sadness mixed with pride. I've been there to document this uniquely Canadian phenomenon since the repatriations first began, when Sergeant Marc Leger, 29, Corporal Ainsworth Dyer, 25, Private Richard Green, 22, and Private Nathan Smith, 27, came home for the final time in April 2002.

Until that time, I don't know if I really understood the meaning of the word *sacrifice*. For me, that first day brought it home, and that understanding stayed with me in the days that followed, and over the years that have passed since. *Patriotism*, *gratitude*, and *pride* are just a few of the other words I truly came to know that day.

I've covered most of our fallen soldiers' homecomings, either attending the repatriation ceremonies at CFB Trenton or from atop one of the bridges along the way. Four times I've had the honour of riding along in the procession, where I was able to document, bridge after bridge, the thousands of people who stand to pay their respects, some openly weeping as they wave Canadian flags and banners that convey messages of condolence and support.

Whether I was working or not, I would go. And so did others — not many at first, but as more soldiers were killed, the numbers

Two men stand along the side of the highway near Quinte-West, March 23, 2009.

swelled. It's been called a "grassroots phenomenon," and it truly is. No organization started it; certainly no town or city started it. It's something distinctly Canadian, something we as a large family from coast to coast do to show our collective grief. It's about patriotism, and about honouring the great sacrifice made on our behalf by the fallen soldiers and their families.

But for me it's also about honouring the soldiers who have survived and those who continue to serve their country. I've met many of these men and women who journey along the highway, soldiers such as Jody Mitic, who lost both legs to an improvised explosive device. The route is also a tribute to their heroism — anyone who goes into a war zone has my gratitude and respect. Not many can imagine the horrors these soldiers have seen and must live with, not only today, or tomorrow, but for the rest of their lives. Their families and friends share the burden of these mental and physical scars of war. I believe the highway is about them as well, for they are also heroes.

As I have had the opportunity to meet with the families of the fallen over the years, I realized there are no words of condolence that seem adequate. I have spoken with a number of families, and I remember each and every one of their stories. I am pleased to be able to share a few of their experiences in this book.

I spoke with the parents of Marc Leger in Cobourg's Victoria Park in August of 2008. Sitting a short distance away from the Cenotaph, Richard and Claire Leger told me about their son — not only how he died, but how he lived. How he was called "King Marco" by villagers while he was serving in Bosnia. They told me about a miscommunication with respect to the repatriation, how they had flown out west to Edmonton where the son was based, thinking that he would be landing there and not in Trenton. I gave them the first picture that I took of their son's procession along the

It was an honour for the author to meet Master Corporal Jody Mitic on January 25, 2008, when he stopped by Cobourg on his way to Toronto. Not only fallen heroes travel along the Highway of Heroes.

highway as it crested a hill in Port Hope in the hope that in some small way it would help to ease the pain of not being able to be there.

On the evening of October 16, 2006, I attended the repatriation of Sergeant Darcy Tedford and Private Blake Williamson at the base at Trenton. Lights had been put up for the ceremony, which in the early years usually took place during the evening hours. I was in a small area designated for the media, but I had moved away from the other photographers so that I could shoot from a different vantage point.

Out on the tarmac, a small child was lifted up at the back of one of the hearses so that he could place a flower on his father's casket. I was really struck by the emotion of that moment, and that feeling returns each time I recall it. I remember feeling the tears rolling down my face as I was taking those photos. I moved back to where the rest of the media were, thinking that somehow talking to the others would make it easier to not think about what I was capturing on film. I won an award for one of those photographs, but what I remember so clearly about that evening was the anguish on the faces of those families. That hasn't changed over the years.

I covered another repatriation at the base on March 23, 2009. Four soldiers who had been killed by an IED arrived at 2:00 p.m., and the members of the families lined the tarmac, along with dignitaries and personnel from the base. Marcie Lane, common-law spouse of Master Corporal Scott Vernelli, was holding the couple's six-month-old daughter, Olivia. When Ms. Lane saw the bearer party carrying the flag-draped casket off the back of the Globemaster aircraft, she screamed, nearly collapsing with the child in her arms. Another woman quickly grabbed the child.

I can't put into words my despair at witnessing that moment. I will never, ever forget it. But seconds later, Ms. Lane was holding the child in her arms again, and after the casket had been placed in the hearse, she carried her daughter over, blew a kiss, and then gave one of the sharpest military salutes I've ever seen. I later learned she was also in the military.

While working at the paper one day, I received a voicemail message that made reference to one of the photographs I'd taken during a repatriation, and which had recently appeared on the front page of our local paper. The woman had called to convey her displeasure with the anguish shown on the faces of the family members in the image. She left her name, but no phone number. After some searching, I was finally able to get in touch with her. She was very polite as I explained that it was the family's decision whether or not to allow media on the tarmac to document the repatriation.

MJ, the wife of fallen Canadian soldier Colonel Geoff Parker, and their two children, Charlie (right) and Alexandria (left), salute the casket inside the hearse during the repatriation ceremony at Canadian Forces Base Trenton on May 21, 2010.

More importantly, I wanted to tell her that these images represent the true face of war. It's not just a dusty battlefield, tanks, soldiers, and a country of beige. This was a war in which people died. The overwhelming heartache of a family during their time of grief is, unfortunately, one of the great horrors of war.

Many of us who stand on the bridges have never lost a friend or family member to war, can never know the hurt, the pain these families feel, but I think it's important that those directly affected know that, along their journey on the Highway of Heroes, they are not alone. That has always been the most important thing in my mind.

People from all walks of life come out to the bridges to pay their respects. Among the crowds can be seen the young and the old, the rich and the poor, cadets, veterans,

Dee Dee Kaczmar holds daughter Rowan as she walks away after paying respects to her partner Sergeant Prescott Shipway during his repatriation at CFB Trenton on September 10, 2008.

emergency services personnel, and Canadians from all different cultural backgrounds — even visitors from other countries who have heard about the Highway of Heroes come out to lend their support.

There is OPP Inspector Earl Johns, who attends each repatriation, standing along the fence line at CFB Trenton. As a detachment commander, Johns has a very busy job, but I've seen him there both in uniform and in civilian clothes. Whether on duty or not, it means a lot to him to be there.

Then there is "Trapper" Paul Cane, the national president and co-founder of the Canadian Army Veteran Motorcycle Units, which hasn't missed sending a representative to the repatriations on the base or the funerals of any soldiers killed in Afghanistan

Crowds filled three overpasses in Oshawa on March 23, 2009, as the procession for Master Corporal Scott Vernelli, Corporal Tyler Crooks, Trooper Jack Bouthillier, and Trooper Corey Hayes passed.

since 2003, the year the CAV was founded. Former Chief of the Defence Staff Rick Hillier and Major-General Lewis McKenzie, along with Silver Cross mother Darlene Cushman, are also members.

There are regulars who attend the bridges throughout the journey, such as Glenn and Catherine Case, Vince Parbery, Ray and Debbie Hellam, Andy McLaughlin, Jan and Deb Bisset, Fred and Marg Salmon, Ron Smith, Mary Sleeman, and Dan McMillan in Port Hope. In Cobourg, Wayne McVeen, Peter O'Donnell, Randy Hall, Joanne Hall, and Lenore Miller always show up in support.

In every town, along the stretch of highway, many residents have made a habit of coming down to pay their respects on a regular basis. Each time a procession passes, Cobourg resident Ron Flindall stands on his property just off the highway, proudly displaying a large Canadian flag as well as a number of smaller flags, one for each soldier killed. He started the practice when the highway overpasses became too full. "When the bridges started to fill, I thought I might just as well come out back, put up my own flagpole, and that would leave two spaces on the bridge for somebody else," he says. Flindall grew up during the Second World War and remembers the stories. "I went to school with kids whose father either didn't come home or came home wounded. You never forget. So I just saw this as my opportunity to show my respect for what these guys are doing."

Ontario Provincial Police Inspector Earl Johns (in white shirt) salutes as the hearse carrying fallen soldier Corporal Nick Bulger leaves CFB Trenton, July 6, 2009.

Over the years, I've met many people on the overpasses, as well as many family members and friends of the fallen. Memories of the people I've met rise up, and then fade with time, but some stand out and remain clearly etched in my mind.

On June 17, 2009, I was introduced to a mother and son from Wisconsin who were vacationing at a resort just north of Cobourg. Willow Bay Cottages owner and Harwood Fire Chief Pete Staples had told Sharon DuBois-Vallman and her 20-year-old son Joshua about the highway and that some Canadians attend the procession of the fallen soldiers as they pass through the area on their way to Toronto. So they

Cobourg resident Ron Flindall pays tribute to Canada's fallen soldiers. He installed a five-metre flagpole along his property line, which abuts the westbound lanes of Highway 401 at Cobourg. Before the repatriated soldiers pass along the highway, Flindall also heads out on his ATV to install flags along the fence line.

decided to make their way to the bridge on Ontario Street in Cobourg to pay their respects; both are in the armed services in the United States. Shortly after the procession for Corporal Martin Dubé went by, Sharon told me how proud she was to have been there. She said she had goosebumps and, considering herself a proud American, she wondered why they didn't do anything like that back home.

Covering processions along the highway, I never knew who I was going to meet. I remember talking to Chuck Vernelli from Sault Ste. Marie, who stood on the Cranberry Road overpass in Port Hope with his friends and fellow Sault residents, Ed Adshead and Randy Fawcett, waiting for the procession of Sergeant John Faught to pass on January 19, 2010.

Vernelli's son Scott had been killed on March 20, 2009, along with Corporal Tyler Crooks. Sergeant Faught had been from Sault Ste. Marie also, and the three men had driven for nine hours to show their support for the young soldier's family. They held a Support Our Troops banner over the bridge. I couldn't believe that these men had driven nearly 1,000 kilometres for something that took less than 30 seconds.

Vernelli told me that he knows how important it is to be a part of the procession on the highway, and to stand on the bridges; he knows first-hand that the Highway of Heroes is part of the healing process.

The war in Afghanistan has brought an understanding of the sacrifice of war home to me. I'm grateful now that I understand, but I still hate to think of the price that so many pay. I respect the veterans and honour them; I envy the courage they have to go into battle — I know I couldn't.

But the Highway of Heroes isn't just about Afghanistan. Royal Canadian Mounted Police officers Sergeant Mark Gallagher and Chief Superintendent Doug Coates were killed on January 12, 2010, along with thousands of others, in the earthquake that

destroyed much of Haiti. They, too, served their country and were honoured with a final trip down the Highway of Heroes, and the people still came out and stood on the bridges, paying their respects.

I'm honoured that the highway passes by my hometown, and I'm glad to have met the many individuals that I have because of the Highway of Heroes — I just wish I could have met them under different circumstances. Although the highway has changed me in many ways, I know it's made me a better person. I now realize what a great country Canada is, and I better understand the patriotism of the diverse community of people who live here.

Many of the families I've spoken to don't realize at the time what kind of experience they are in for when they leave the base to take that long journey to Toronto. I can only hope that the healing begins for them as they travel down the Highway of Heroes, and that when they look back, along with the pain, they can take comfort in the fact that so many Canadians stood beside them in their time of sorrow.

A *Los Angeles Times* journalist once interviewed me about the Highway of Heroes. When two Canadian soldiers were killed while he was embedded with them in Afghanistan, he was told how the two would be making a journey along the highway. When he asked me about the process, I explained all about the highway, how it began, and how the phenomenon has grown.

I'll never forget his words to me that day: "You guys do it right up there."

My answer: "It's not that we do it right, it's just the right thing to do."

I've always believed that.

LEFT: *People stand by the Highway of Heroes sign on Hamilton Road in Trenton as the procession for Master Corporal Scott Vernelli, Corporal Tyler Crooks, Trooper Jack Bouthillier, and Trooper Corey Hayes passes, March 23, 2009.*

RIGHT: *Charles "Chuck" Vernelli (left) and two friends travelled down from Sault Ste. Marie to Port Hope when another soldier from the city was repatriated. Vernelli's son, Master Corporal Scott Vernelli, was killed on March 20, 2009, while serving in Afghanistan.*

LEFT: *A woman gathers her thoughts as she watches the repatriation ceremony for Private Demetrios Diplaros, Corporal Mark Robert McLaren, and Warrant Officer Robert John Wilson.*

ABOVE: *Two of the dedicated stand in the extreme cold as the procession for Gunner Jonathan Dion passes by, January 2, 2008.*

CHAPTER 1 ❦ THE FIRST FOUR

Since the day those first four Canadians were repatriated at Canada's largest military air base in 2002, the stretch of highway between Trenton and Toronto has been a gleaming example to the world of a nation's grief — and its pride.

The Highway of Heroes was officially named in the summer of 2007, but long before that, the people turned up on the bridges and stood on the overpasses of Canada's busiest highway to make a connection, if only for a few brief moments, with a fallen soldier's family. All along the 172-kilometre stretch they waited, in the blistering heat of summer and the bone-chilling cold of winter, to honour their country's heroes.

The expressions on the faces of the people show a variety of emotions as they watch the procession for Corporal Michael Starker pass by from an overpass in Northumberland County, May 9, 2008.

It was not a political statement, nor was it a show of support either for or against the role of Canadian soldiers in Afghanistan. It was simply ordinary people paying their respects. It has always been a grassroots movement. People young and old — emergency services workers, Legion members, military personnel, friends and family members of fallen soldiers, and ordinary citizens — came to stand, with pride and sorrow in their hearts, on the bridges along the highway.

On that first solemn day, Sergeant Marc Leger, 29, of Lancaster, Ontario; Corporal Ainsworth Dyer, 25, of Montreal, Quebec; Private Richard Green, 22, of Mill Cove, Nova Scotia; and Private Nathan Smith, 27, of Tatamagouche, Nova Scotia, came home for the last time. It was April 20, 2002.

The four Princess Patricia's Canadian Light Infantry soldiers had been killed

RIGHT: *Charlotte Rath (left) of Port Hope and her mother, Starr Rath, of Cobourg hold Canadian flags as they stand on a side road in Port Hope to catch a glimpse of the procession for Private Alexandre Peloquin, June 11, 2009.*

BELOW: *People lined the Cranberry Road overpass in Port Hope on April 20, 2002, when the procession for the first four fallen soldiers — Sergeant Marc Leger, 29, Corporal Ainsworth Dyer, Private Richard Green, 22, and Private Nathan Smith, 27 — passed by.*

two days earlier in a live-fire training exercise near Kandahar Air Base when a 225-kilogram bomb from an American F-16 fighter jet accidently struck the area they were patrolling.

Regrettably, in the nine years since that day, they would be followed by more than 150 others, casualties of Canada's military mission in Afghanistan.

In an age of technology, that first repatriation at CFB Trenton was broadcast by a wide variety of media, and satellite trucks lined County Road 2 outside the base to cover the ceremony live. People stood along the south fence of the base, and thousands of citizens across Canada watched the coverage on their televisions at home.

That Saturday I was working as a photographer for the local paper, and, although I had been given several specific assignments, I was also told to keep an eye out for other stories of interest.

I can remember my father calling to let me know that the repatriation ceremony was on television. Both he and my mother were watching from their home in Grafton, just east of Cobourg. My father

Lenore Miller from Cobourg stands on the Ontario Street bridge awaiting the procession of Sapper Sean Greenfield, February 3, 2009.

Crowds line the embankment in Durham Region on March 23, 2009, as the procession for Master Corporal Scott Vernelli, Corporal Tyler Crooks, Trooper Jack Bouthillier, and Trooper Corey Hayes travels along the highway.

had been a reservist with the 33rd Medium Artillery Regiment in his younger years, and had retired in 1996 as Deputy Chief with the Cobourg Fire Department after a 40-year career. One of the things he mentioned to me that day was that the procession would most likely be coming along Highway 401, through Cobourg and Port Hope, on its way to Toronto, where autopsies would be performed on the soldiers before they were released to their families.

Like most people across Canada, I'd heard the terrible news about the four soldiers, but at the time Afghanistan seemed a world away from Northumberland County, where I lived, one hour east of Canada's largest city.

I didn't know the soldiers' names, or where they were from, but, knowing that there was a brotherhood behind the uniforms of military and emergency services, I phoned Cobourg dispatcher Bob Jenkins, who was on duty that day. I've known Jenkins for a number of years, and I can tell you that he's the type of person who would give you the shirt off his back. As a dispatcher, he knew his job inside and out, and he volunteered with several community organizations. He had also spent 42 years with the Canadian Forces Reserves as a captain.

Jenkins has since retired after 18 years as a dispatcher with the Cobourg Police Service, but he remembers that day vividly. As a dispatcher, Jenkins was responsible for handling police calls and dispatching area fire departments. On this particular Saturday, he was listening to the repatriation ceremony over the radio at work.

When we spoke, I mentioned to Bob that it might be nice to have a show of support from the local police service on the bridges. Bob agreed and phoned CFB Trenton to see if the procession had left the base yet. A Military Police officer (MP) answered the phone but informed Bob that he didn't have time to look into the matter. Jenkins phoned back about 15 minutes later and spoke to a commissionaire who was working on the south side of County Road 2 — CFB Trenton's airport is on the north side of the roadway, and most of its offices are located on the south. Jenkins again asked if the procession had left the base. When the commissionaire asked why he wanted to know, Jenkins explained the idea of having officers on the bridges in the Cobourg/Port Hope area when the procession passed.

"I told him, 'I am a member of the Canadian Forces Reserve, I have officers here that have served in the military. These [soldiers] are fellow brothers.'"

Immediately, the commissionaire informed him that the motorcade was leaving the base. Jenkins then contacted a number of officers who were on patrol to let them know that the procession was headed toward Cobourg.

"I spoke with Dave [Periard] about setting up over the 401 at Division Street, and he said he would do it," Jenkins told me. (Cobourg Police Constable Dave

Durham Regional Police officers salute beside the highway near Oshawa, March 23, 2009.

Periard had served as an MP with the Canadian Forces for 11 years before becoming a police officer with first the Peel Regional Police Service, and later the Cobourg Police Service.)

No one knew precisely what time the procession would pass through the area, but the distance from Trenton to Cobourg is approximately 60 kilometres — about a 30-minute drive.

Jenkins then phoned the neighbouring police service in Port Hope to ask if they could also have officers posted along the on-ramps and overpasses: "When the procession came through [Cobourg], I remember our guys contacted me by radio and said, 'They're here.' That's when I contacted Port Hope, who arranged for a cruiser to be along the highway."

I was in contact with Jenkins at the dispatch centre and with my father, who was listening in on a police scanner and watching the events unfold on television at home in Grafton, so I was made aware as soon as the procession had passed Cobourg. I decide to park along the shoulder of the highway just east of the Cranberry Road overpass, where I would have a clear view of the procession approaching from the west. I was far enough away that I couldn't see the faces of those on the bridge, but I could tell there were about 40 individuals standing at the top of the span, including two people who were holding a Canadian flag. I also noticed that there were two Port Hope police cruisers there.

The minutes ticked by but the procession did not appear. I phoned Dad again and he told me he had heard that they had turned off the highway and were stopped at a service centre near Port Hope. I didn't know why they would be there, but I thought that if something was wrong, I should be there too. Making my way to the nearest exit, I sped back to the service station.

When I pulled in, I saw something I will never forget: four hearses were parked by the main building, along with several other vehicles from the procession. A military officer approached me; I had my cameras around my neck and it was obvious to him that I was with the media. He asked that I not take pictures of the hearses or the other vehicles, and I asked the obvious question: why did they stop? He said it was because family members, soldiers, and others in the procession had to use the washroom.

I can remember actually smiling and thinking, *why not, of course. Why wouldn't people have to go to the bathroom?* Then I glanced to my left at the four black hearses.

Through the window of one, I could see that there was a Canadian flag draped over one of the caskets, and the reality of why I was there suddenly hit me. I assured the officer that I would respect the privacy of those in the procession, and headed back out onto the highway. I parked along the same stretch of road where I had stopped earlier, and waited.

Family members wave as they pass by the Cranberry Road overpass in Port Hope during the procession for Private Simon Longtin on the morning of August 22, 2007.

Catherine Case and her husband, Glenn, a Port Hope firefighter, were having lunch in their kitchen that day, watching live coverage of the repatriation, like so many other Canadians. Catherine had heard the recent news reports and knew that these were the first four of our country's soldiers killed in Afghanistan. Knowing that the procession would be making its way along the highway past Port Hope, she had an idea.

"We knew the route they were going to take, and out of the blue we … talked about how Trenton is only 45 minutes away … we [could] be at the bridge when they [went] by," said Catherine. She also told me that her mother's maiden name was Dyer, the same last name as one of the four soldiers, although they were no relation. "I thought, I've got a connection to this. We have to go."

So they got in their car and drove the few blocks from their home in downtown Port Hope to the Cranberry Road overpass. When they arrived, they were surprised to see so many other residents of the community there. "I was amazed at the fact so many people were thinking alike. We were all just so upset that we [had] lost four lives at once, and everybody [was thinking] along the same lines — that we wanted to pay our respects to the families."

While there, the couple ran into retired Port Hope firefighter Andy McLaughlan, and the three spoke of the peacekeeping mission in Afghanistan, of the great tragedy of the Canadian soldiers' deaths, and why they felt they had to come to the bridge, how it somehow felt more "real" to be there rather than just watching it on television.

The Cranberry Road overpass is one of the best vantage points from which to view the highway, due to the fact that it is located at the top of a hill. From here, one can see buildings as far away as Cobourg, seven kilometres away. So it wasn't long before everyone could see the emergency lights of the procession

Peterborough firefighter Robert Lloyd, who was in the military for 18 years, mounts a Royal Canadian Regiment flag on top of the Peterborough fire truck that travelled to Port Hope for the procession along the Highway of Heroes for Peterborough resident and RCR member Private Michael Freeman, 28, Sergeant Gregory Kruse, and Warrant Officer Gaetan Roberge, December 30, 2008.

The final salute. A Toronto police officer salutes as the first of four hearses enters the final turn before heading into the coroner's building in Toronto. The procession was for Trooper Corey Hayes, Trooper Jack Bouthillier, Master Corporal Scott Vernelli, and Corporal Tyler Crooks, March 23, 2009.

approaching. As the four hearses, followed by the other vehicles in the procession, crested the hill, Catherine noticed that a soldier in the passenger seat of one car was waving at them. "That was moving, because we knew they were acknowledging us," said Catherine. Several people waved back from the bridge, and the police officers stood at attention, saluting; most just stood silently.

Catherine and her husband, like many others, still travel regularly to the bridge to honour the fallen soldiers as they pass by. She feels as if it's their duty: "As long as we're capable … we go. The only reason we haven't is if we are out of town."

It doesn't matter whether the repatriations happen on the coldest day of winter or the hottest day of summer: "We just go, and always will."

Catherine's husband, Glenn, always stands with his fellow firefighters, who bring two vehicles — usually an aerial and a pumper truck — to the bridge each time. Unless it is too windy, the firefighters will stand atop the ladder truck, saluting, as the procession passes under.

With each subsequent procession, the emotion increases for those present. As Catherine told me, "We leave, thinking *we don't want to see you up here again, but we*

Rush hour on Friday at Bloor and Yonge Streets in Toronto. Police had blocked off the intersection to allow the procession to continue through. One man was holding a Canadian flag, but it seemed others didn't quite know what to do, so they started clapping. It was a very moving and spontaneous gesture. May 9, 2008.

will. But let's just hope we won't be here again. It's ... very satisfying to know [that] the people of Canada are coming together to honour these soldiers. And the people who come to the bridge, come from all over the province, not just ... from Port Hope. I go for the families, and to pay my respects. I can't imagine losing my son or daughter." During that first solemn trip along the highway, members of the Port Hope Police escorted the procession along the highway up to the border of the municipality, where Durham Regional Police took over, accompanying the line of cars up to the border of Toronto. From there, the Toronto Police accompanied the motorcade to its final destination.

As other fallen soldiers arrived home over the course of the war, those involved in escorting the motorcade along the route eventually got the process down to a science. Today, members of the Ontario Provincial Police (OPP) escort the procession up to the border of Toronto. At that point, members of the Toronto Police Service take over and lead the procession through the city to the coroner's office, located at the Centre of Forensic Sciences on Grenville Street, near the intersection of Yonge and College Streets.

Carolyn Mrakava lives just north of the Highway of Heroes and made the trek over the hill to the Ontario Street bridge in Cobourg to pay her respects to Sapper Sean Greenfield, February 3, 2009.

When I think back to that first repatriation and procession in 2002, I couldn't have imagined the great outpouring of support that would follow in the years to come. I couldn't foresee the sheer number of people who would come out to stand on the bridges and overpasses along this remarkable stretch of highway to honour the brave men and women of this country and the great sacrifice made by their friends and families here at home. The sentiments and emotions felt by those who come out have not changed since that first procession, but this stretch of asphalt linking Trenton and Toronto will never be viewed the same again. It will live on as a symbol of Canadian patriotism and pride.

CHAPTER 2 ❦ THE NAMING OF THE HIGHWAY

The route that the procession takes between Trenton and Toronto wasn't always called the Highway of Heroes. But the meaning behind the stretch of the MacDonald Cartier Highway that runs for 172 kilometres through southern Ontario has been there since 2002, when those first four fallen soldiers came home for the final time. Spontaneously, people came out to show their support for the grieving families.

In the three years after those first four casualties, only four other soldiers were killed. But in 2006 that changed, with 37 soldiers killed in action in Afghanistan that year. And with that, a growing number of Canadians came to out to the bridges and lined the base outside CFB Trenton.

In 2007, another 13 fallen heroes came home, but it was not until Private Joel Wiebe, Corporal Stephen Frederick Bouzane, and Sergeant Christos Karigiannis were killed by an improvised explosive device (IED) that the highway got its unofficial name.

The words *Highway of Heroes* were blazoned on the front page of the *Toronto Sun* on June 27, with a picture I had taken of the three hearses cresting the hill at the top of the Cranberry Road overpass in Port Hope. The image showed six Port Hope firefighters atop a fire truck, standing at attention, saluting as the procession passed (front cover image).

It was early evening, the sun was setting, and the firefighters, along with the other people on the bridge, were illuminated by a beam of sunlight. Some waved and others stood silently as the motorcade crested the hill. One of the escorting officers was waving from a passenger window as the procession passed the bridge.

Veteran columnist for the *Toronto Sun* and strong supporter of Canada's military Joe Warmington said the words came to him as he was travelling back to Toronto from a weekend at his cottage north of Kingston. It was just after the announcement that Canada had lost the three soldiers, and Warmington had just passed Trenton on the highway: "Coming home from the cottage, I was thinking about the highway … and the phenomenon of how people wanted to be a part of it. I thought, *we have to give it a name*."

A few ideas, such as the "Road of Heroes," went through his head, but it only took a few minutes to realize the headline he wanted if there were to be another fallen soldier coming home. "It just popped in my head. I thought of [the name] Highway of Heroes, and I knew right away it would be a good headline."

Warmington didn't share his idea for the headline with anyone until the last moment, in case word got out: "It really was grassroots. It just blows me away every time I see a soldier come home — the support." The name quickly caught on, not only in the *Sun*, but in other media outlets across the province, and soon across the country.

"The Highway [of Heroes] has almost been a part of the coping process," Warmington adds. But it is the procession's final turn onto Grenville Street and that last few hundred metres to the coroner's office that is the most emotional for Warmington, who lives in the heart of Canada's largest city. Here, what began with about eight people standing along the road has now grown to hundreds of individuals paying their respects. Emergency service workers wearing every type of uniform stand shoulder to shoulder with members of the public. Officers on horseback, fire trucks, police cars, and ambulances line the street — honour guards from the Toronto Police, Fire, and EMS stand at attention.

In the area where the procession ends, the city comes to a virtual standstill. It is eerily quiet. Warmington remembers attending once with Canadian music legend Gordon Lightfoot: "It's very, very moving. The escorting officers get out and shake the hand of everyone there. The Highway of Heroes is obviously the bridges, the overpasses, and the motorcades, but it's also the end. There is something … surreal when you stand at the end. I think it's something every Torontonian should experience, because you really get the feeling of what has been sacrificed."

THE HIGHWAY OF HEROES BYLAW

Though it's been well-documented how the Highway of Heroes got its name, the two cities where the procession starts and ends had differing views on naming their streets to honour the fallen.

The City of Quinte-West, where aircraft carrying the fallen touch down at CFB Trenton, passed a bylaw to change the name of the roads that run from the base to the highway. Mayor John Williams originally brought forth a motion shortly after the Province of Ontario officially recognized the stretch of roadway as the Highway of Heroes.

After three readings, Quinte-West designated the repatriation route through Trenton as the Highway of Heroes on September 17, 2007. The route starts at the base, then travels along roads that include portions of Highway 2, RCAF Road, Hamilton Road, Sidney Street, Glen Miller Road, and finally the on-ramp to Highway 401 (MacDonald-Cartier Freeway) — the entire stretch is now known as the Highway of Heroes.

An honour guard of emergency service workers, including police, fire, and medical services, stand shoulder to shoulder as the procession arrives at the coroner's building in Toronto, March 23, 2009.

After the image and headline appeared on the front page of the *Sun*, it was obvious that the name struck a chord with many people. Word quickly spread, and more people started to talk, not about "going to the bridge," but about going to the "Highway of Heroes."

Growing up as the son of a firefighter, I had the opportunity to get to know many of the local firefighters. When I became a reporter and photographer, I met others from fire stations across Northumberland County.

Ken Awender has been a full-time firefighter with the City of Toronto for 15 years. He also served as a member of the Cramahe Township Volunteer Fire Department for five years. He emailed me on July 10, 2007, stating that he had read the headline in the *Toronto Sun* a few weeks before and that the image and headline had stuck with him.

Just a few days earlier, on July 8, Canadians had gathered on the bridges that marked the route to mourn Canada's greatest single loss of the war in Afghanistan. The long procession of emergency service vehicles, limousines, and the six hearses carrying the remains of Captain Matthew Dawe, Master Corporal Colin Bason, Corporals Cole Bartsch and Jordan Anderson, Private Lane Watkins, and Captain Jefferson Francis passed through Cramahe Township, where firefighters, citizens, and Legion members covered the bridge.

Members of the Brighton Legion stand atop a bridge as the author travels along the Highway of Heroes, January 2, 2008, during the procession for Gunner Jonathan Dion.

The Ontario Street bridge in Cobourg is crowded with people waiting for the procession of Sapper Stephan Stock, Corporal Dustin Wasden, and Sergeant Shawn Eades to pass along the Highway of Heroes on August 23, 2008.

Awender was a member of the volunteer fire department at the time: "I thought, it's true, you guys are our heroes. I thought it would be fitting for it to be named the Highway of Heroes and I thought we should do something about it."

Awender and the others on the bridges feel a great deal of respect for the soldiers and their families. "We can never understand what the families are going through, but I think it's like going to a visitation service. We're letting the families know that their [loved ones] were heroes and the respect we have for the sacrifice they made on behalf of this country."

Although I don't often write columns, when I feel very strongly about a subject I make an exception. When Awender brought the idea of officially naming the highway to me, I thought it was a brilliant one. I had covered most of the repatriations from the highway or the base since 2002, and I could certainly attest to the fact that the name Warmington came up with fit the stretch of road perfectly.

I've never claimed to be a strong writer, but the words just seemed to flow. And within 30 minutes I'd written a column calling for the renaming of the highway. It appeared in the July 20, 2007, editions of the *Cobourg Daily Star* and *Port Hope Evening Guide*. It was also posted on the papers' website. With the Internet being a portal to the world, it didn't take long for the column to also be picked up by a website called *Army.ca*.

Jay Forbes from London, Ontario, read my article online and took the idea to the next level by creating an online petition calling for the provincial government to officially rename the highway. "It's already called [the Highway of Heroes by] the thousands of people who line the bridges along the way, and it should be remembered as such in the future, for generations to gather and pay their respects," wrote Forbes on the petition site.

Forbes, who is a military history fan, said he'd never even been to Trenton for repatriation, but knew the meaning behind the highway. "People [go] to the bridges … to show [their] support, to let families know that our thoughts are with them … and that we support everyone in a uniform risking their life so we don't have to."

Looking back, Forbes said he never realized that so many people from all corners of the world would sign the petition. "I thought I'd get a few thousand [signatures] and the government would look at it and forget it. I spent my day off … randomly checking how many people signed it, and there [were] a few new names every minute … it was amazing to watch that number grow and grow. I'm really glad it happened, as I never expected it would. [The more than] 60,000 people who signed, and the media who reported it, all did something great." When the media got hold of the story, it garnered national attention. The number of names on the petition grew by thousands each week.

It was around this time, in August (2007) that I was assigned to cover the local Liberal Party barbeque in Brighton, Ontario. Lou Rinaldi is the Northumberland–Quinte West MPP. I'd known Lou on a professional basis since he was elected to office for our riding in 2003. He's always been very approachable on issues and very easy to talk to.

The following is the column that the author wrote that appeared in the *Cobourg Daily Star* and *Port Hope Evening Guide*, Friday, July 13, 2007, calling for the official naming of the highway:

HIGHWAY OF HEROES: LET'S MAKE IT OFFICIAL?

What began quietly, spontaneously in Northumberland County has now extended along the 172 kilometres of Highway 401 the Canadian soldiers killed in Afghanistan travel when repatriated. People standing on bridges have become a powerful expression of support by fellow Canadians for the soldiers and their families. We all pray there will be no need to come together again on a bridge to honour our fallen but, with the war in Afghanistan continuing, it's naive to think there won't be more casualties. Starting from the first procession for Sergeant Marc D. Leger, Corporal Ainsworth Dyer, Private Richard Green, and Private Nathan Smith, who were killed in April 2002, people have stood on bridges in Northumberland County.

I remember there were approximately 30 people, including two police officers saluting, on the Cranberry Road overpass in Port Hope watching the four hearses pass below. People had been watching the live coverage of the repatriation service at CFB Trenton on television and saw the hearses leave the base. Wanting to show their support, they spontaneously went to the bridge to wait for the procession to pass. Once a funeral procession leaves CFB Trenton, it heads west along Highway 401 to Toronto, then goes south on the Don Valley Parkway, ending at the Centre for Forensic Sciences on Grenville Street. To date, 66 fallen heroes have made the journey. Since then, on various bridges along the Highway 401 route, there have been people on bridges, sometimes fewer and, of late, more — many more.

Every person who stands on a bridge will tell you they experience a feeling like no other. As you wait, you talk with people who have been there before, who you've come to know. People smile, share feelings, talk about how many times they've stood on various bridges. It's a mix of pride and sadness. When the convoy of vehicles is seen approaching, murmurs in the crowd can be heard: "Here they come." There's silence as people get ready. Then, there's a sudden sea of arms waving Canadian flags, wanting to let the soldiers' family members in the procession know we are there for them, that we share their pain, and are proud to be Canadian. It's not unusual to see a soldier's hand waving a beret from a hearse, or a family member waving from a limousine to acknowledge the people on the bridge. Those waves are simple gestures, but more than enough for everyone on a bridge to know that, in that split second, everyone has made a connection to the people in those vehicles. Five years after the first procession went through Northumberland County, hundreds of people — farmers, businesspeople, firefighters, paramedics, police officers, Legion members, kids — pay tribute to the husbands, fathers, brothers, sisters, sons, and daughters who have given their lives for their country. People have lined bridges on cold winter evenings, rainy nights, and evenings when the sun is setting behind them. People have stood for hours on the bridges with their flags, with their homemade signs, some with red Support the Troops shirts. Everyone by now knows someone, or someone with a relation, who has been, or is, in Afghanistan. Canadians are not trying to conquer a country. They are trying to help the people of Afghanistan. Soldiers say we are there for the right reasons. They give firsthand accounts of the good Canada is doing. And out of tragic times come good things.

In his June 25 column in the Toronto *Sun*, Joe Warmington described people standing on Highway 401 bridges from Trenton to Toronto as a "Highway of Heroes" phenomenon. Since then, the name has taken on a life of its own. On July 10, I received an email from Cramahe Township firefighter Ken Awender. He, like so many, said it's beautiful that scores of people come out to pay tribute. Then he said something that was so simple, I wondered why it hadn't been thought of before. He suggested a petition should be started to rename the stretch of Highway 401 from Trenton to Toronto as "The Highway of Heroes." He's right. The section of highway is 172 kilometres long. It's already unofficially known as the Highway of Heroes. And it's time we find a way to make it official. It would be a fitting tribute to all the people who stand on the bridges, and for all the families who have lost loved ones. Most of all, it would honour our soldiers who die so others can live a better life.

At the barbeque, I asked him if he'd heard about the name Highway of Heroes, and we chatted briefly about the idea of officially renaming the highway. I explained to him that the movement was quickly growing and told him that whatever he could do to make it happen would be greatly appreciated, and, in short, that it would be the right thing to do. He agreed.

Rinaldi spoke with the minister of transportation, Donna Cansfield, a few days later about the idea: "It was out of the realm, but I remember talking to Donna about it. Donna is one of those folks who are very enthusiastic about things, and after we talked, she said, 'Let's do it.'"

A the time, Rinaldi thought the idea was going to take a lot more than just words to get off the ground, but he smiled at Cansfield and asked, "Where do we start?"

The author proudly displays one of the new Highway of Heroes shields, west of Port Hope, September 7, 2007.

While meeting with the transportation minister and the premier of Ontario, Dalton McGuinty, Rinaldi felt that, although the response was generally positive about the renaming of the highway, there remained some trepidation: "It was just prior to the 2007 provincial election. There were some worries within our party that this might look like some political gamesmanship. I remember saying 'I have no problem defending something when we do it for the right reasons.' Frankly I don't give a hoot what some people might think. For me it was for the right reason, and if somebody else [saw] it differently, more power to them."

Rinaldi characterizes the province as being a bit "guarded" about the idea, but there was no doubt it would move forward with the idea of the renaming. "I didn't have to argue very long," recalls Rinaldi. "But I did have to put [forward] a case."

Rinaldi recalls the first time he saw people standing along the bridges. It was in 2006, while he was driving home from Toronto. "At first I thought, when I saw the fire trucks and other emergency services, [that] there must have been an accident. Then I came across the same thing at the next bridge and I wondered what was going on — then [at] another bridge."

Just after he had passed Cobourg, he saw the lights of the procession approaching from the opposite side of the highway. "I obviously knew what was happening then. I pulled off to the side

THE ROUTE OF HEROES

The City of Toronto has designated its own name for the section of roadway that runs through the city to honour the fallen soldiers.

The Route of Heroes is a fifteen-kilometre stretch of roadway that runs from the exit of the Highway of Heroes (Highway 401) to the coroner's office in downtown Toronto.

Fort York Royal Canadian Legion member Peter Moon wrote to Mayor David Miller on May 31, 2007, requesting that the city re-name the Don Valley Parkway the "Parkway of Heroes." Moon stated in his letter that three provincial highways are now designated Veteran's Memorial Highways. He also pointed out that Toronto has only two significant public monuments honouring our veterans — the Cenotaph at Old City Hall and the new Memorial Wall at Queen's Park.

His argument was that a Veteran's Memorial Parkway would be a major and significant daily reminder for hundreds of thousands, even millions of people, whether they use it or not, of the debt of honour we owe to our veterans. "Without their sacrifices," he wrote, "Toronto could not be the city it is today."

But City Council thought that changing the name would confuse motorists. There was a concern that it would share a name with Highway 416, and that all maps and signs would have to be rewritten. They felt Torontonians might be slow to adopt the new name.

Legion representatives from across the Toronto area expressed their dissatisfaction, and the issue was then escalated to the District level, representing 9,000 members in 28 branches. In January 2009, a motion was put forward to pursue the movement, and a committee formed to develop a course of action.

One report indicated the Legion should abandon the request for the name change and consider asking the city to give the Don Valley Parkway a designation honouring veterans. It would still be called the Don Valley Parkway and no maps or directional signs would be changed. Signs would be erected identifying the roadway as the "Parkway of Heroes."

David Adamson, the District D chairman, said members felt that it was a different type of relationship once the procession left the provincial roadway and travelled on city-owned roads: "We wanted something distinctive to recognize the Toronto nature of the route."

At a meeting held on February 23, 2010, the city proposed to the Legion the wording "Route of Heroes." Toronto would be the first city in North America to adopt a street recognition of this kind for the fallen. One of the reasons given for the suggestion was the argument that "Route of Heroes" is more appropriate because the route the fallen take is an urban one after it leaves the Highway of Heroes and includes a number of city streets, not just the Don Valley Parkway.

On April 8, 2010, members of the Legion met again with City of Toronto staff and it was agreed that the name adopted would be the Route of Heroes. Signs would be posted where the procession leaves the provincial highway and enters onto city streets.

On June 7, 2010, the Route of Heroes was unveiled by dignitaries and members of the military in downtown Toronto. "It is important for the City of Toronto to pay tribute to these heroes, and providing signage along this part of a soldier's final journey is a fitting honour," said the mayor. "The courage and sacrifice demonstrated by all of our soldiers in conflicts around the world helps to ensure the freedoms that all Canadians enjoy today."

The Route of Heroes starts south of Highway 401, and runs along the Don Valley Parkway to the Bloor/Bayview exit ramp to Bloor Street. It then travels westbound on Bloor Street to Bay Street, where the procession heads south to the coroner's office on Grenville Street.

A sign just south of the Highway of Heroes measures approximately one metre by one metre: it is blue with a red poppy, and it reads "Lest We Forget." The top of the sign is curved, and "Route of Heroes" is written across it with a faint image of the Canadian flag.

Smaller versions of these signs have also been erected at major interchanges, at the exit at Bayview, and at the major intersections leading to the coroner's office.

of the road just east of Cobourg — which we now know you're not supposed to do. It was a feeling I've never experienced. I'm not sure who the soldier was, whether there was one, or two, or three, but it was very, very emotional."

As an immigrant, Rinaldi knows first-hand the sacrifices soldiers have made. "I think as you get older … you come to appreciate more what we have in this country, the best country in the world, by far." Rinaldi's father had been a prisoner of war during the Second World War, but had escaped and made it safely home. His father-in-law had fought for Canada in that same war. "And because of what they did, and the suffering they both [endured], I am able to be here today. So when you see these men and women who go to these missions, not just for Canada, but for the freedom of the world, to me it has a special meaning. I'm proud of my heritage, but even more proud to be Canadian."

Rinaldi describes the Highway of Heroes as "keeping the flame burning." As he see it, "Anytime you see those signs, [you] teach our up-and-coming generations what made Canada, what made Ontario, and what made our community. [It's] a good thing. And anything we can do to remember those people who are in the trenches that give us what we have today. Anything to support those men and women who are in the forces, to let them know we care, is an honourable thing…."

Premier Dalton McGuinty gave credit to Rinaldi for approaching him about the idea of the renaming of the highway: "It struck me as inherently sensible and important thing to do. When I heard about it, I thought, *let's find a way to make this happen — the sooner the better*."

Because the provincial Liberal Party was at a caucus retreat, McGuinty was able to discuss the idea with other members of his party, which isn't always the case: "You have to remember, a caucus consists of a group of

A SIGN OF REMEMBRANCE

Once it was announced in August 2007 that the section of the MacDonald-Cartier Freeway, or Highway 401, would be officially named the Highway of Heroes, members of the Ministry of Transportation worked with the Royal Canadian Legion to come up with a symbol for the roadway.

Head of Traffic Operations for the Ministry of Transportation (MTO) Roger DeGannes said it didn't take long to come up with the symbol that would be displayed on highway markers along the 172-kilometre stretch from Trenton to Toronto — a poppy.

DeGannes said it was simply a matter of removing the numbers *401* along with the word *Ontario* and installing the poppy with the words *Highway of Heroes* over top and *Support Our Troops* across the bottom.

MTO had to get permission from the Royal Canadian Legion to use the poppy on the highway marker because it is copyrighted by the Legion. Because there were so many requests to use the shield, the Province of Ontario has also copyrighted the Highway of Heroes markers.

The day before the official naming of the highway took place on September 13, 2007, MTO staff unveiled eleven large highway signs measuring two and a half metres tall by almost five metres wide.

In the days that followed, 106 route markers were placed on the on-ramps to the highway between Trenton and Toronto.

This portion of the Don Valley Parkway in Toronto was later renamed the "Route of Heroes." Seen here is the procession for Corporal Michael Starker, May 9, 2008.

people from varying backgrounds, from varying cultures and faiths and traditions — and from different parts of [Ontario]. So it's not that usual for us to find common ground so quickly."

But on the renaming of the section of highway, McGuinty said the response was overwhelmingly positive: "It was instantaneous. There was a profound understanding that this was the right thing to do."

The media was informed by the premier on August 24, 2007, that the 172-kilometre stretch of Highway 401 would be officially known as the Highway of Heroes, in honour of the fallen men and women who travel along it on their final journey. The section of the MacDonald-Cartier Freeway would not lose its designation, but signs along the route would be erected from Trenton to Toronto. Members of the provincial government then worked with members of the Royal Canadian Legion to design the appropriate logo for the signs.

McGuinty says that he feels both proud and humbled when he thinks of the fallen men and women who have travelled along the highway, but also of the people who line the bridges, who come out to support the families of the soldiers. "When I'm on the Highway of Heroes, I remember these young men and women, filled with a sense of purpose and idealism, placing themselves in harm's way."

Although the province did not have an official unveiling of the name, Rinaldi stood alongside firefighters, police, paramedics, Legion members, ordinary citizens, and other dignitaries to officially announce the

Branch 133 Legion members walking to the Ontario Street bridge in Cobourg, August 23, 2008, for the procession of Sapper Stephan Stock, Corporal Dustin Wasden, and Sergeant Shawn Eades.

Northumberland-Quinte West MPP Lou Rinaldi speaks at the official naming of the Highway of Heroes on the Cranberry Road overpass in Port Hope, September 7, 2007.

dedication on the afternoon of September 7, 2007, from the top of the overpass in Port Hope, the place where I took that first picture back in 2002.

Rinaldi remarked during his speech that it was my "tireless advocacy" and "personal passion" that brought the Highway of Heroes to his attention. "Today we honour the sacrifices of the brave men and women who so nobly and unselfishly have given the ultimate gift to defend the interests of democracy abroad," Rinaldi continued, his voice rising above the constant drone of vehicles passing under the bridge. "In dedicating this stretch of highway as the 'Highway of Heroes,' as a permanent memorial, we forever honour their legacy and pay tribute to those [to whom] we owe so much.

"For me, what is so touching is the outpouring of compassion for the fallen by hundreds and … thousands of their fellow citizens who come out to stand on overpasses like this to pay their heartfelt respect to those who are no longer with us, and to show their support for the families left behind. Every time a child passes, sees these signs, and asks, 'What is the Highway of Heroes?' it will be an opportunity to explain what real heroism is. What real heroism means to us all, and, most importantly, what

Patrol supervisor Steve Savage installs a Highway of Heroes shield at the on-ramp in the Municipality of Port Hope, September 10, 2007.

Cruickshank Construction Ltd. employees Steve Savage (up ladder, out of sight) and Paul Phillips unveil a large sign in Trenton, September 6, 2007, the day before the stretch of highway was officially unveiled as the Highway of Heroes.

the ultimate sacrifice of the truly heroic is. Our Highway of Heroes will forever stand as a testament of selflessness."

A day prior to the dedication, four signs had already been unveiled — one by the Don Valley Parkway, one at the Glen Miller Road exit in Trenton, and one on either side of Highway 115/35. Small markers were also erected at all on-ramps to the highway along the route.

Before the dedication, Lou Rinaldi had asked if I wanted to say a few words. I was working at the time and am definitely more comfortable behind the camera than in front, so I graciously declined. Besides, this wasn't about me; it was about the highway, and about doing the right thing.

During his speech, Lou again asked me to get up and share my thoughts. Reluctantly, I said a brief few words. As I have said many times, I wish that there wasn't a need for the highway at all, but I am grateful that it is there, grateful to the men and women who come out to honour the heroes, and mostly I'm grateful to those who serve their country with such bravery.

I had travelled to Trenton the day before the ceremony to watch the workers in the twilight hours unveil one of the new signs, and as the tarps were slowly removed from the large sign, the reality of what had been accomplished really hit home. I can't say I was happy, I know the cost involved, but I did feel satisfaction that our hard work had paid off. The highway and the memories and gratitude it invokes would now live on.

THOUGHTS FROM SOUTH OF THE BORDER

Before I travelled to Ontario last week, I thought of Canada like a neighbour who I had never really met before. Always next door, but I had never really had the time to introduce myself. When I came to Toronto to produce the Highway of Heroes story, I quickly learned how my unassuming neighbour was someone I greatly admired. To see Canadians' pride for their country and utter respect for their soldiers — it is evident everywhere you look — I was astounded by every symbol of salute and every form of recognition. I learned about the poppies; I even took a bag home with me to pass out to all my friends.

But it was the people wearing those poppies who especially struck me. And hearing about the Highway of Heroes made me wish we did something like that here in America.

When the spot ran, the responses were immediate. People told me tears were brought to their eyes. One colleague said that when the spot began, she was thinking, "Why do I care what Canadians are doing on our veterans day?" By the end of the piece, she had learned why, as tears streamed down her face.

I know why I now care about my once unknown neighbour. And I hope to visit again soon, when there is no longer a need for the Highway of Heroes.

— HILARY GUY, Producer, *NBC News*

It was a late summer afternoon when I was driving toward Toronto along the 401 from a vacation in the Charlevoix region of Quebec when I started noticing people standing on bridges and along the side of the highway with Canadian flags. At first I paid no attention; but by the fourth or fifth bridge I realized the crowds were getting larger and that something must be going on. It struck me as odd and interesting; and I started to wonder what it was all about. Had Canada won a summer hockey tournament? Was there are new holiday I hadn't heard of? Had there been a sudden outburst of spontaneous patriotism? (Well, not that! This was Canada, after all!)

When I arrived at my parents' home outside Toronto I mentioned what I'd seen, and my mother responded; "Yes, there is another soldier coming home today." They then explained the "Highway of Heroes." I couldn't get this compassionate grassroots phenomenon out of my head for the entire trip back to Chicago; and once back at work I pitched the story to my senior producers at *NBC Nightly News* with Brian Williams. I believe the folks at NBC were just as touched by the story as I was; and we set out to return to that stretch of highway between Trenton and Toronto. Our story ran nationally in the United States and was soon being forwarded via email throughout North America and around the world. The response I received was tremendous. Ordinary people taking the time to stand with those who'd made the ultimate sacrifice. It was a story of compassion and loss and honour and remembrance. It was a way for complete strangers to stand together and say "Lest We Forget"; and a way for the families of the fallen to see that they are not alone in their grief. Standing along the Highway of Heroes made me proud, not of my reporting, but of those anonymous Canadians who braved the elements to show their respect.

— KEVIN TIBBLES, Correspondent, *NBC Network News*, Chicago

NBC correspondent Kevin Tibbles speaks with Cobourg Fire Chief Al Mann, Deputy Chief Mike Vilneff, and Captain Todd Wilson, November 7, 2008.

CHAPTER 3 ❧ ONE HERO'S STORY: WAYNE JOHNSTON

A repatriation ceremony at CFB Trenton is something that has been perfected by the military since 2002.

The person who is in charge of the conduct and logistics of the repatriation is known as the Officer of Primary Interest (OPI), whose official title is Casualty Administration Officer. They are commonly referred to as repatriation officers.

Since the beginning of the war in Afghanistan, there have been four repatriation officers who have all been reservists. One of those repatriation officers was Captain Wayne Johnston.

Johnston has been in the Canadian Forces for nearly four decades. He started off as an infantryman and rose to the rank of Master Warrant Officer. He commissioned from the ranks as a logistics officer and has commanded a support squadron of engineers with the 32 Combat Engineering Regiment, with whom he went on an overseas tour. Since June 2010, he has been the officer commanding HQ Squadron of the Ontario Regiment (Royal Canadian Armoured Corps) in Oshawa, Ontario.

I've known Johnston for years, mostly through a charity he started, Wounded Warriors.ca. He created the

Captain Wayne Johnston, who has been in the Canadian Forces for nearly four decades, started the charity Wounded Warriors.ca after a soldier who he had recruited was critically wounded in Afghanistan.

organization after a soldier who he had recruited was critically wounded by a suicide bomber on September 18, 2006, while stationed in Afghanistan.

The bomber had ridden a bicycle into an area 30 kilometres west of Kandahar where there were both soldiers and Afghani civilians. The blast killed four Canadian soldiers and wounded 16 others. A large number of Afghanis were also injured, including several children. Twenty-year-old Sapper Mike McTeague was one of the soldiers who were critically injured. Johnston was the recruiting officer who had signed McTeague up a year earlier. Johnston had also known McTeague's father for more than 30 years, as they both served in the military.

McTeague was flown from Afghanistan to Germany, where he received life-saving treatment for his injuries, but his family was told that their son was not expected to survive. They were flown from their home in Orillia, Ontario, to Landsthurel Regional Medical Centre in Germany to be at their son's side. Johnston accompanied them, along with the padre of the 32 Combat Engineering Regiment, Captain Phil Ralph. It was here that Johnston began his three-year role as an assisting officer (AO), helping McTeague while he recuperated.

The Canadian Forces assigns an assisting officer to a soldier and his or her family in a situation where the soldier has incurred an operational or domestic injury, or to the family in the event of a death that occurs in theatre or domestically. The AO's job is to take away as much of the burden of stress as possible. "Basically, the AO's main job is to make sure the family doesn't have any additional stresses and that everything is looked after," Johnston told me from his home in Brooklin, Ontario. "In Mike's case, given the severity of his wounds, he and I worked toward setting him up for success [once he was] released from the Canadian Forces." Because the soldier's and the family's needs may be great, the AO is assigned to only one family at a time.

The emotional experience of seeing the cost of war, combined with witnessing McTeague's courageous struggle to survive and seeing all the other wounded soldiers lying in hospital beds, led Johnston to create the charity that he called the Sapper Mike McTeague Wounded Warrior Fund (*www.woundedwarriors.ca*).

While in the hospital in Germany, Johnston and McTeague's father both noticed that soldiers rarely had any personnel effects, such as entertainment items — even something as simple as a portable DVD player to help them pass the time while recovering. With Johnston's leadership, they set about remedying this oversight. Since that initial effort, the charity has blossomed, having raised close to $1.5 million in aid of Canadian soldiers. When I spoke with Johnston in 2009, he was extremely busy — he was acting as AO to McTeague and administering and raising funds in his role as president of the charity, in addition to performing his primary role as Casualty Administration Officer (CAO), a position that he accepted in 2008. I sat down with him to speak about the demands of both his jobs and the charity.

What immediately strikes you when you meet Johnston is his long, thin handlebar moustache. He is a collector of historical metal toy soldiers and owns a pristine 1966 Ford Mustang. His home in Brooklin, Ontario, is filled with military memorabilia.

"I was basically the orchestra conductor of a great team of Canadians bringing back the fallen," Johnston tells me. He uses the past-tense "was" because the toll that the war has taken on soldiers in the field has also taken its toll on him and on his fellow repatriation officers. He is now being treated for a form of Post-Traumatic Stress Disorder (PTSD).

Crew of a Globemaster aircraft salute during the repatriation of Sapper Mathieu Allard and Corporal Christian Bobbitt, CFB Trenton, August 4, 2009.

Johnston may have been the conductor, but he's quick to point out that there are many individuals who play equally important roles in bringing our heroes home. "In that team of great Canadians, I include 8 Wing in Trenton, the folks in theatre in Afghanistan, a number of Canadian Forces folks in Ottawa and Toronto, Assisting Officers, in-theatre escorts, peer escorts, Liaison Officers, civilians [such as] the terrific folks from MacKinnon and Bowes mortuary services, and the Ontario Provincial Police."

Another group of people he considers a key part of the team are the people who stand along the bridges each time a fallen soldier returns home. He is very appreciative of each and every one: "I cannot tell you the solace it brings a mother or a father, a husband or a wife, when they bring their loved one home and they travel down those horrible 172 kilometres. It lets them know the nation cares. I've spoken to a number of mothers of the fallen, and they see the mothers with their kids on the bridges and they make this connection."

A number of people stand along the fence line at CFB Trenton watching the repatriation ceremonies for Private Demetrios Diplaros, Corporal Mark Robert McLaren, and Warrant Officer Robert John Wilson, December 8, 2008.

Johnston's son is with the 3rd Battalion of the Princess Patricia's Canadian Light Infantry. "If I were to lose my son, I'd need every person in Canada to help me through that day."

While he says being a repatriation officer has been the best job he's had since being a member of the Canadian Forces, "it's also ripped my soul from me. I'm not the person I was." Despite the cost, Johnston says he is privileged to have been able to perform these duties.

He explains the process when a soldier is killed in theatre. Canadian Expeditionary Forces Command (CEFCOM) in Ottawa, which is responsible for overseas operations, is the first to be notified, followed by Land Force Central Area Ontario. They in turn notify Johnston. "[T]he phone would usually ring around 3:00 a.m. [I'm] a 52-year-old man [who's] afraid of phone calls after 10:00 p.m.," says Johnston. "It just got to be [that] I'd say 'How many, and where are they from?'"

And then the arduous task begins. "There is a lot of coordination. Everything from the notification team going out, starting up a situation report ... notifying people in the governor general's office and many others." Johnston informs me that the situation report contains essentially a "military resume" of the fallen soldier and as well lists the timing of the arrivals, what they call the scheme of manoeuvre, and the names of the family, friends, and VIPs attending the repatriation and the funeral. The file remains active until interment, keeping those who need to know informed.

Staring out his kitchen window, Johnston tells me that the "demons" of the job finally got to him. "I never knew any of them [the soldiers], but I sure miss them.... You get to know a lot about them. You get to know the family dynamics. You see these folks at the worst moment of their lives. You deal with many people during the process.... [It's] a very sad time indeed. It's odd, but in some strange way I feel like a family member.... I mourn each and every one, every day. I have been privileged [to work] with assisting officers, who help the family in so many ways.... They embody the very essence of 'service before self.' Each and every AO, for both the fallen and [the] wounded, should be officially recognized by the nation."

For obvious reasons, the military does not release the names of the fallen until all the immediate family have been notified. "Being in Canada, many families are spread apart.... We've had to wait because family members are sometimes travelling. I'm pulling and pushing the AOs to get information — calling the staff of the Governor General, the Minister of Defence, and the Chief of the Defence Staff [CDS]. The minister and the CDS then call the next of kin.... Those calls are unique in the way [that] we, as a nation, handle our fallen. The minister and CDS, to me, demonstrate real courage, kindness, and decency ... I cannot imagine how difficult it is to make that call."

Usually within three to four days the fallen soldier is on his or her way home from Afghanistan. "There are a whole bunch of things that have to happen," explains Johnston. First, a ramp ceremony takes place at Kandahar Airfield (KAF) for each fallen soldier. Canadians and other coalition forces line the tarmac as the soldier is carried by his or her comrades to the plane.

Canadian soldiers at KAF are notified the day of the ramp ceremony. Other coalition forces stand shoulder to shoulder with the Canadians, paying their respects to the fallen. Soldiers at KAF have often said that Canada should be proud, not only of how we treat our fallen when they return home but also of how they are treated before leaving Afghanistan. Soldiers from other countries have told their Canadian counterparts that Canada is a shining example of how the military should treat their fallen. During Canadian ramp ceremonies held at KAF, there is often a much larger turnout than for those of other countries.

When the fallen are returned home to CFB Trenton, the aircraft used to transport them can be either an Airbus or a Globemaster. Johnston explains that in the past a C-130 Hercules would fly the fallen to Camp Mirage in the United Arab Emirates (UAE), then on to Germany. Since the Canadian Forces have recently been asked to leave the UAE, and Camp Mirage is no longer in existence, he was unclear at the time what would happen in the future. Once they have landed in Germany, the flight crews are usually changed before they begin the last leg of the journey to Trenton.

Up until the summer of 2007, repatriations at CFB Trenton occurred during all hours of the day and evening. Lights were set up at the base if needed. When the procession would pass along the highway during the evening hours, people on the bridges would hold lights or lanterns to let the families of the fallen know that they were watching over them on their journey.

The time was eventually switched to 2:00 p.m. for all repatriations, primarily out of respect for the families, many of whom had to travel great distances to attend, explains Johnston. Having it at a specific hour allows them time to collect themselves in the morning before travelling to the base in Trenton. Another benefit to having the repatriations take place at the same time is that it allows those who wish to turn out to pay their respects from the bridges and overpasses along the route to do so more easily.

Soldiers carry the flag-draped casket of Lieutenant Andrew Richard Nuttall off the Globemaster aircraft, CFB Trenton, December 28, 2009.

Chief of the Defence Staff Rick Hillier speaks with the citizens gathered at the fence line at CFB Trenton as they wait for the plane to land before the repatriation of Major Raymond Ruckpaul. In the photo, Hillier is looking at a Canadian flag with all the names of the fallen soldiers on it. September 2, 2007.

Fallen Canadian soldiers have been repatriated since the days of the peace support mission in Bosnia. "To be sure, General Rick Hillier brought some transparency, and that's a good thing," says Johnston.

MacKinnon and Bowes Ltd. has been the mortuary service in charge of bringing each fallen soldier home from Afghanistan since 2002. In fact, MacKinnon and Bowes Ltd. has been repatriating Canadian soldiers since Bosnia. They have also handled the affairs of a Canadian diplomat and a journalist who were killed during the

Afghanistan mission, as well as those of the two RCMP officers who died in the earthquake that hit Haiti on January 12, 2010.

Johnston says there was some initial debate in the case of Michelle Lang, the journalist who was killed, but because she had died alongside several soldiers, it was decided that she should be brought back with them.

"Two gentlemen [who served] with the RCMP died in service of the nation [while on] a United Nations mission," he says, referring to the two officers killed in Haiti. "The criteria would be [that if one dies] in service

ABOVE: *Editor-in-chief of the* Calgary Herald, *Lorne Motley, composes himself after paying his respects to journalist Michelle Lang at CFB Trenton, during her repatriation on January 3, 2010, alongside four soldiers.*

LEFT: *Royal Canadian Mounted Police members and others salute as the hearses carrying RCMP officers Sergeant Mark Gallagher and Chief Superintendent Doug Coates leave CFB Trenton on January 22, 2010, on their way to Toronto.*

A soldier salutes at the repatriation for Michelle Lang, Sergeant George Miok, Corporal Zachery McCormack, Sergeant Kirk Taylor, and Private Garrett Chidley. CFB Trenton, January 3, 2010.

of the nation [they should be given the honour of repatriation] ... Michelle Lang was definitely in service of the nation."

Johnston says MacKinnon and Bowes offer an "extremely unique service." Although they are not a funeral home, Johnston calls them "logisticians to funeral homes." From the moment a Canadian soldier is killed, MacKinnon and Bowes is a part of the service, and they send a representative overseas to assist the Canadian Forces personnel with preparation and transport of the remains. Johnston points out that, unlike the U.S. military, the Canadian military does not have a mortuary service. "They [MacKinnon and Bowes] prepare the fallen. The family makes the selection of the casket, but that casket will be shipped from MacKinnon and Bowes."

After the autopsy, the fallen soldiers are placed in the care of MacKinnon and Bowes and prepared for their final journey by road or air to the family's funeral home of choice. "I consider them a de facto part of the Canadian Forces in this process. They treat our fallen as if they were their own [family]." They look after the family, providing intimate support at a most difficult time, and organize everything from the number of limousines to booking the hotel rooms in Toronto for the families and friends of the fallen.

"Trenton is the hub of Canadian air transport, [and] 8 Wing is the busiest wing in the country," Johnston tells me. Combined, there are nearly 4,000 people who work on the 833-hectare base, including regular army personnel, reserve personnel, and civilians. Each day, there are as many as 15 passenger and cargo planes taking off and landing at the base. "They are sustaining various missions, not just Afghanistan, but others, including Haiti. That's where all our major strategic air transport lifts are."

Because the aircraft carrying the fallen land at the nation's largest air base, they must then be transported to the coroner's office in Toronto. "[T]he coroner of Ontario is legally bound by Canadian law [to] treat [a death in theatre] as a violent death," Johnston says. He adds that the military calls this process "lessons learned." In other words: What can the military learn from a death in theatre? How can they better protect their people in the future?

Johnston explains. "We have learned a lot of things. We [now] have better protection, body armour, and vehicle protection."

The procession as it travels along the highway is led by several police vehicles, followed by the hearse, then the limousines carrying the family members. Johnston says there is no limit on the number of family members that may attend the ceremony, but that the question has come up many times.

"There are criteria .... Generally, immediate relatives [attend], including aunts, uncles, and cousins under the age of 16." But it's not only "blood relatives" who are allowed on the tarmac for the repatriation. "If there is a close family friend or a neighbour ... it will be allowed."

Johnston points out that this is one of the reasons why AOs are so important. They are there to help coordinate all of these details on behalf of the grieving family. The "orchestra," as Johnston refers to it, needs to work together. On the worst day that any family can endure, everything must go smoothly, and knowing how many members of a soldier's family are attending is important, even when it comes to something as simple as the catering inside the terminal for the family and dignitaries.

A simple message on the Deer Park Road overpass states "We Will Remember Them." Members of the Municipality of Port Hope Fire Department salute as the procession for Private Demetrios Diplaros, Corporal Mark Robert McLaren, and Warrant Officer Robert John Wilson passes, December 8, 2008.

In the end, it is about respect and support, and Canada has always done it right. "We've never pushed back on numbers," says Johnston. He recalls one situation where the parents of an In-Theatre Escort, there to accompany a fallen soldier, drove 18 hours to CFB Trenton just to see their son. Though the parents weren't on "the list," Johnston knew it was important for them to see their son. "There was no way I was going to come between … a mother and son and I knew how important it was to [them] both. She gave her son a hug … to make sure he was alright. I got some push-back, but I thought, *that mom and dad drove a long way to see their boy*. To this day I stand by that decision. Frankly, it was one of the few happy moments I remember during a repat."

As Canadians, Johnston points out, we all have differing views, but when it comes to honouring our fallen, the Highway of Heroes is something unique and magical: "I call it quintessential Canadian patriotism — without a doubt. And it's a horrible thing to be the envy of the world — quiet, unassuming, but oh so effective."

Johnston says that a simple, unorganized, spontaneous outpouring of respect is something Canada is known for throughout the world: "It's the coldest day in February, and people take their children to show them the sacrifice that one family made.… When a family from Quebec sees the Canadian flag side by side with the fleur de lis, being waved from Port Hope or Cobourg, that says everything. We as Canadians feel their loss."

In the decades to come, Johnston says, whatever historians write about the Afghanistan mission, about "the rights and the wrongs, the concept of the Highway of Heroes will be one of our defining moments, when the nation came together through horrible individual tragedies."

Johnston continues: "Mothers and fathers should never [have to] bury their sons or daughters. Sons bury their fathers. But unfortunately, in war, fathers bury sons. I do believe, if there is anything good that's come out of this mission and these tragic losses, the Highway of Heroes has redefined us as a nation, and given us back some pride that I don't think we knew we had."

In the end, it's all about providing support, dignity, and respect.

Six hearses approach the Burnham Street overpass in Cobourg, July 8, 2007.

CHAPTER 4 ❦ ONE FAMILY'S STORY: PRIVATE MILLER

Over the years, a few parents have been gracious and allowed me to interview them. I've sat with them, I've cried with them, but I could never imagine what it's like to lose a child. I've listened to proud parents telling stories of their children growing up. Most times they've said it was a calling that brought their son or daughter to join the military, many at a very young age.

I've always felt that the Highway of Heroes is a way of letting families know that we, as Canadians, will never forget their sacrifice, that they are not alone, and that, although those wounds will never fully heal, we share in their grief as a country.

From their home in Sudbury, the family of Private Andrew Miller, 21, spoke to me through the mixed emotions of pain and pride that they feel about the loss of their son. Although the Millers agreed to speak to me, their story is echoed by family members of many other fallen soldiers across the country.

Private Miller and Master Corporal Kristal Giesebrecht, 34, were killed by an improvised explosive device while travelling with other soldiers who were on their way to defuse another IED that had been planted in the doorway of a home on June 26, 2010. Both were medics based out of Petawawa, Ontario: Miller with the 2 Canadian Field Ambulance and Giesebrecht with the 1 Canadian Field Ambulance.

Miller's mother, Wendy, told me that she loves talking about her son — he is her favourite subject. The adventurous boy was born on New Year's Eve, 1988. Wendy was just 18 at the time. She remembers being thrilled that she had had a boy and says she tried to raise him the best way she knew how: "He lived large, as people say."

She told me that her son was destined to be a soldier all his life, and that she knew in her heart that he would die as one.

At the time of his death, Andrew also left behind his fiancée, Staci Jessup, his stepfather, Ray Ealdama, who had been a father to him since he was 12 years old, a sister, Emma (now age 14), and two other children from Ealdama's first marriage — sister Jordan (18) and brother Justin (16).

Since he was about seven years old, Wendy remembers her son wanting to join the military. While other boys had pictures of girls or cars hanging in their rooms as they got older, her son had recruiting posters and camouflage netting. Andrew's stepfather, Ray, had been in the Canadian Forces for several years. For the past two decades he has been a member of the Greater Sudbury Police Service, and holds the rank of sergeant.

"Andrew grew up with the military as a foundation, and I tried to raise him with that standard," says Ray. "He always knew what he wanted — and he worked for that."

Ray remembers going for walks in the woods with his son, with Andrew wearing military gear — a hunting rifle, the boots, the camouflage jacket. So it was no surprise when, at the age of 16, Andrew came to his parents and asked them to sign the papers so that he could join up.

Ontario Provincial Police officers stop westbound traffic along the Highway of Heroes as the procession for Private Andrew Miller and Master Corporal Kristal Giesebrecht prepares to merge onto the highway. June 29, 2010.

Because Andrew was nearsighted, he was not accepted for the infantry. "So we said, 'Why don't you do the next best thing — be a medic,' and that's what he did," says Ray. When Andrew was younger he used to tear apart the first-aid kits and play with all the different items in them. If he couldn't join the infantry, being a medic would be a perfect fit. "He wanted to follow in my footsteps," says Ray.

In 2007 and 2008, Ray was seconded from the Greater Sudbury Police to Afghanistan as part of the United Nations Police Contingent, deployed to train Afghan police officers and help set up security zones and build police stations. He was ranked as a colonel and went on many patrols. Posted to the Kandahar Provincial Reconstruction Team (KPRT) out of Camp Nathan Smith in Kandahar City, Ray patrolled alongside Afghan police officers in the surrounding District of Kandahar.

"Andrew was very jealous." Ray's voice trails off as he reminisces about his son. "He was a great son, and we shared many hobbies and interests .... I don't have that anymore."

After lobbying to go to Afghanistan, Andrew was finally accepted. He left CFB Petawawa on May 15, 2010. It was something he'd been looking forward to since he began dreaming of the military life. His dream would last only 43 days.

The determination of Andrew and other soldiers to help the people of Afghanistan to lead a better life was evident, in part due to the sheer courage demonstrated, not only by the fallen, but by each soldier who passed through the relative safety of the compound. Kandahar Air Field, or KAF, is regularly shelled by the Taliban. There is not only danger outside the wire, but inside as well.

Just six days into his tour, Andrew was hit by shrapnel from a rocket attack at his first Forward Operating Base (FOB). He sustained a leg injury from the flying debris and was transported to Role 3 Hospital in KAF, where he was stitched up. He was offered time away in Germany to convalesce, but opted to stay in Afghanistan.

Wendy tells me she had a rule: her husband and her son couldn't be out of the country at the same time. It was too much for her to worry about — to even contemplate. "My role was [to ensure that] one was in and one out of the country, because I couldn't handle it." Although she admits she was worried when her husband left in November 2007, when Andrew left it was different. "I had a feeling when I left my husband at the airport that he was coming back. Whereas, when I put Andrew on the bus to go to Trenton, I told my husband, I whispered in his ear, that he wasn't coming home."

Ray told her to not think like that, but "you just kind of know, as a mother," says Wendy. Just over a month later, she was told that Andrew was dead. It is a day Wendy goes through in her head again and again.

It was about two o'clock in the afternoon, and Wendy was at work at the local department store, where she is the manager, when her husband walked in with a military chaplain and another soldier. Ray was visibly distraught, and, just looking at him, Wendy knew in her heart what had happened.

"I went into mother military mode right away because it was too much for me to handle," she says. "My husband hugged me and I cried, and cried, and cried."

The notification officer was a major from the 49th field Artillery (RCA) reserve unit out of Sault Ste. Marie. Wendy said she could tell he was shaken up after he gave

The procession carrying Private Andrew Miller and Master Corporal Kristal Giesebrecht proceeds over the final bridge on Glen Miller Road in Trenton before entering onto the Highway of Heroes. A number of paramedics from across the Province of Ontario attended the ceremony.

her the devastating news. "I grabbed his face and said, 'it's okay. I am not angry at you. I don't wish this job on you. It's probably the hardest thing you've done in your life.' I kept saying to him, 'I don't hate you.'"

It is standard practice that each family of a fallen soldier is provided with the services of a chaplain and an assisting officer, whose job it is to explain all the details and what to expect over the coming days. Every family I've spoken with has told me that these officers were a tremendous support to them, assisting with everything from dealing with the media to helping with funeral arrangements.

Wendy left work and drove home with her husband and the military personnel. Along the way, thoughts raced through her head and she says she felt more and more numb. "I cried a little bit, but your mind is going and going. I said 'I don't want this sugar-coated, I'm his mother, I need to know what happened and I know you have the details.'" The soldiers explained to them that Andrew had been killed by an IED. "When they said he didn't feel anything, that was a relief to me."

After calling a few close friends, the couple arrived home and began talking about the funeral arrangements. Ray says he knew where Andrew was going to be stationed when he was in Afghanistan, but Wendy and Andrew had kept some information from him: "I didn't know that he was going to be a designated driver for his medical section."

"Andrew disclosed to me his main role in theatre would be an Armoured Bison Ambulance driver," Wendy admits. Ray remembers telling Andrew that the most dangerous thing in Afghanistan was driving from point A to point B. Subsequently, Andrew and his mother had told Ray that he was going to be attached to a platoon patrolling on foot, so Ray wouldn't worry as much.

"I was furious when I initially found out the news that he had been driving the whole time. Both Andrew and Wendy kept that from me because I had been in three motorized patrols while deployed that had been subjected to IED attacks."

Only two weeks before his death, Wendy remembers getting a call from her son from Afghanistan. They were open about everything in their lives, and even spoke of what would happen if he was killed. "He said he didn't want to be viewed, even if he was viewable, because it's not him, and he didn't want to upset his sister. He didn't want his fiancée to see him, and I'm glad."

She asked her son what he would want her to do if the worst happened. "He just asked me to take care of things. He said, 'Make sure Emma goes to school.'"

Andrew told his mother he wanted everyone to be treated equally and not [to] fight over his belongings.

"When I think of Andrew, I always think of him when we [were] saying goodbye. I think of when we were in my house and drinking a beer and [when he was outside] walking with me, smoking."

As next of kin, Wendy said one of the main things she has tried to do is to make sure Andrew's fiancée, Staci, is taken care of. "That was his wish."

The Miller/Ealdama family were told what they could expect in terms of the repatriation at CFB Trenton in the days ahead, and Wendy could not say enough about the assisting officer who had been assigned to the family. In her words, he was "truly amazing." Tragically, so many families have had to deal with the final journey of their loved one that the people involved have become expert at executing the process in a seamless and timely fashion. Everything is made as easy for the families as is humanly possible.

Wendy said she wanted everything to be bright and cheery. "I had a few requests.... I didn't want people wearing dark colours. I wanted them to wear red. I was welcoming my son home." But she knew, her family knew, and the country knew that this wasn't the way she wanted her son to come home.

Just two days after they had received the terrible new about Andrew, as the family was about to board the plane to Toronto, Wendy said the reality of the situation suddenly became overwhelming. She knew that if she boarded that plane, there was no turning back — she would have to attend the ceremony, and she didn't want to. Everything just became all too real at that point.

"I didn't want to go get him ... that was my son. I couldn't get on the airplane. I started screaming in the airport in Sudbury. I scared everyone, until my sister ... told them who I was."

Everyone has the greatest compassion for a fallen soldier's family, and this day was no different. Staff at the airport told Andrew's family to take as long as they wanted to board the plane. When the flight finally arrived at Pearson Airport in Toronto, Wendy had to be supported from both sides as she left the flight.

As the family left the terminal, they were met by a limousine with Canadian flags on the front. Wendy says that this gesture is usually only reserved for two dignitaries: the queen and the governor general. The family was then driven to a hotel, in preparation for the journey to CFB Trenton. But Andrew's mother couldn't sleep. She'd never been to Canada's largest military air base, but she knew what this trip meant.

On the morning of June 29, Wendy remembers getting ready, dressing up in order to welcome her son back home. "I put my hair exactly the way he would want me to. We gathered all the kids together and told them 'this is going to be awful, spectacular, and devastating all at the same time … you'll never forget this.'" She remembers Emma saying that it looked as if her mother was getting married.

Before they left for CFB Trenton, Wendy and Ray had a private moment together at the hotel, reassuring each other and trying to find the strength to get through the day.

The family and close friends were then picked up by numerous limousines from their hotel and driven from Toronto to Trenton. As they rode along, Wendy says it was all very surreal. The trip lasted just over an hour. Inside the car, few words were spoken, and the family held one another for support.

When they pulled into CFB Trenton from County Road 2, they were met by the Military Police officers, who saluted the line of limousines. Wendy said it was at that point that it all became "real" again.

Military Police salute as the hearse carrying Private Tyler William Todd leaves CFB Trenton to begin its trip down the Highway of Heroes to the coroner's office in Toronto, April 14, 2010.

The family was then escorted inside the terminal, where they were greeted by numerous dignitaries. Governor General Michaëlle Jean normally attended each repatriation ceremony, being flown in approximately one hour before the service began. But unfortunately, on this particular day, the governor general was out of the country. Numerous other dignitaries and politicians were there, and offered condolences and hugs to the family.

"I hugged every person I met," said Wendy. "I just thought, my son is gone, and I'm going to hug you." The wife of Chief of the Defence Staff Walt Natynczyk told her she was a good military mother.

Defence Minister Peter MacKay and Chief of the Defence Staff General Walt Natynczyk walk onto the tarmac, at the repatriation ceremony for Corporal Joshua Caleb Baker, February 15, 2010.

Over the last several years, aircraft carrying the fallen have touched down at the base at precisely 2:00 p.m. If there is more than one fallen soldier aboard, rank dictates who is brought off the plane first.

"I could feel the excitement of Andrew. It was almost like he was saying, 'I'm home, I'm home,'" says Wendy.

Before the ceremony, each family is asked if they would like to permit media on the tarmac to photograph the repatriation from a distance. In a case where more than one soldier is being repatriated, only one family has to decline for the media not to be allowed on the base. If this is the case, reporters and photographers must watch the ceremony from the fence line, outside the base, along with the other members of the public.

Although Private Miller's family consented to the media being allowed on the base, the family of Master Corporal Giesebrecht declined. Though she respects the decision made by the Giesebrecht family, Wendy thinks that the public has a right to see the homecomings: "This child, this boy, gave his life.... You don't push that to the side." Of course, the wishes of the families in these circumstances come first. It is solely their decision, and the vast majority of those in the general public and the media respect that.

Clutching flowers, families and close friends of both soldiers walked out onto the tarmac from the terminal. Personnel from CFB Trenton, along with the bearer party and a piper, were already in place for the ceremony.

A lone bagpiper waits on the tarmac for the flag-draped caskets of Corporal Thomas Hamilton, Private John Curwin, and Private Justin Jones to come off the Globemaster aircraft, CFB Trenton, December 16, 2008.

Walking out, Wendy remembers helping her husband, who was having a more difficult time: "It was absolutely mind-boggling ... when you walk out onto the tarmac and there are hundreds of people there, but you can't hear anything. It was so silent."

Ray says he spoke with Andrew after his son had been a casket-bearer for one of his stepfather's good friends, a man Ray had served with in Afghanistan, who was killed in May of 2008. Corporal Michael Starker had been a medic and had died very close to where Andrew was later killed.

"I had asked Andrew if he would welcome Mike home for me to Canadian soil," said Ray, who had to remain in Afghanistan. "He petitioned his superiors, and they

Just outside the gates of CFB Trenton, a Legion Honour Guard stands while the procession for Corporal Michael Starker proceeds along the streets of Trenton, May 9, 2008. Private Andrew Miller was one of the soldiers who carried Corporal Starker's casket off the plane that day.

allowed him to carry Mike off the plane during [the] repatriation in Trenton. Little did I know then that we'd be carrying Andrew off the same plane only a few short years later."

Wendy promised her son that she wouldn't "lose it" if the worst ever happened. "I said, 'Andrew, I'd be very dignified and be very proud. I'd lose it behind the scenes.'"

Andrew had answered, "Yeah, I kind of figured so."

After everyone was in place, and the two families of the soldiers were standing in a line parallel to the aircraft, Master Corporal Giesebrecht's flag-draped casket was carried off the plane by a bearer party, who then walked slowly to one of the two hearses waiting on the tarmac.

"I stood there with my flower and watched as Krystal's body went by, and I cried for her."

Then came the realization that her son was next. "I kept saying, *he's not in there, it's not him*. And then the bagpipes start[ed]. You just cry and cry and cry."

Gripping one another for support, all clutching flowers, Wendy, Ray, and their children slowly walked over and gazed at the back of the hearse. Wendy says, "[I] wanted Andrew to know I wasn't angry. Because I know he would have been thinking, *My God, my poor mom, what have I done to my mom?*"

Wendy put her left hand on the casket and whispered, "It's Mom. You're home, Andrew, and I'm going to be okay. I'm not angry, and I'm proud of you." She and her family then stood off to the side while other family members and close friends placed flowers in the hearse, embraced, and shed tears for the young man who'd lived a lifetime in just 21 years. The family then slowly walked away, and the driver closed the back door.

Both families were then escorted back to their limousines for the ride to the coroner's office in Toronto. As base personnel saluted, the hearses carrying the two fallen soldiers and the escort officers drove off the tarmac, followed closely by the limousines with the families inside.

From the base, family members could see the throngs of people lining the street on the other side of the fence. "All of a sudden, we go through the gates of the base and there are thousands of people there. My

BEARER PARTIES

The bearer party slowly carries the fallen soldier's casket on their shoulders — base personnel on one side, dignitaries and family members on the other. Depending on which type of aircraft brings the soldier home, the casket is either carried off the back ramp of a Globemaster, or lowered into the arms of soldiers from an Airbus. The bearer party then carries their comrade to a hearse parked a short distance away on the tarmac. The casket is always covered with the red and white flag — the flag of a grateful nation that mourns each loss.

Depending on the wishes of the family, either a bugler or a bagpiper plays a lament while the soldier is transported to the waiting vehicle. As the soldiers reach the hearse, they turn and lower the casket from their shoulders, before gently placing the casket inside. Then, with one final salute, the bearer party marches off the tarmac.

ESCORT OFFICERS

An escort officer accompanies each fallen soldier from Afghanistan, and stays with them right up until the time of the funeral. The escort officer is to be of a rank no lower than that of the deceased. When the EOs arrive at Trenton, they wear their camouflage uniforms, which they continue to wear throughout the process, right up until the soldier is interred.

Several people place Canadian flags along Hamilton Road in Trenton. This is done for each repatriation, so that, as the procession reaches the crest of the hill, the people in the cars encounter a sea of Canadian flags flying from the street poles and guard rails.

mouth dropped, and I said, 'Oh, my God, they're here for us, for Andrew.'" At that point, Wendy told everyone to roll down their windows: "They came to say thank you. They came to see Andrew."

As Wendy remembers that day, she starts to break down. It was such an incredibly emotional time, and months later the wound is still fresh. "I wanted to thank everyone," she says. "You're so heartbroken, but you're so proud. Andrew would have given you the shirt off his back, and for him to be welcomed home by everybody was an honour. My son was a hero, and I was so proud."

As they continued around the perimeter of the base, firefighters from the base stood alongside their equipment, saluting; other people were holding flags; there were children and veterans — people from every walk of life were there to support the families.

As the procession passed a subdivision, mailbox after mailbox had Canadian flags sticking out of them, and residents came to the end of the driveways and stood silently watching the procession pass by. The connection between the grieving families and the people along the road was evident. Each time a fallen soldier comes home, tears are shed, not only by family and friends of the fallen, but by complete strangers — those who have come to show their support, to grieve, and to let the family know they are with them.

Wendy says she noticed every one of them, but the ones who stood out the most for her were her son's extended family — the paramedics. "It was phenomenal," she tells me. Bridge after bridge, dozens of individuals from the emergency services had come out to show their respect for her son. "I couldn't believe it."

Although it takes more than an hour to travel the route from CFB Trenton to the coroner's office in Toronto, Wendy said it felt like only 20 minutes. "I was just awestruck," she remembers. "People were in the fields, and they were far away, and I'd wave, and they'd wave back to me. I wanted to acknowledge them. They took a day off work, or they know someone, or their dad was in World War One or Two. Just because they're Canadian and they wanted to say thank you. It was [as if they were saying] he's home, the heroes are home."

A couple stand at the end of their driveway as the procession for Private Demetrios Diplaros, Corporal Mark Robert McLaren, and Warrant Officer Robert John Wilson passes by on Hamilton Road in Trenton, December 8, 2008. Tragically, this brought the number of Canadian soldiers killed in Afghanistan to 100.

Traffic was at a standstill on the Don Valley Parkway northbound as the procession was passing by in the southbound lanes when Wendy noticed a woman had gotten out of her car and was holding her hand over her heart. "As cars were slowing down on the Don Valley, one lady [who] I said thank you to said, 'No. Thank you.' She said 'you gave the ultimate sacrifice.'"

As the procession exited the parkway onto the streets of downtown Toronto, businessmen and women were waving Canadian flags as they stood outside the buildings.

As they turned onto Grenville Street for the final few metres before reaching the coroner's office, Wendy says there were rows of people lining the street, along with fire trucks, police cars, and police on horseback.

"My husband was so upset." Wendy says. "[H]e was upset because he was so proud." Ray then leaned out the window, showing the people a picture of Andrew and telling them, "This is my son."

"You want everyone to know, this is my son. Andrew Miller is my son," says Wendy.

After the autopsy was performed, the coroner released Private Miller's body, which was met by the family and driven to Sudbury by police escort. It was July 1 — Canada Day.

"We laughed because Canada Day was better than Christmas Day for Andrew. We are all very proud Canadians," Wendy says. The Millers have four Canadian flags and a Support Your Troops flag on their front lawn, and, since their son's death, members of Ray's police platoon have also planted a maple tree here in honour of Andrew.

To show her support for the troops, every Friday, even before her son died, Wendy would wear red. She now wears the Silver Cross of Honour medal presented to her by the Surgeon General. "I tell people [that] my son was awarded this because he was a hero for our country."

Miller was buried with full military honours on July 3 in his hometown of Sudbury. Wendy told me that Governor General Michaëlle Jean phoned her after the family had arrived home after the repatriation and spoke to her like a mother would speak to a daughter. "It was so comforting. She knew exactly how I felt."

The Chief of the Defence Staff, General Walt Natynczyk, had called the family before the repatriation to offer his condolences but to inform them that he would be unable to attend because he was tasked to be with Queen Elizabeth during her visit. Wendy said it was the first time in the history of Canada that soldiers had been repatriated when the queen was on Canadian soil. But to the family's surprise, General Natynczyk walked through the doors of the base the day of the repatriation. "He said the queen told him to come," explains Ray.

The queen herself sent a fax through the military to the family, conveying her sympathies. Prime Minister Stephen Harper also called to personally offer his condolences.

Since Andrew's death, his family has received many phone calls, letters, and emails of support. One soldier emailed Wendy to tell her that she felt that Andrew was watching over them while they were in Afghanistan. "She emailed me saying she was supposed to turn right, but that 'Miller kept telling me to turn left.'" They later discovered that a roadside bomb was buried on the roadway to the right.

Wendy said her love and admiration for her son's bravery will last a lifetime. "You're looking at people who are willing to lay down their lives for this country, and he did. And I know, if he was alive, he'd do it all over again."

The pain of losing her son left her inconsolable; but travelling along the Highway of Heroes left her with something else. "I miss him, but along the highway was different. If we were so sad, then why [were] we screaming and thanking people."

Looking back, Wendy said the ride down the highway felt like a hero's welcome. It was something the fallen soldiers deserved after serving their country, and she sees it

The procession carrying the remains of Private Andrew Miller and Master Corporal Kristal Giesebrecht crests the final bridge on Glenn Miller Road in Trenton, which is lined with emergency service workers, before heading onto the Highway of Heroes for the journey to Toronto, June 29, 2010.

as an extremely important part of the healing process for families. "We owe it to them. It helped me out in an amazing way. It's extremely important for us to have that — as a country, and as a family. It's the least we can do for these men and women. That was the starting point for the rest of my life … to be proud."

Wendy displays a card and picture of her son and a large Support the Troops ribbon at the store where she works. When people ask if it is her son she says yes, but many times she finds it makes people uncomfortable. "I always tell people, 'thank you very much for letting me talk about my son. He's my favourite subject.' I'll guide them and grab their hand and say, 'I'll do all the talking; you just listen' — because I'm proud of him. This boy lived more in his 21 years than you will in your lifetime."

Andrew Miller's mother, Wendy, waves to the people along the route in Trenton, June 29, 2010.

CHAPTER 5 ❦ FLYING THE FLAG: A PROUD CANADIAN

Like soldiers who serve their country, Canadians are there to serve their soldiers.

I've met many soldiers over the course of the past decade who have told me stories of battle and of courage. I've also met many civilians from this country who go above and beyond to honour those who serve.

The procession for Major Michelle Mendes passes by the Lyle Street overpass in Grafton, April 26, 2009. This is the nearest bridge to her family's home in Wicklow, Ontario. Firefighters, friends, and Legion members came out in honour of Mendes and her family.

A young family show their support along RCAF Road in Trenton, March 23, 2009.

As a member of the media, I would occasionally be notified of a soldier's death before it became public. Once it does become public, I've usually been able to find out, tentatively, when the repatriation is scheduled to take place at CFB Trenton.

Through a growing list of email contacts, I've compiled a list of people who are notified across the province of the tentative date of a repatriation ceremony. As the military usually doesn't release the repatriation date until the day prior to the ceremony, any advance notice to members the public helps if they are planning to attend a gathering at one of the bridges.

Although I've never met, nor even talked to, most of my Internet contacts, they are part of a family of sorts — people from across this nation who grieve every time a soldier falls.

Some have asked not to be recognized, though they are all worthy of recognition. But I would like to introduce you to one person who exemplifies how many of these Canadians honour their own. When a soldier falls, we all hurt, we all come together as a family. Most of us don't know the soldiers or their families personally, but that doesn't make the pain any less — we still hurt, we still shed tears.

Arnie Williamson is an associate director of IT who lives and works in the Greater Toronto Area. I've only met him once — while at an awards ceremony in Toronto, he stopped by the hotel where I was staying and presented me with several now-cherished keepsakes from of his nephew, a reservist from the Moss Park Armoury who had served a tour in Afghanistan.

Williamson recalls seeing the coverage on the news of the first four soldiers killed in April 2002 and of two soldiers killed in October 2003. "It was absolutely heart-wrenching watching them make this drive, and I thought *somebody should do something*."

Since 2004, Williamson has gone to the Victoria Park overpass to pay his respects as the line of black vehicles passes by. The overpass is the last bridge the procession travels under before it heads south on the Don Valley Parkway toward downtown Toronto and the coroner's office.

The first time Williamson went to the bridge to watch a procession — that of Corporal Jamie Murphy — he brought along a single Canadian flag. Each time since, he has brought along that flag, and others. "I started with a Canadian flag. One [at first], then two, then three, and it went from there." Soon, family members and friends began joining him, standing along the span of the bridge as the cars passed below.

Citizens and firefighters pay their respects as Corporal Steve Martin passes by the Cranberry Road bridge in Port Hope, December 22, 2010. The flight was scheduled to arrive a day earlier, but was delayed due to severe weather in Europe.

Since his nephew did a tour in Afghanistan in 2007, Williamson thinks even more about the cost of war. Matthew Clark is a reservist out of the Moss Park Armouries in Toronto. He's been a reservist since he was 18 years old, but when he told the family that he would be heading to Afghanistan in February 2007, the realization of what could happen hit home with his uncle. The two are very close, as are the other family members, and they all live within a few blocks of each other.

"I thought, *I hope I'll never [be] on the bridge for him*. It's everybody's worst nightmare. I said [to Matthew], 'Do you understand what you're getting into?' He said he did, and we all supported him in his decision."

While deployed, Clark would phone Williamson any chance he could. One time he told his uncle how proud he was that he had been put in charge of his first convoy. Williamson, who was always grateful to hear his nephew's voice, said with a laugh, "You stupid son of a bitch. You're in the lead vehicle — and guess who's been taking the brunt of the punishment."

"But he's in his twenties, and thinks he's invincible," Williamson says.

Clark made it safely home from his tour in August 2007.

Members of the Peterborough Fire Department travelled to Port Hope to pay their respects to Private Michael Bruce Freeman, Sergeant Gregory John Kruse, and Warrant Officer Gaetan Roberge. Private Freeman was from Peterborough.

Although the building that houses the coroner's office is closer to where Williamson works in downtown Toronto, he attaches special meaning to that last overpass at Victoria Park. When Corporal Mark Robert McLaren, Warrant Officer Robert John Wilson, and Private Demetrios Diplaros came home for the final time on December 8, 2008, Williamson decided he would do something different.

His father gave him the idea that, along with flying the Canadian flag on the overpass, he should also fly the flag of McLaren's hometown — Peterborough, Ontario. "He thought it would be a nice gesture to fly the Peterborough flag on the Highway of Heroes when the procession passed," said Williamson of his father, who also lives in Peterborough.

So Williamson took his father's advice and did just that. He also flew the flag of the city of Toronto, representing the hometown of the other two soldiers, and an Ontario flag.

A few days later, Williamson met a mutual friend of both his father and the McLaren family. "I was bringing the flag to give to him, to give to the family, when he asked if I could go on an errand with him."

Williamson agreed and hopped in the car. Minutes later, they pulled up in front of the McLaren home. "I didn't know what to say," said Williamson. "I made that long walk from the car to the front door and I was thinking, *what do I tell them*? All I could really say was, 'I'm so sorry.' It only took a few seconds to make the walk, but it [felt like] one of the longest walks I'd ever made."

When he gave the flag to McLaren's father and stepmother, they were both very grateful. When Williamson saw the family's reaction to the flag, he made a promise to himself that he would try his best to fly a flag in honour of each fallen soldier that passed, and afterward send it to the family. "It went from there. We started flying flags and sending them to the families as best we could."

Since then, Williamson hasn't missed a procession. Although it's been hard, logistically, getting flags to the families, he has relied on help from friends, friends of friends, and the power of the Internet to ensure they reach the intended recipients.

With the connection of the flags and the fallen, Williamson doesn't think of any of them by numbers. "Number 99 was just as well-loved as number five. You can sometimes get caught up in the numbers without understanding these were people."

With each flag sent to the family, Williamson also includes a letter. In part, these letters read as follows: "Enclosed is a flag which was flown from the final bridge of

Courtesy of Arnie Williamson.

The flags wave proudly from the Victoria Park overpass, where Arnie Williamson attends.

the Highway of Heroes during your passage with your loved one from Trenton to Toronto. While simple words cannot hope to alleviate the emptiness and hollowness you must feel within, we hope that this flag at least lets you know that Canadians do care about the sacrifices other Canadians make in defence of this country."

If the fallen soldiers are from the Greater Toronto Area, Williamson tries his best to get a flag from the soldier's hometown. If they are from outside of Ontario, he'll try to get a hometown flag. Failing that, he will get a provincial flag.

When a soldier from Mississauga was killed, Williamson phoned Mayor Hazel McCallion's office. He was astounded when a flag arrived 20 minutes later at his office in downtown Toronto. "To this day, I still don't know how she did it," Williamson says with a laugh.

The outcome of a similar situation still baffles Williamson. It was the time that he tried to get a Newfoundland flag after Private Justin Jones was killed on December 13, 2008. He knew that the best-quality flags came from the offices of the provinces, so Williamson decided to phone the Newfoundland premier's office directly. He explained what he was doing, and about the current situation as it related to Private Jones. "[An] hour later a flag showed up at my place of work," Williamson told me. "It came in by bicycle courier."

In April of 2009, when Trooper Karine Blais was killed by a roadside bomb, Williamson phoned the mayor of her hometown in Quebec to try to get a flag: "I don't speak French and the mayor there didn't speak English, but a person from [my] work spoke both and managed a rough translation for me so I could speak with the mayor. I told him we were looking for a flag, and we managed to get one sent to us. We flew it on the overpass and sent it to her family."

By phone, Williamson got to know a gentleman from Halifax by the name of Tim Dunne, who now receives flags from Williamson and sees that they are delivered to the fallen soldiers' families in Eastern Canada.

In early January 2010, Williamson tried to get two provincial flags from Alberta when Corporal Zachery McCormack and Sergeant George Miok, both from Edmonton, were killed on December 30, 2009, by an IED. Dunne put Williamson in touch with a member of parliament for Edmonton-Spruce Grove, Rona Ambrose, the Minister of Public Works and Government Services Canada. The parliamentary office apparently had only one flag available, so one of the people working there at the time simply went outside and took down the one that was flying on the flagpole.

However, there was not enough time for a courier to pick up the flags in Edmonton and get them to Toronto. So an employee at Ambrose's office called WestJet airline to see if something could be done. It was decided that one of WestJet's pilots, Captain Paul Atterly, would keep the flags in the cockpit of the aircraft he was flying from Edmonton to Toronto that day.

Williamson says he then got the arrival times mixed up and wasn't there to get the flags. Luckily, Captain Atterly had dropped them off at the WestJet duty office at Pearson Airport, and Williamson was able to pick them up a short time later. "We got

[them] the night before [the repatriation] … if the plane didn't make it, we were going to be scuffered," says Williamson. "We were extremely grateful to the MP from Alberta and [to] WestJet, because they both did a bunch of things they didn't have to do … it was great how everyone came together."

Even Williamson's coworkers have helped him out — they always remind him when it's time to get going in order to get to the bridge on time. Because he works in the heart of downtown Toronto, it can take him as long as 45 minutes to get to the bridge overlooking the Highway of Heroes. He is very grateful and says they've always supported his cause.

Once, when Williamson couldn't find a flag fast enough when a soldier from New Brunswick was killed in 2008, a neighbouring business stepped in to help out. "For whatever the reason, we had a difficult time getting a flag," he explains. "I'd mentioned it to the hotel manager at the Royal York Hotel in Toronto. The person running the front desk … had [the staff] take one down from a flag pole in front of the hotel. We flew that one and sent it off to the family." A few days later, Williamson replaced the New Brunswick flag for the hotel with a new one he received.

The letter that Williamson sends along with the flag informs the family that it flew on the last bridge along the highway, but only tells the recipients that it is from an anonymous Canadian family — he signs the first names of his family members only. "That way, they could look at anybody [but] aren't sure who it came from," Williamson explains. "I think everybody, given the opportunity, would probably do it. But not everybody is in that position."

Williamson hasn't missed a ceremony since December 2008, but he has occasionally had problems finding the connections to get the flags to some families. Often this is more difficult than getting the flags in the first place. But a number of people he's met over the years have helped out on both fronts.

For example, the MP for Peterborough, Dean Del Mastro, stepped forward and offered to send 15 flags out that Williamson was having trouble connecting with the family members, and MPP Jeff Leal offered to supply flags from the province of Ontario when needed.

Although most people have been very supportive, Williamson tells me that in the beginning he went to a number of flags stores in Toronto asking if they would be interested in donating a flag from each of the provinces to fly on the bridge. "Nobody seemed to want to donate them."

But a chance meeting with a gentleman from the United States solved that problem. The man had heard about the Highway of Heroes and had come to the bridge to pay his respects. As the two were conversing, while waiting for the procession, Williamson mentioned that he couldn't get anyone to donate the flags from the Toronto area.

That brief conversation apparently stuck with the man, because a few days later Williamson got a call: "He called me to say a person would be [contacting me] from the States and [that it was] legit. A flag company … was going to send up a flag from every province and some extra Canadian flags!" Although he was thrilled and very grateful to the man, he says, "It took the Americans to do it, for crying out loud."

In some cases, Williamson says, people did not understand the well-meaning behind the gesture. When he called the premier's office in Saskatchewan, for example, "he thought we were a bunch of crackpots," although they later sent several provincial flags to him.

Other than the McLaren family, only one other fallen soldier's family has met him — and that was by accident. Private Kevin McKay was killed on May 13, 2010. On September 18 of that year, Pat Burton, a regular at the Victoria Park bridge, held a small ceremony in the backyard of her home in Richmond Hill. A special group of friends who attend the bridge were there, along with Private McKay's parents, Mayor David Barrow, and various other dignitaries and neighbours.

Burton had had several portraits done of Private McKay, which were to be given to McKay's parents. The artist, Keith Chaplin, was also in attendance that day. While conversing with the mayor of Richmond Hill, where McKay was from, Williamson requested that the mayor not say anything about the flag from the city. Unfortunately, when the mayor spoke to the assembled guests, he did mention Williamson's efforts on behalf of the fallen soldiers.

"They were quite emotional," says Williamson.

As far as Williamson is concerned, he's just trying to do his part in some small way to help the families realize that their sons and daughters will always be loved by the ordinary citizens of a grateful nation: "If you're in a position to help, you should help, and that's just the way I feel."

He's heard through the grapevine that in the case of some soldiers who come from split homes, one family keeps the flag that was on top of the casket, and the other keeps the one flown from the highway.

I've been honoured myself to have been able to help facilitate two flags reaching the appropriate families. One I gave to a friend to deliver to one of his neighbours near Cobourg who had lost a family member in Afghanistan. Editor-in-chief of the *Calgary Herald*, Lorne Motley, was kind enough to pass on the flag flown by Williamson to the family of journalist Michelle Lang. He sent me an email after he received the flag:

> ... thank you for passing along the flag flown following the repatriation of Michelle Lang and the four soldiers at Trenton in early January.
>
> Heartfelt gestures such as this mean a tremendous amount to the family, her friends, and her newsroom colleagues. I will also say, Peter, that it's a very kind gesture you are helping facilitate.
>
> We will be delivering it to the family in Vancouver on your behalf and [on behalf of] the "Anonymous Canadian family" in the coming days.
>
> You have my deepest gratitude.

Although Williamson has been asked many times, he has granted only one other interview since he has undertaken this personal mission. I am grateful he agreed to speak with me. His explanation for why he does what he does is simple. He doesn't do it for the recognition; he does it because it's the right thing to do.

Though we don't know each other very well, I know he's always been there to support our troops, and he goes above and beyond for the members of our military and their families. I consider him a proud Canadian and good friend.

CHAPTER 6 ❦ THE QUEST FOR A COIN

What started out as a visit to the Royal Canadian Mint in the summer of 2009 turned into something I hoped it wouldn't — a fight.

It was August of that year, and my family and I were visiting the nation's capital. I love Ottawa — the history, the cleanliness of the city — we all do. We try to visit Ottawa at least once a year, and when there we endeavour to spend time in the various museums or exploring someplace we've never been before.

I had been to the Royal Canadian Mint on other occasions, but had never been on a tour of the facility. So, off we went for the roughly 30-minute tour. It was a "behind the scenes" look at the facility, and our guide showed us various examples of the coins that were manufactured there. One item I found interesting, though I thought it rather useless, was the mint's world-record, 100-kilogram, 99.999% pure gold bullion coin with a $1 million face value. Nice to look at, though I couldn't imagine anybody going shopping with it!

From the general circulation coins to the specialized collector coins, the guide provided us with a lot of information about the mint and what they do. Of particular interest to me was the fact that the mint produces currency for several other countries.

Anyway, during the tour, I asked him how the mint decided which specialized coins to produce. By specialized, I am referring to the collector coins that are specially minted for events such as the Olympics, or the Remembrance Day poppy coins. He informed us that often the ideas for the coins came from suggestions made by members of the general public.

As the Highway of Heroes has always been close to my heart, and the mint produces many coins that celebrate Canadian culture, I decided that a depiction of the highway would certainly be a worthy and patriotic symbol to appear on the country's currency. So I picked up a business card on my way out, with the plan in mind to inquire about the prospect of minting a coin.

When I returned home, I sent an email asking where I could send my suggestion regarding a Highway of Heroes coin. On August 14, I received a reply from an

The procession for Private Michael Freeman, Sergeant Gregory Kruse, and Warrant Officer Gaetan Roberge travels along the Highway of Heroes near the Cranberry Road overpass in Port Hope, which is filled with people who have come out to pay their respects to the fallen soldiers.

administrative assistant at the Royal Canadian Mint. She informed me that she worked for the marketing department and that she would be happy to forward my suggestion to the director of the department. Less than four hours later I wrote back, explaining who I was, and giving a short history of my experience with the highway. I told them that I thought it would be a tremendous honour to have a representation of the route travelled to be emblazoned on a coin from the Canadian Mint, and that it would be a lasting tribute to everyone who attended the bridges along the route, but more importantly, to the families and friends of the fallen soldiers.

For months I heard nothing. I had hoped that they would embrace the idea, but I didn't hold my breath. Finally, on February 11, 2010, I received an email from the mint's communications coordinator thanking me again for my proposal and letting me know that they had received a favourable response from coin consumers and were quite keen on the idea. She assured me that they were in the process of considering how best to honour the route and the people who travelled it, as well as those in the public who came out to support our heroes, and promised to get back to me as the process went on.

To say I was overjoyed, thrilled, and honoured was an understatement. I emailed the mint back right away, stating "words cannot express my gratitude for your email." I asked if there was a timeline for the process and asked what the next step would be.

I told a few of my close friends, though I never felt that it was something that I should take credit for — it was simply the right thing for the mint to do. But was I grateful? You bet.

Several days later I received another email from the coordinator, informing me that they appreciated my passion and support for this project, and offering assurance that they would indeed be in touch again soon regarding the next steps to be taken.

But several months went by, and I heard nothing more. Periodically, I would email to check in about the progress of the coin. After asking for an update in April of

2010, I finally received a response informing me that they had nothing new to report and that the coin would not likely be out that year. They explained that the process was a lengthy one, but assured me that my suggestion was still one that they planned to develop.

Nearly a year had passed since my last visit to Ottawa, and my family and I were planning another trip, so I decided to email the mint once again to ask if any progress had been made. I informed them that I would be in town, and that I was very interested in seeing anything that was taking shape with regard to the coin. The response this time was much less positive, and I was told that, although they were still considering various options for honouring the Canadian Forces, a Highway of Heroes design was just one of the options being considered.

At the start of November that same year, I read that the mint was producing a coin in honour of Remembrance Day. Wondering if it would be a Highway of Heroes coin, I once again emailed the mint. To my shock and disappointment, I was told that the mint had decided not to produce a coin in commemoration of the Highway of Heroes.

I received a formal email from the coordinator on November 4, 2010, stating that the 2010, 25-cent poppy coin was something that the mint had been planning for a while but that it was not intended to replace any other military-themed coins that they were considering producing.

It was at that moment the bubble burst on what I thought would have been something all Canadians would have embraced.

The email went on to say that it was not likely that they would be doing a specific Highway of Heroes coin, and that, although they felt that the sentiment behind this theme was an honourable one, designing a coin which accurately depicted the Highway of Heroes while honouring the sentiment had proven difficult. She then apologized and informed me that they were working on several other products for the coming years that would honour the Canadian Forces, past and present, and their sacrifices.

I couldn't believe it. How could it be "difficult?" They can put a schooner on a dime, a beaver on a nickel, and other images, *but they found this idea too difficult?*

I explained in an email that the outcome was unfortunate, especially after the initial response I had received from the mint was so positive. I told them that I would have thought a coin representing our country's heroes and those who support them would have been something they would be honoured to produce. A simple image of people on a bridge with Canadian flags would have been more than enough to show support for the highway.

Later, I spoke with several friends, debating the pros and cons of going public with my experience with the mint. The last thing I wanted was to cause any type of scandal that would negatively affect the military or the morale of the soldiers in any way. They have enough on their plates.

But, shortly after sending a reply to the mint, I sent out a copy of my correspondence with the mint over the past year to everyone on my Highway of Heroes contact list. I also included a short email. In it I said, "I don't want to 'ruffle' feathers, but if they can make coins for things like whales and Canadian rock stars, I thought making them for something like the Highway of Heroes was certainly an honourable thing to do. Again, just throwing this out there …"

All but one reply advised me that I should go public and to continue to push for the coin to be made. But despite my feelings about the mint's decision, I didn't want to blindside them, and decided it was only fair to let them know that I was going to be following up on it. I knew this wasn't going to be an easy battle, but I phoned up the mint and spoke with one of the representatives I'd previously corresponded with.

It was a polite conversation, but I informed her that I wouldn't be dropping my fight for the coin and that I would be going forward and making the situation public. She told me that another representative would be calling me about my concerns. I told her that I had no problem with that, but that, frankly, there was really nothing more to discuss.

During the conversation, she told me that she understood my disappointment, but in reality I felt not so much disappointment — I just felt that their decision was wrong. And the more I looked into it, the more I knew it was wrong. The mint over the years has produced various coins depicting whales, dinosaurs, Santa Claus, a variety of birds, as well as one to commemorate the 100th anniversary in 2010 of the Saskatchewan Roughriders football team. On the mint's website they state that the latter was "for the millions of Saskatchewan Roughriders fans across Canada."

Now, although I don't follow the CFL, I'm fairly sure that there are not "millions" of Roughrider fans — if there are, great. I have nothing against the CFL, or Canadian wildlife, for that matter; my point is that I couldn't grasp the concept of how they could produce a coin representing these entities yet deny one for our country's genuine heroes.

The next day I received a call from the director of communications at the Royal Canadian Mint. Needless to say, it was a lengthy conversation. She explained that since 2004 the Royal Canadian Mint had produced more than 30 coins honouring veterans and Remembrance. I thought, *that's wonderful, and here's one more you can do!*

I consider columnist Joe Warmington a good friend, a great supporter of the troops, and someone who looks objectively at any situation. When I told him about the mint declining the idea for the coin, he was one of many who couldn't believe it — mostly he couldn't believe that the reason given was that it was "too difficult."

Soon after I contacted Joe, he wrote in his column about my request that a coin be minted. On November 6, 2010, he wrote, "Who got to the Royal Canadian Mint? And why?" In the article he stated that I was "like a dog with a bone" when I thought something was unjust: "Good luck getting him to heel. [W]atch for the reaction of Canadians in the next few months. You'll learn something about patriotism."

As usual, he was right.

Just a couple of days later, on November 8, the director of communications at the mint sent a letter to the editor at the *Toronto Sun*, in response to the column written by Mr. Warmington. The email explained that Canada Post was at that time circulating thousands of the new 25-cent poppy coins that were unveiled by the mint to commemorate Remembrance Day and our Armed Forces, past and present. A special collector card and coin were also available of which five dollars from each sold (which represented all profits) would be given to the Military Families Fund. She went on to say that more than 30 coins had been minted since 2004 that commemorate our veterans and Remembrance, and that the idea for a Highway of Heroes coin, although it was not chosen for 2010, was still possible for consideration in the future — some definite back-pedalling from their earlier communications with me. She also stated that that the mint is a commercial crown corporation, and is operated at "arm's length" from the Government of Canada.

I've stated this before, but a fight like this is hard, very hard. It's emotionally draining, and you get doors slammed in your face left and right; but you have to keep pushing. It's one step forward, two steps back sometimes, but you just hope that at the end of it the right thing will be done; but there are no guarantees.

Fortunately two saviours came to the rescue. The first was Caroline McIntosh from Mississauga; the second was Hector Macmillan, the mayor of the municipality of Trent Hills. When I sent out the general email asking what the next step would be, Ms. McIntosh wrote back, "If we, the grassroots of this country, could instigate the renaming of the Highway of Heroes, I see no reason under the sun that we can't do [it] again with the coin.... Can we start a petition again? ... just say the word and I am there."

And she was — from start to finish.

We talked about what should be on the petition, and I suggested that my correspondence with the mint be included. I wanted to let the people know all the facts surrounding the push for the coin. Ms. McIntosh also wrote a few paragraphs explaining how she felt about the situation and why she felt it was important for people to sign.

It read, in part:

> In honour of those fallen soldiers, their families and all of the good people of Canada who choose to stand and honour on bridges, overpasses, and along the roadsides each time we must repatriate those who paid the ultimate sacrifice, I am asking you to sign this petition and send a clear and strong message to the Royal Mint and the Federal Government that "we shall never forget" ... we want a coin that commemorates our passionate support of our soldiers. This is NOT a political statement; this is simply the ways and means to have our voices heard. We did it once before in a simple, powerful way, let's do this again. Our soldiers, their families, past and present, deserve nothing less.

And with that, yet another petition was off and running.

Immediately, people began posting their comments. Sergeant Todd Cane (Retired) CD from Cobourg wrote, "Nothing against Santa ... but if the mint is producing a 50-cent coin [with] snowflakes with inlayed tanzanite ... then SURELY a coin pressed in honour of the highway of heroes would be the RIGHT thing to do ..."

Scott Powell, an Alnwick/Haldimand Township firefighter, wrote, "For those that have not experienced the Highway of Heroes, you cannot imagine the feeling and emotion that is felt from standing on a bridge. There is a sense of community, patriotism, pride, sadness, respect, grief, gratitude, and honour that all happens in the blink of an eye. It is nearly inexplicable and needs to be experienced to be understood and appreciated. This is the first time that casualties of war have been repatriated to Canadian soil. That alone is worthy of commemoration. The fact that thousands of Canadians stand on the bridges along the Highway of Heroes to pay their respects to

A couple holds a poppy blanket by the Hamilton Road overpass in Port Hope as they await the procession of Corporal Karine Blais, April 16, 2009.

our fallen Canadians is also a phenomena that is very worthy of commemoration as well. Please do the right thing and mint this coin."

And the comments weren't just coming from Ontario, but from across Canada, and from across the world. Justin McKee from Abbotsford, British Columbia, wrote, "I believe after being over here in Afghanistan and seeing the sacrifices that our soldiers make that one of the least things that we could do as Canadians is [to] commemorate them with a 'Highway of Heroes' coin. They have made a coin for Paul Henderson commemorating his goal; that was hockey, this is life or death."

And from Whitehorse, Yukon, Corporal R. Wayne Wannamaker CD1 (Retired) wrote, "I am fully behind those for having this coin struck as soon as possible. This coin also would respect ALL those that attend the overpasses ... along the Highway of Heroes for the support of our Fallen Comrades."

"As an Australian ex-Navy Vietnam Veteran, I salute your heroes and pray that one day peace will come, and when that day comes this coin will remind us all of the

Construction workers in Durham Region pay their respects by standing silently as the procession for Trooper Corey Hayes, Trooper Jack Bouthillier, Master Corporal Scott Vernelli, and Corporal Tyler Crooks passes by on the Highway of Heroes, March 23, 2009.

sacrifice of those who made it happen," wrote Vern Bechaz from Victoria, Australia. "May God rest their souls."

Needless to say, the support for the coin was very strong.

Before emailing back and forth with Ms. Caroline McIntosh, I'd never spoken to her. She was on my email list that notified people of the dates and times of the repatriations, but I didn't know who she was. But she was amazingly committed to this cause and always remained positive. Whatever was asked of her, she did it without hesitation, whether it was sending emails to various media outlets, fire and police chiefs, and politicians across the province, or keeping me informed about the status of the petition. Her energy was something I wish I had, and I was honoured to finally meet her when I was in Toronto doing a radio show in December of 2010. She is a great person and most dedicated to the cause.

In early November, I had been in Campbellford covering another story, and the situation with the coin at the time was getting a tad "heated." After I filed my photos to the paper, I met with and shared my views on the situation with Municipality of Trent Hills Mayor Hector Macmillan.

At the time, Macmillan had his hands full with other issues, but he listened. At that time, I didn't realize what was to come. Macmillan thought that as a municipal politician it might be within his powers to help us out with our cause, and said that he would ask the local council to endorse the idea. He recalled that previously council had passed a resolution for a local ratepayers group, which in turn was passed by 135 other councils throughout the province.

"With the coin it sounded to me like there was some disconnection. Either they didn't understand the proposal, or somebody there (at the mint) didn't understand the process," Macmillan said. "Either way, it was unacceptable."

So he came up with a resolution, which he submitted to the Trent Hills Council on November 15. It was the last session before a new council would be sworn in following the municipal election. "Our council was going to endorse it no matter who the players were," said Macmillan. "It had nothing to do with council members leaving, or new members coming in. It was just that obvious [that] it was a wrong that needed to be corrected. I made the pitch to council and they agreed unanimously that there was something wrong and we needed to send a message."

The proposal read as follows:

> Please be advised that the Council of the Corporation of the Municipality of Trent Hills has passed the following resolution at a recent Regular Council meeting:
>
> WHEREAS the Highway of Heroes plays a significant role honouring our fallen Canadian soldiers;
>
> AND WHEREAS the Highway of Heroes provides a remarkable venue for Canadian citizens to pay tribute to our fallen soldiers;
>
> AND WHEREAS the Highway of Heroes has become a significant component of Canadian culture;
>
> NOW THEREFORE the Council of the Municipality of Trent Hills unanimously endorses the production of a Canadian coin depicting an image of Canadians honouring our fallen soldiers from bridges that span the Highway of Heroes;
>
> AND FURTHER supports the circulation of this resolution to our MP, MPP, the Royal Canadian Mint, AMO, FCM and the City of Toronto for distribution to all Canadian Municipalities requesting support of this initiative;
>
> AND FURTHER respectfully request all Canadian Municipal Councils make it known to their MP, and encourage the Royal Canadian Mint in writing to produce a Canadian coin to recognize the Highway of Heroes.
>
> AND encourage all citizens to contact their MPs and sign the on-line petition and to send a written letter to the Royal Canadian Mint supporting the development of a commemorative Highway of Heroes coin.

Macmillan told me that because the endorsement was sent to the Association of Municipalities of Ontario, it would be received by over 400 municipalities throughout the province. Even though the Municipality of Trent Hills is not along the Highway of Heroes, Macmillan says he knew it was the right thing to do for the fallen, the families, and for all Canadians: “There are very few municipalities that are along the Highway of Heroes. It had nothing to do with geographic location. It was just the … right thing to do!”

The next day I did an online search for the coin and noticed that the Corporation of the Town of LaSalle, Ontario, had also agreed to write to the mint expressing the hope that they would reverse their decision. To be honest, I wasn't even sure exactly where the town of LaSalle was in Ontario! I know it now.

LaSalle councillor Sue Desjarlais presented a letter to council asking them to endorse a special request that the Canadian Mint go ahead with the minting of the commemorative coin.

Desjarlais promptly received a response: "I am proud to say my Council agreed to send a letter to the Canadian Mint asking them to reconsider their choice and will be forwarding that to our other County and City of Windsor councils asking them for support as well."

So the ball was now rolling; it was just a matter of maintaining support and keeping the public informed.

One thing I've always maintained is that if the public wants something, it will happen. I just wanted to ensure that the public had all the facts that would allow them to decide for themselves what was right. From that point on, whatever happened, I was okay with it; it was up to the people. Their dedication had spearheaded the creation of the Highway of Heroes, and it would be the same with the coin — if they chose to back the movement.

My only fear was that Ottawa and the mint wouldn't listen. But in the end it was the strength of people, the many emails, the signing of the petition, and the support from Macmillan, McIntosh, and the councillor in LaSalle that would make or break the decision. The momentum was growing, but was it attracting the attention of the right people, people who could make it happen?

The support was growing, and the word was getting out, but we had to keep the pressure on. On November 20, I emailed members of Cobourg Council to ask for their support, and sent them the information about the movement.

As I was covering the Cobourg Santa Claus Parade on November 21, I happened to see Mayor Delanty and his wife, Suzanne, riding in a convertible in the parade. As this is my family's hometown, and has been for three generations, people know me. So, I thought, *why not approach him just to share my ideas*? I didn't know if or when I'd see him again. As soon as there was a stoppage in the parade, I approached them and quickly explained the situation: why I felt that it was so important to do the coin, and how the mint, in their infinite wisdom, had originally thought it was a grand idea, also, but later said they wouldn't be following through.

Angela MacIsaac (left) and Jennifer Thompson hold up a Canadian flag on the Ontario Street bridge in Cobourg, September 2, 2010. Veterans, fallen soldiers' family members, and ordinary citizens have signed this flag, which she hopes to eventually place in the Royal Military Museum. She has made several such flags, all of which flew on the Ontario Street bridge in Cobourg then were shipped out to locations throughout Canada. MacIsaac called them "The Travelling Flags" because they have been sent to hundreds of locations over the years, including many military bases and Legions.

"I didn't understand why they would refuse," admitted Delanty later. "We had commemorative coins on many things and I couldn't understand why we couldn't produce a coin for people who have made the ultimate sacrifice on behalf of Canada. I thought, *let's get on with it, it's the right thing to do*. It speaks much to the values that we, as Canadians, put on the sacrifice, put on the soldiers in Afghanistan. For those soldiers on their last journey on the Highway of Heroes, they have made the ultimate sacrifice to protect the values that we, as Canadians, cherish. I don't think we have words strong enough to say thank you and a coin lets the families know [that] we are thinking about [them]. It's a symbol of what Canada is all about."

The very next day, Cobourg City Council endorsed the proposal unanimously during one of the last council sessions before Delanty retired from politics. It was something he says he will always remember.

Northumberland Ontario Provincial Police Constable Robin Reinke salutes as the procession for Private Alexandre Peloquin passes by Port Hope, June 11, 2009.

The day after that, on November 23, the Municipality of Port Hope approved the motion to support the coin unanimously at their council meeting.

It was during this time that I found out the Government of Canada doesn't accept online petitions. I thought about creating a "hard copy" petition and placing it in various financial institutions throughout the area, but the logistics involved in getting it distributed across the country, or even the province, would have been too time-consuming. I thought, the way it was going, we could certainly keep the online petition going, regardless of whether or not the Feds thought it was "acceptable." It showed how Canadians felt, and that's what it was all about.

But with the support of the various city councils that were coming aboard, I thought that it might also be worthwhile to try to get more municipalities on-side. After all, the municipalities represented the citizens, and if they supported it, they spoke for the thousands of people in their communities.

We were at the point where we would accept all the help that we could get.

As I have already said, Caroline McIntosh had a passion for the cause which went above and beyond what I'd ever have expected. She was scheduled to appear on December 15 at the City of Mississauga Council session to request their support.

One area where I observed the mint may have made a mistake in their response when emailing me is that they closed the door by saying they would not likely be producing a Highway of Heroes coin.

I never thought of it before, but I would guess it's best to always leave the door open when dealing with the public. If the mint would have initially stated that they wouldn't be producing the coin this year, but will be looking at it in the future, it would have been hard to argue with their decision, but the response I got was along the lines that they would not be producing one — at all. Now, the Director of Communications was telling me that the door was indeed open; but in my opinion, the floodgates were already wide open.

On November 24, I spoke with MP Rick Norlock, who informed me that he would take up my concerns with the Minister of Transportation, who oversees the mint, but that he would have to stay at "arm's length" so it wouldn't be viewed as interference.

Karl Walsh, from the Ontario Provincial Police Association, was also instrumental in the cause. He threw his support behind the fight for the Highway of Heroes coin and encouraged association members to sign the petition.

With more municipalities and associations coming onboard, the movement was gaining the steam we'd hoped for. Though Mayor Macmillan kept telling me that I worried too much, I knew that when dealing with Ottawa, anything could happen. I had been here before.

On November 30, the president of the Toronto Professional Firefighters Association, Ed Kennedy, announced that they would be supporting the initiative. Around the same time, I also received a call from MP Peter Stoffer, representing Sackville-Eastern Shore, Nova Scotia. He spoke of how he appreciated the cause and told me that the Federal NDP fully supported the idea of a Highway of Heroes coin.

Also in late November, I heard that the Minister of Transportation had asked the mayors of Port Hope, Cobourg, and Trent Hills to attend a meeting in early December in Ottawa that would also include the head of the mint. Due to the Christmas season, however, it was decided that they would engage in a conference call instead. The telephone meeting took place on December 8.

There was some indication that the coin may go forward, but as I knew, anything could happen. At the time I wondered why I hadn't been invited to the meeting, but it didn't bother me for long. It was all about the end results, the important thing was that the right people were there to convey the message of what the Highway of Heroes meant to Canadians.

Throughout November and into December, radio show hosts Roy Green and Ted Woloshyn were absolutely onboard. I appeared on their shows along with Warmington and Macmillan. Locally, the paper I work for, *Northumberland Today*, was fully supportive and kept the story in the headlines, and CHEX television in Peterborough did numerous stories on the effort to get the coin produced — with the power of the Internet these days, there is no such thing as "local" news.

During that time, I also spoke with Northumberland–Quinte West MPP Lou Rinaldi, who indicated that he fully supported the minting of the coin. He wrote a letter to the mint himself in December:

A LASTING MEMORIAL

The City of Quinte West is currently partnering with a group of community volunteers to create a lasting memorial to the fallen Canadian soldiers in Afghanistan.

Mayor John Williams said a portion of Bain Park, a city-owned park located beside CFB Trenton, will be utilized in the development of the memorial project. It will be located less than one kilometre from where the repatriation procession exits the base en route to the highway.

Part of the design features the image of a soldier against a black granite maple leaf, looking at members of a grieving family. The names of all the fallen Canadian soldiers will be carved on a wall of the memorial. Planted between the walls will be hundreds of poppies.

The design is the creation of James Smith, a sculptor with Campbell Memorials in Belleville. The committee is comprised of community members along with members from CFB Trenton. Mayor Williams says the committee is not looking for any government funding for the project; however, the committee will be looking for donations from the community as well as from people from across the country. It is hoped that the project will be completed by 2012.

> It is with great pride that I have been given the opportunity to support Mr. Pete Fisher with his request to have a coin minted to support the Highway of Heroes. The Highway of Heroes begins in Northumberland–Quinte West as the fallen soldiers make their way along this stretch of the highway to Toronto. I have proudly stood with many residents of the small communities [who] pack the overpasses of more than two dozen bridges that span across Northumberland–Quinte West from border to border. Minting a coin to commemorate the Highway of Heroes is one more way [to honour] the Canadian soldiers that have sacrificed their lives … [it] is an everlasting tribute and memory for those that support the work that the soldiers do for the betterment of our country.… A Highway of Heroes coin will be a permanent keepsake in remembrance of the sacrifices our soldiers made for all of us and the final journey they took after they returned home. I wholeheartedly support Peter Fisher's efforts and it is my hope the Royal Canadian Mint will proceed with a Highway of Heroes coin.

On December 7, the Ontario Professional Firefighters Association unanimously approved the resolution to support the coin along with the International Association of Fire Fighters, and the Mississauga Fire Fighter's Association. Gaining the support of the firefighter associations was due again to the dedicated work of Caroline McIntosh.

Hamilton Township endorsed the proposal on December 7, and the next morning, the day of the meeting at Northumberland County Council in Cobourg, Macmillan brought the motion forward. It was endorsed by the council — and, as with the others, it passed unanimously.

It was no longer a case in which hundreds of people were in support, it was now thousands; it would be hard for the mint to ignore the growing outcry. Success seemed imminent; at least I hoped so.

So I waited on pins and needles for word to come out of the meeting. What would they say? Would they "see the light" and reverse their decision, or would they continue to play hardball?

Around noon I received a text from Macmillan. He asked that I meet him for coffee in Cobourg. I had a million questions for him, but he didn't give me any details over the phone. My heart was racing, but I didn't want to get over-confident just to be let down.

When I arrived, Macmillan was already there. I was so excited that I felt like blurting out the words, *tell me, tell me!* After what seemed like minutes, but was likely only a few seconds, he told me, "It's going to happen." — The mint would be producing a collector coin in honour of the Highway of Heroes.

I let out a sigh of relief, hung my head, and shed a few tears. It felt as if the process had taken so much out of me. I felt drained — as if I had been in a prize fight, with an endless number of rounds.

I stood teary-eyed and hugged him. It meant so much to me that this wrong was finally righted. And I also knew what it meant to so many others. It had been just over a month since the mint had informed me that they wouldn't be doing a coin. And now they had reversed their decision. A press release posted later that evening on the mint's website stated:

> In keeping with its proud tradition of issuing coins honouring Canada's veterans and Remembrance, the Royal Canadian Mint today advised members of the Northumberland County Council that a collector coin commemorating the celebrated "Highway of Heroes" and Canada's fallen in Afghanistan will once again illustrate these themes in 2011.
>
> Further to our intention to introduce this coin at a future date, we are pleased to assure supporters of the "Highway of Heroes" that their tribute to those who have made the ultimate sacrifice during Canada's military mission in Afghanistan will be immortalized by the Mint in 2011. This will open yet another window on the milestones, people, places, and events which shape Canada's rich and diverse identity, and which the Mint consistently celebrates on its coins.
>
> The Mint will report on the status of this project to the Northumberland County Council in the next four to five months and we look forward to the addition of this collector coin to a long line of Royal Canadian Mint coins honouring the men and women who proudly serve the Canadian Forces.

THE T-SHIRT

A T-shirt given to me by a friend helped convince me that to keep pushing for the coin was the right thing to do.

Paul Beyette was born and raised in Cobourg. Throughout high school we were best friends, and have always been like brothers. Paul is a Senior Biomedical Electronics Technologist Western Region with 1 Field Ambulance at CFB Edmonton. He's spent over two decades in the military, and is currently a warrant officer. He's been to Bosnia, and has done two tours in Afghanistan. During his career, he's been posted throughout Canada.

Another high school friend of ours, Carol Young, went to visit Paul in Edmonton in November 2010. When she returned, she brought me a T-shirt. On the front was an image of a bridge overlooking a highway —the Highway of Heroes!

Young said she purchased the T-shirt at the Canex store on the base in Edmonton. Canex (The Canadian Forces Exchange System) is a retail operation that was started in 1968 to meet the needs of the military community. The T-shirt was one of the official items from the Support Our Troops line sold at the store.

It surprised me that the Canex was selling Highway of Heroes merchandise, but it made me realize that the highway is well-known throughout Canada, not just in Ontario. This helped me make up my mind about going public about the mint's decision, and it was the very next day that I got the ball rolling by making that call to the mint to inform them of my decision.

When I received the response from Caroline McIntosh, after she got word of our success — although it's hard to convey emotion in an email — I understood her words: "I cannot type with tears in my eyes. We certainly did make a good team."

I'm pleased to report that the coin is scheduled for release in October 2011.

My thanks go out to all those individuals who lent us their support in our quest to have the Highway of Heroes coins minted, and I would also like to thank the following municipalities for their backing of the cause: City of Toronto; Town of Rainy River; Municipality of Neebing; City of Belleville; Township of Gillies; Municipality of Huron East; Township of Faraday; Township of Evanturel; Municipality of Tweed; Township of O'Connor; Township of Pickle Lake; Township of Enniskillen; City of Hamilton; County of Peterborough; Township of Malahide; Township of Mapleton; Town of LaSalle; Municipality of Trent Hills; and of course the cities of Cobourg and Port Hope.

KANDAHAR CENOTAPH

AFPP-international — formerly the Armed Forces Pride Programme — is a Calgary-based company that has expanded from imprinted and embroidered sportswear to the design and production of laser-engraved granite, coins, and medallions, as well as award and presentation plaques. In addition to their established product lines, they also have ability to design and produce decals, signs, banners, and vehicle wraps.

Shortly after the first four Canadian soldiers were killed by friendly fire in April 2002, Rod McLeod says he felt compelled to create an engraved memorial plaque to honour them. Copies were made for Princess Patricia's Canadian Light Infantry Regimental Headquarters (PPCLI RHQ) and Land Force Western Area Headquarters (LEWA HQ) in Edmonton.

In preparation for the Remembrance Day ceremonies at Camp Julien in 2003, McLeod sent a copy of the plaque to them along with another honouring two other fallen soldiers. The engineers there prepared a large granite memorial stone cairn to which they affixed the two plaques.

In November 2005, Camp Julien was closed and the Canadian troops moved south to Kandahar … along with the stone cairn. As casualties began to mount, it became clear that a larger cenotaph would be needed.

McLeod varied each plaque a little bit to reflect each soldier's unique personality. In August 2006, it was decided that each soldier should be memorialized on his own plaque. Until this time, if there was more than one casualty at the same time, all would be included on the same plaque.

The plaques' journey begins in Calgary. They are then shipped to Montreal, Trenton, and on to Camp Mirage, and eventually into theatre. The entire process takes about 15 working days.

The cenotaph is located just behind the JTF Afghanistan (Canadian) Headquarters. It was designed and built by the Canadian Military Engineers (CME) with a view to expansion if and when required. Each plaque is placed in order of sequence in a wooden grid. This enables fellow soldiers and visiting family members an opportunity to affix a memento if desired. Following the Remembrance Day ceremonies, many soldiers remove the poppy from their head dress and position it on the memorial in remembrance of a fallen comrade.

The cenotaph is said to be visited every day by a number of soldiers — to pay their respects. It is maintained daily, and each plaque is individually dusted, cleaned, and cared for. This responsibility is ably carried out by designated member of the Canadian Forces and a staff of representative members from air, land, and sea.

It was decided that the KAF Cenotaph should be expanded to include Americans who serve under our command. AFPP has been contracted to design and produce twenty memorial plaques to commemorate the passing of American soldiers. It is likely that the entire cenotaph will be removed to the War Museum in Ottawa once our troops come home.

A young girl waits with hundreds of others for the procession carrying six fallen soldiers to pass under the Ontario Street bridge in Cobourg, July 8, 2007.

CHAPTER 7  THE GRASSROOTS SUPPORT

The people who make their way to the overpasses and bridges, or to stand along the route called the Highway of Heroes, are patriotic and proud. These individuals come from all walks of life, all professions, all cultural backgrounds, and all faiths. They live in the big cities, the suburbs, and the small towns. They are rich and poor, young and old. But they all share a love of country and a deep respect for the sacrifices made by a few for so many.

By now, I'm sure everyone in Canada knows someone who has served or does serve in the military, and hence knows that it could very easily be someone they know who is travelling along that highway for the last time.

On the coldest day of winter up to that point, a genuinely Canadian image appears on an overpass during the procession of Gunner Jonathan Dion, January 2, 2008.

ABOVE LEFT: *Air force veteran Colin Stillwell stands saluting as a procession passes; a fitting tribute from one generation of heroes to another.*

ABOVE RIGHT: *A man with his hand on his heart stands on the median wall as the procession for Trooper Corey Hayes, Trooper Jack Bouthillier, Master Corporal Scott Vernelli, and Corporal Tyler Crooks goes by on March 23, 2009.*

RIGHT: *Ministry of Natural Resources officers stand alongside the Highway of Heroes in the area of Quinte-West, March 23, 2009.*

Although there are many of these dedicated citizens, I would like to highlight just a few who I have come to know over the years, individuals who have gone above and beyond to show their support for this, the Highway of Heroes.

WAYNE

Wayne McVeen is a retired Cobourg gentleman who I've known since first attending the Ontario Street bridge in Cobourg, what seems like so many years ago. As a member of the media, I always try to show up at different bridges each time, or to go to the base and take photos of the repatriation from the tarmac.

Every single time I've been to the Ontario Street bridge, McVeen has been there, standing in the same position on the bridge. He has told me that, even though he could arrive later, he always shows up when the aircraft is expected to land. And for the last several years that's been at 2:00 p.m. It then takes nearly two hours before the repatriation is done and the procession makes its way along the highway to Cobourg. And that's if one soldier is repatriated. If there is more than one, it takes longer. But McVeen will always be there, like others, no matter the weather.

But it wasn't always that way.

Though some showed up for that first procession that passed through in April 2002, most didn't know about the other repatriations until, unfortunately, there were casualties on a more regular basis.

McVeen himself feels bad that he didn't go to those first seven processions. But since then, he's only missed five, and then only because he was out of town.

Cobourg resident Wayne McVeen stands in his usual spot on the Ontario Street bridge, June 11, 2009.

McVeen's nephew, Chris Barker, had brought his son to one of the bridges, and happened to stop by his uncle's house on the way home. Barker explained about the procession passing by on the highway, and from then on, whenever available, McVeen has made the journey to the bridge.

"At that point there was nothing in the paper and it was up in the air how to find out what time the soldiers were coming home," McVeen told me. After searching on the Internet, however, he was finally able to find a military website that listed the times of repatriations.

When McVeen and members of his family first started going to the bridge, there were few, if any others there. "At least eight times my wife, Judith, and I were there by ourselves and waving the flags. Then our daughter would come. Then as it became more and more [known] to the people, and the press got involved in it, then the crowds started to come."

There were then usually 15 or 20 people who came out to the Ontario Street bridge on a regular basis. As more and more people started to show up, McVeen could usually tell who the "first-timers" were. "They were the ones who were crying," he says.

And anyone who has ever been to a bridge to watch a procession pass knows why. It's something you can't easily put into words. Once you see the long line of black vehicles with the emergency lights and flashing headlights you know what is approaching. "When we can see them approach … off come the hats, and the flags go up, and people … put their hands over their chests."

He says that the first-timers always seem to become the long-timers, though.

Surprisingly, the weather doesn't seem to factor in. People come to the bridge no matter what the weather. I've covered repatriations in teeming rain, I've covered them at times when I can't feel my fingers — and that's with gloves on. I've walked through poison ivy in a field to get the picture I wanted. And all the people who go on a regular basis say the same: "It's the least we can do."

McVeen agrees. "From freezing rain, to hot summer days … nobody will leave. If a thunderstorm came in, we'd stay on the bridge. Others would go to their car, but they'd come out when it was time. We have a responsibility, and we are dedicated to that. There is no stopping us."

I think there is a calling for people who join the military, and I almost think there is a calling for the people who go to the bridges. McVeen, like most people, has never

The procession for Corporal Mark McLaren, Private Demetrios Diplaros, and Warrant Officer Robert Wilson travels along the Highway of Heroes during a snowstorm. Despite the weather, a crowd gathers on the overpass to pay their respects.

met any of the family members who've been in the processions, but he's read the media reports about how those families are thankful for the dedication of those who come out to the bridges.

He hopes it brings the families some small solace, but can never imagine the heartache of losing a son or daughter. McVeen's son was in the military for a decade, during which time he served in Bosnia. Every once in a while he'll throw on a video of the Canadian Forces coming under fire during that mission and it brings it all home. "I play that once in a while to remind myself of what my son went through [during the peacekeeping mission]. These guys in Afghanistan are doing peace*making* and there's a hell of a difference."

McVeen has collected a lot of memories during the time he has stood on the bridge. One summer day, while he was waiting, a car pulled over and two bagpipers got out. After standing and watching the cars pass by for a short while, the two pipers got in their car and left. Lucky enough for them, they did, because, less than 15 minutes later, someone yelled, and as people looked along the highway they saw a truck wheel that had come off a transport truck. It went rolling up over the hill, hit the fence, and rolled back down into the berm — the path of the wheel passing right where the two pipers had been standing. "Nobody mentioned anything about it," Mcveen told me, "but it was one of the strangest things."

Another time a woman approached McVeen after the procession had passed by. She was crying. "I hugged her, but I didn't know what was going on." It turned out that the fallen soldier had been a good friend of her son.

But the heartfelt thanks from one particular soldier is a memory McVeen especially cherishes. While waiting on the bridge one day, a Canadian Forces vehicle pulled over along the highway. Three soldiers got out and climbed up the embankment. One by one, they shook hands with the people on the bridge and thanked them. Several soldiers in uniform who were already on the bridge saluted them as they went from person to person.

"He shook our hands and thanked us. We soon found out [one of the soldiers] was a general. He [walked] all along the bridges thanking people for their support. That perked us up — that a general would take the time and do that ..."

Canada has been a world leader in the way they show their respect to the fallen, and McVeen is one of many people who proudly tell the story of the Highway of Heroes, no matter where he is. On a trip to Scotland, McVeen, who is a retired factory worker,

THE ROAD TAKEN

A young man with dreams of a life fulfilled
Talks of engineering, flying and adventure.
There are midnight beers with friends and family
And many conversations about the meaning of life's work.
His talents are numerous, everyone says ....
A natural leader, a level headed young man,
No challenge abandoned, no watered down purpose or response.
The many choices, the many possibilities
Roll and roll in his head.
Then, with strong determination,
A decision is made.
And in his wide-eyed youth, he steps on foreign soil,
Having merely skimmed the depths of life's complexities and
emotions.
He looks ahead to living
Pride and family
Love and hate
Duty and remorse
Humour and fear.
In a flash, he becomes an observer of life around him.
In an unforgiving land, a lifetime of anticipated exploration is in
cinders.
He speaks ... no one hears
He cries out ... no one consoles
He reaches out to touch ... no one responds.
He is alone ... for a short while....
For, on the journey home,
There are proud Canadians who recognize the loss of a life unfulfilled.
They stand by the hundreds to momentarily share the pain, the
sorrow, the grief, the emptiness,
To momentarily acknowledge and thank a hero.
The young men who no longer talk of engineering, flying and
adventure are never alone on the Highway of Heroes.
May they rest in peace.
May the world find peace.

— Madeleine Thibault-Smith,
Cobourg, Ontario, November 2007

Cobourg resident Madeleine Thibault-Smith, who was inspired to write this poem about the Highway of Heroes.

Taken during the author's ride-along, May 9, 2008, in the procession of Corporal Michael Starker. This banner shows how far some people travel to pay their respects to the fallen soldiers.

filled in another Canadian traveller with great detail when asked about the Highway of Heroes. "I told him, you couldn't have talked to a better person, so I unloaded all the information on him." Three years later, the two still exchange emails and have become friends. "He hadn't been out to a bridge before but he hasn't missed one since."

McVeen talks about two women he met who have driven more than two hours to come to Cobourg from Kitchener a number of times. Their sons were both in the military and had served in Afghanistan.

In covering repatriations or processions since 2002, I think I myself have missed approximately ten, but McVeen brings up a good point when I'm talking to him about the highway. He tells me that he feels guilty when he's not at one. "I feel ashamed when I'm not there, because I'm retired, and that's what I do. I've changed appointments for a number of things. Anything I can change I do, so I can go the bridge."

McVeen is just one of thousands who attend the bridges each time a fallen hero comes home. His story is echoed from Trenton to Toronto, with ordinary Canadians doing their part to let not only the fallen soldier's family know, but, through the media coverage, through word of mouth, to let others who are in harm's way know across the world that we as Canadians care and that we mourn their loss.

Cobourg resident Wayne McVeen raises the flag from the Ontario Street bridge, January 9, 2009.

JOHN

John Prno, Director of Medical Services for the Region of Waterloo, drives for an hour and a half to attend a bridge in Toronto. He sat down to share his thoughts on the Highway of Heroes with me:

> My son Justin was on tours in Afghanistan in 2006 and 2008, first as a Reservist with the Royal Highland Fusiliers of Canada out of Cambridge, then with Regular Force 3RCR out of Petawawa. I don't recall when I started going to the bridges, but it was [sometime] during his first tour in 2006.
>
> I remember driving down with my wife, Deb, for the first time, on a warm summer day, and ending up at Warden and 401. [There] was a narrow sidewalk on the overpass and the bridge shook with each passing truck. (Not the most comfortable place to be!) I think there were five of us there that day — an older veteran and his wife, along with a regular force soldier, and Deb and I. Even without the crowds that show up now, it was a very emotional day.
>
> We were hooked. The vet told us he'd heard there was a group that gathered on Victoria Park [bridge], so we went there the next time — and ever since. For the longest time, I made it to pretty well all of the repatriations. I've lost count how many, but in 2008, Paul Filsinger, another Kitchener member of our family support group, FOCSIA (Families of Canadian Soldiers in Afghanistan), started coming with me. His son Ryan was with PPCLI in Shilo and had been deployed, as well. Neither of our wives could bring themselves to come once our kids were in the midst of the fighting, so it was nice to have someone to go with. Because he worked in Markham at the time, he was also able to make the weekday repatriations that I couldn't always get to. I always felt better knowing there was someone there from our group, and we brought along many other family members over the years.
>
> We met some amazing people on that bridge ... family members of fallen soldiers who came back to say thank you — even Brian Williams

from TSN, who lives nearby and is a great supporter of our troops. He and Paul actually struck up quite the friendship, corresponded regularly, and Brian came out to speak to our support group last year.

Sadly, I've slipped up the last few repatriations. I've had work commitments and recently weather postponed the repatriation from a day I could go to one I couldn't. Hopefully, there won't be another one, but if there is, I'll make every effort to be there. I've always been extremely proud of what the Highway of Heroes means … of course, in respect to our fallen and their families, but also to what a ground swell of genuine public support it really is. This is nothing the government came up with and asked people to show up for. They come because they want to, or, as in our case, just [because they] feel they have to be there. I can't think of any other initiative like it that has joined regular citizens [and] our military and emergency services into one mass cause. Even those that do not support the war understand that the Highway of Heroes is about supporting our troops.

LARRY

Though it was six years before he went to a bridge, Toronto resident and firefighter for the city for more than 30 years, Larry Lalonde has felt for every soldier who has travelled along the highway.

Through newspapers, radio, and television, Lalonde saw the faces of the young men and women who gave their lives for the betterment of the people of Afghanistan. "One thing led to another and we just missed it, or I was working."

Although he feels guilty about it, nothing was going to stop him from going to the bridge for the procession of 21-year-old Corporal Étienne Gonthier on January 27, 2008. Since that day when the 78th Canadian soldier came home for the final time, Lalonde has only missed attending a bridge if he has had to work.

Lalonde remembers that first time vividly. "It was really very special to me. My wife [Sue] and I went out to my sister-in-law's for a visit and I said 'I'm going to the bridge today.' I didn't care if anybody else was coming, I was going to go."

Lalonde brought a Canadian flag with him and travelled to his in-laws', the Britts, in Ajax, east of Toronto. "I went out … and told them what I was going to do, and they said, 'we're coming along,' … that was their first time."

The Britts took their Canadian flag off the front lawn of their home and went with the Lalondes to the bridge in Ajax. "It was super, super emotional, standing up on the bridge, all of us crying. We were totally overwhelmed … never have seen anything like it. It is something I'll always remember."

Cheryl and Randy Britt stand on the Harwood Road bridge in Ajax, January 27, 2008.

Photo courtesy Larry Lalonde.

A few months afterward, in the spring of 2009, Lalonde drove past a McDonald's near his home at Port Union and Lawrence Avenue in Toronto. He noticed something that bothered him so much that when he got home he phoned the restaurant and asked to speak to the manager. The Canadian flag had been at half-staff, and being a member of the community, Lalonde wondered if a neighbour or employee had been tragically killed.

The manager explained that, since the restaurant could be seen from the highway, the flag was lowered in honour of the fallen soldier coming home. Lalonde was so taken by the gesture of the restaurant that he phoned and spoke with the owner.

Dale Bartlett owns six McDonald's restaurants in Scarborough, Ontario, but the most highly visible is the one just off the highway near the Port Union Road overpass. "I've rarely ever been touched by war," said Bartlett. "I've watched it on television, and read it in the paper, but actually seeing the effects of war, I've never experienced."

What hit home was when Bartlett, who has a wife and three children who work at the restaurant, happened to be sitting in his car in the parking lot when he witnessed a procession pass by along the highway. "I'll tell you, I've never felt that much emotion [as] when I saw the hearse go by, and witnessed everyone on the bridge — it was packed. I said to myself, now I get it. I know what war is about."

Feeling the need to do something, he thought of his friend who owns a McDonalds in the city of Kingston, Ontario. Kingston has a population of over 120,000 people and is home to CFB Kingston. Knowing his friend was actively involved in supporting the military in many ways, Bartlett also felt the need to show his support for the military and came up with the idea of lowering the flag each time a procession passed along the highway.

"We're a highway store, with an 80-foot flagpole with an 18-foot ... flag. So I thought, in honour of the fallen soldiers, I'm going to lower my flag to half-mast."

Bartlett's wife took a picture the first time manager Ali Tayebi lowered the flag of the restaurant. Whenever a soldier passed, the flag was lowered. Over time, people would periodically call, or ask at the store why the flag was lowered. When staff told them, Bartlett said people were surprised and thought it was a nice gesture. Lalonde was one of the people who contacted Bartlett over the phone.

A few months later, the two met. "I told him it was in respect of the fallen soldiers," said Bartlett. "I could tell when I told him he was choking up. Although he said he couldn't believe what we were doing, I told him it's not much, but it's the least we can do."

Photo courtesy Larry Lalonde.

Larry Lalonde, his wife Suzie, and their granddaughter Lily-Anne Lalonde stand on an overpass in Toronto.

Lalonde then said it would be nice if other businesses along the highway did the samc to show their respect. Lalonde says that as soon as he got home that day he started looking up businesses along the highway, and sending out emails and making phone calls.

Over several weeks of frustration, and many phone calls looking for the "right" person who could make the decision, Lalonde managed to get most companies along the highway onboard, many agreeing to lower their flags when the processions passed.

First on his list was Toyota Canada headquarters, located in Scarborough. "A couple of times they said they'll look into it, but after … three or four weeks I phoned and asked for the president of the company. I thought, I might as well go to the top of the ladder."

But Lalonde could only get as high as the secretary to the president. After explaining in-depth his plight over the phone, frustration turned to jubilation, and a few days later the secretary phoned back to tell him that their flag would be lowered.

"The security centre at Toyota is amazing. They get the notice and it's red-flagged on their bulletin board … that flag is down for sure that day."

During that time, Lalonde was also busy with other businesses along the stretch of highway throughout the Greater Toronto Area. He says it was a "slow process," but knowing it was the right thing, he didn't give up, and settled for nothing short of full participation.

Contacting the vice president of corporate affairs, Sandra Kaiser, at SmartCentres, he once again explained the importance of lowering the flags to honour the fallen soldiers, and showing respect to the soldiers' families.

"She was a wonderful lady and was very, very helpful," says Lalonde.

Kaiser remembers the same about Lalonde, as well as his passion for getting businesses along the highway to lower their flags. "He said that although the government of Canada had a different policy about lowering the flags, he was asking [that] we lower them when a soldier passes. I told him, you're talking to the converted. My mom was a veteran."

Kaiser's mother was a Second World War veteran who passed away in November 2009. A few years prior to her death she was honoured to be asked to join the governor general of Canada in laying a wreath during Remembrance Day services in Ottawa.

"I told him [Lalonde], of course we would participate … tell us what you want us to do and when do we do it?"

Kaiser notified members of her staff about the new protocol with respect to the flags. Lalonde responded to her co-operation: "I am so glad that you agree to this lowering of our flag to bring our fallen home. It's like our flag is bowing its head in honour. I realize that Ottawa has some protocols but sometimes I feel that we have to refine some of these protocols, for not all of them are carved in stone. This is why this grassroots movement is growing."

But SmartCentres took the initiative one step farther. When Kaiser discussed lowering the flags with owner Mitchell Goldhar, he proposed another idea. "I told Mitch we were lowering the flags along the Highway of Heroes and he said, why aren't we lowering all of our flags along the highway?"

Soon after, all the SmartCentres along the 400-series highways in Ontario began lowering their flags whenever a fallen soldier came home. "It's the least we can do," said Kaiser. "You have men and women who are serving in Afghanistan and other dangerous places. It's a simple gesture to show respect to the fallen soldiers who are coming back."

Kaiser says Lalonde is "incredible … very passionate about getting the flags lowered along the highway. I can certainly understand why so many people are supporting him."

When Lalonde went by one of the busy shopping centres only hours after it was announced that another soldier was killed, their flag was already lowered. "I hadn't even sent a message out and their flag was down!" It was that commitment that spurred Lalonde on.

He then phoned up CTV, but the person who answered informed him that they followed the Canadian flag etiquette rule, meaning they only put their flag at half-mast twice a year.

Lalonde later saw a story that veteran reporter Tom Hayes had done about a woman in Toronto who had hung a flag on a bush in a townhouse complex, and the manager had forced her to remove it because it wasn't on a flagpole. And in August of 2009, after a CTV camera operator was killed along with another person in a helicopter crash north of Montreal, things changed. The CTV building lowered their flags in honour of their colleague.

Lalonde called Mr. Hayes after he saw the lowered flag. "I phoned Tom Hayes a couple of days after I saw the flag lowered, because I knew we had two more soldiers coming home in the next few days." Corporal Christian Bobbitt and Sapper Matthieu Allard had been killed on August 1, 2009, by an IED.

After Lalonde explained the situation and what he was asking CTV to do, the reporter said he'd call him back. Five minutes later Lalonde received a phone call. It was Hayes: "Consider it done," he said. Less than an hour later, Lalonde drove to CTV to get pictures of the flag at half-staff.

He then went to one of the bridges nearby to show friends and Legion members the respect CTV was showing for fallen Canadian soldiers. "I said, hey guys, I want to show you something. I showed them the pictures of the flag on my camera and everyone was thrilled. I give 100 percent credit to Tom Hayes for that."

Hayes remembers the phone call but downplays his role, saying CTV was on board from the start. "I remember one day I got a phone call from Larry because there were two soldiers coming along [the highway] that day and I was doing a story. We had lowered the flag and joined the collective salute and I actually used the background of our flag out front in the story. CTV was all over it and glad to take part.... It was a huge initiative along the 401."

Like the thousands of people standing on bridge after bridge, Hayes said, businesses along the highway also did their part. "It's these individual efforts of these huge companies all on side, all on board doing their individual part in order to create a collective thank you and salute to these soldiers. I think we are all passionate about the Highway of Heroes. It's our backyard, but the entire country appreciates it."

Bud Lauria of Lauria Hyundai in Port Hope has a 25-metre flag pole with a flag measuring five by nine metres. Though others had tried to get Lauria to lower the flag over the years, he said his biggest concern was if he wasn't able to do it for one of the soldiers for some reason, it might be perceived as disrespectful.

Lalonde told him, "If you can put it down this time, put it down. If you can't put it down due to weather conditions, you can put it down the next time. You're putting it down for the sole purpose for the respect of our fallen soldiers."

After speaking with Lalonde, Lauria had a change of heart: "Within a couple of days I came to the conclusion that it's the right thing to do, and ever since we've lowered the flag."

Photo courtesy Larry Lalonde.

The first time CTV lowered the flag in front of their offices facing the Highway of Heroes, September 9, 2009.

Lauria used to put the flag at half-mast later in the morning on the day that a fallen soldier came home, but after seeing the procession of stretch limousines heading east from Toronto, he started lowering the flag earlier so that the families could see it as they passed by on their way to CFB Trenton. "Out of respect for the family, I want them to see it at half-mast on their way to Trenton [as well]."

When Lalonde hears that a soldier has been killed, he sends out a standard email to all the businesses along the highway that he's contacted. Also, he will try to add at least one news story to the email. "I always make sure there is a picture of the soldier included in the email."

Like other businesses along the highway, Dale Bartlett, owner of the McDonald's location, does his very best to ensure the flag outside his restaurant is at half-mast whenever a procession passes. Because the flag is in a highly visible area, people notice when things aren't up to the standard they are used to. "Larry notices everything, and one time, when we lost a halyard off the top of the flagpole, he asked why the flag wasn't flying." Bartlett said he tried to get it fixed before the next

repatriation, but had to bring in specialized equipment to reach the 25 metres up into the air to repair it.

Although lowering the flag is sometimes a "make-work project" — the store is located near the top of a hill and it is often extremely windy there — they do it, and, as Bartlett says, "We do it [out of] respect for the soldiers."

He says that Lalonde's dedication amazes him. "He's a great guy and very passionate about everyone lowering the flags."

Companies that Lalonde contacted and who have agreed to lower their flags include: McDonald's (Port Union/401); SmartCentres (throughout 400-series Highways Company); Scarborough Town Centre (Oxford properties, McCowan/401); Loblaw Super Centre (Scarborough Town Centre); Toyota Canada (Bellamy and 401); the Armenian Community Centre; CTV News (McCowan and 401); Zellers Distribution Centre; Ironstone Media on Whites Road; Howard Johnson (Warden and 401); Gervais Rentals (McCowan and 401); Lauria Hyundai in Port Hope; SmartCentres at Brock Road and 401; and Golfour Property Services on Brock Road.

Fire departments honouring the soldiers as they pass along the route are from Quinte-West, Municipality of Brighton, Municipality of Cramahe, Alnwick/Haldimand Township, Hamilton Township, Town of Cobourg, Municipality of Port Hope, Bowmanville, Oshawa, Ajax, Pickering, and Whitby.

Although the City of Toronto doesn't allow for any of the fire equipment on the bridges due to safety issues because of the volume of traffic, Chief William Stewart told me that

Bud Lauria, of Lauria Hyundai in Port Hope, lowers his 30 by 15-foot Canadian flag that flies atop an 80-foot pole each time a fallen Canadian soldier travels past.

four commands from the fire department are represented once the procession leaves the Don Valley Parkway and enters city streets. The procession passes by one fire hall, and its members stand shoulder to shoulder along the roadway. At an intersection where the procession turns south, just a few blocks from the coroner's office, another pumper is placed on the roadway, and firefighters stand by, saluting. Finally, outside the coroner's building, an honour guard of firefighters stand alongside other emergency services as the long line of black vehicles arrives at its final destination.

Photo courtesy Larry Lalonde.

ABOVE: *The Armenian Youth Centre at Victoria Park and Highway 401 has been lowering its flag during the processions since Larry Lalonde spoke to staff about the importance of paying their respects to the fallen soldiers and their families.*

LEFT: *Two firefighters from the Ajax Fire and Emergency Services unfold a Canadian flag as we pass during the procession for Gunner Jonathan Dion, January 2, 2008.*

One of the escorting officers shakes hands with a member of the Toronto Fire Department after a procession arrives at the coroner's building in Toronto, March 23, 2009.

CHAPTER 8  A VIEW FROM THE HIGHWAY

For two retired Ontario Provincial Police (OPP) officers, the milestone of their careers was participating in the procession along the Highway of Heroes.

Sergeant Harry Carrigan and Constable Chris Johnson both worked out of the Whitby OPP Detachment, Highway Safety Division. Carrigan retired in 2008 after 25 years of policing and Johnson retired on June 30, 2010, after a 30-year career with the force.

The two officers were an integral part of the processions along the Highway of Heroes between 2002 and 2010: Carrigan participated in all but one procession between 2002 and 2008, and Johnson in all but two from 2007 until 2010. The officers led the procession of vehicles from CFB Trenton to Toronto. From there, Toronto Police took over, leading the procession to the coroner's office. The police always have one cruiser at the front of the procession and one at the rear.

OPP Constable Harry Carrigan at the repatriation of Gunner Jonathan Dion, January 2, 2008.

Johnson clearly remembers the day Carrigan mentioned that he needed assistance because of the scope of the procession — it was in July of 2007, and sadly, six fallen soldiers were coming home. So he offered to help. "Because I was the court officer and working straight days, it was the perfect opportunity to give Harry a hand — I felt strongly about it, as well." From that point on, Carrigan led and Johnson took up the position at the rear of the procession.

When Carrigan first started participating in the processions, he says that the majority of people who came out were on the bridges in the Cobourg and Port Hope area, but that today the crowds cover bridges all along the route from Trenton to Toronto.

Ontario Provincial Police Constable Chris Johnson salutes during a repatriation at Canadian Forces Base Trenton.

When I rode with Carrigan for the procession of Gunner Jonathan Dion on January 2, 2008, we chatted about how much the highway meant to ordinary citizens, as well as to emergency services. He told me that once, on the way into Toronto during the evening hours, a police helicopter lit up the bridges along the way so that the people in the procession could see the throngs of people standing on the spans.

As Carrigan and I were nearing the base that day, just after exiting the highway, we passed a number of houses. He pointed to one and told me that every time the procession passed by the house, he noticed a family with a number of children standing at the end of their driveway paying their respects. As we left the base on our way to Toronto after the repatriation, I noticed a woman and several children standing by the roadside outside of the house Carrigan had indicated, despite the fact that it was the coldest day of the year to that point.

Several days later, as I was passing through Trenton on my way to Belleville, I decided to pull off and see if I could talk with the woman. I couldn't remember the exact number of the house that they had been standing in front of, but thankfully my camera still held the images I had taken that day. I found the one I was looking for and was able to locate the house. I drove up, parked the car, and knocked on the door. A woman answered — the same woman I had seen a few days earlier. We conversed and I told her who I was. I explained that I had been in the procession a few days earlier and asked her if she had family in the military. When she answered no, I was a bit shocked. Of all the people standing along the bridges and roadways, Carrigan noticed her, and yet she had no ties to the military. I know, hundreds do not, but I just thought that with Trenton being a military community, she would have.

During the procession for Gunner Jonathan Dion on January 2, 2008, the author was moved by the patriotism of this man. Although it was dangerous for him to be parked on the median lane of Canada's busiest highway, he was standing, and saluting, and paying his respects to the fallen soldier and his family.

I told her what Carrigan had said as we were driving by her house — that he always noticed her and the children standing along the roadway, and that it was appreciated. I'm not really sure why I felt compelled to journey off the highway to tell her that, but I've thought of it often since, and I'm glad I did.

I'm privileged to have had the opportunity to go on a number of ride-alongs down the highway with the Ontario Provincial Police. I've ridden with Whitby Detachment Commander Staff Sergeant Rob Kobayashi, and with both Carrigan and Johnson on different occasions. During my rides we have spoken on a number of issues, and I can

Until the summer of 2007, repatriations at CFB Trenton occurred during all hours of the day and evening. Hearses carrying Corporal Nicolas Beauchamp and Private Michel Levesque pass through Northumberland County in the early evening hours as a truck honouring the Canadian Forces provides a backdrop for civilians on the bridge.

say that all three men are fine representatives of policing, and that I was honoured to ride with each of them.

Johnson continued to participate in the processions after Carrigan retired in 2008. The last procession he participated in was for Master-Corporal Kristal Giesebrecht, 34, and Private Andrew Miller, 21, when they came home for the final time on June 29, 2010. That day Johnson took his usual position at the rear of the procession as it made its way from the base at Trenton along the route to Toronto. The next day, the officer, who had spent more than three decades policing, retired.

A young family stands at the end of their driveway, December 8, 2008, as the procession for Corporal Mark McLaren, Private Demetrios Diplaros, and Warrant Officer Robert Wilson passes by. During the author's first ride-along, one OPP officer said that it meant a lot to him to see the family out there each time. The author stopped in one day and told the family how much it was appreciated by those in the procession that they came out to show their support.

But it was those 55 escorts, helping bring home over 120 fallen Canadian heroes between July 8, 2007, and June 29, 2010, that Johnson is most proud of in his career. The only two processions he missed were the day he found out his mother had died, and when he had to undergo an operation.

One memory that is etched in his mind is of a family with two young girls who had lost their father. They were all dressed up just as if they were going to church, wearing pretty little dresses. "They were skipping along," he says, "and I heard one of them ask 'Where's Daddy?' It just rips your heart out." Witnessing repatriations at the base is something that resonates with anyone who has ever been to one. After the casket is placed in the hearse, the families start that slow walk toward it, flowers in hand — it's a moment you never forget. Families embrace, children cling to teddy bears.

Johnson related to me the story of his first procession. It was Sunday July 8, 2007, a sad day because the procession represented the most casualties that had come along the Highway of Heroes together since 2002. Captain Matthew Dawe, Corporal Jordan Anderson, Private Lane Watkins, Private Cole Bartsch, Captain Jefferson Francis, and Master Corporal Colin Bason were all killed on July 4 when a powerful roadside bomb blew apart their vehicle.

Johnson recalls it was a hot day. Being at the base, and seeing one by one the fallen soldiers carried to each hearse, with inconsolable families walking up each time to place flowers inside, was overwhelming for him. I can say after witnessing many repatriations myself, it never gets easier.

Even though it was his first time witnessing a repatriation, he remembers thinking that it seemed to take a very long time. But considering it takes approximately 20 minutes for each, it took upwards of two hours before the procession got underway. As always, thousands of people lined the bridges, only this time, there were more — lots more.

I was on the Ontario Street bridge in Cobourg, waiting for the procession to pass. The overpass had to be shut down because of the sheer number of people on the bridge. It was a tremendous show of support.

Because it was a summer Sunday evening, the highway that day was also jammed with cars heading back to the city. "Traffic was horrendous, and we actually had to go up the median shoulder around the Oshawa area," Johnson recalls.

It was just after 5:00 p.m., and they were nearing Salem Road in Whitby, when Johnson could see from his position at the rear of the procession that one of the hearses had started to fall back out of the long line of vehicles. "We are not in contact with the hearse drivers, so I had no idea what was going on. I could just see the rest … proceeding. Then I noticed the hearse come to a complete stop on the median shoulder, and that changed things a bit for me."

The hearse had a flat tire.

Protocol for the processions dictates that they are not to stop for anything; so, as the long line of hearses and limousines slowly disappeared out of site, Johnson was left to deal with the situation.

One of the six hearses passes the Ontario Street bridge as hundreds stand to pay their respects, July 8, 2007. The bridge was so crowded that day that police had to block the roadway.

There were at least three lanes of traffic, and Johnson turned his cruiser sideways to try to get cars travelling behind him either stopped or redirected around him. He immediately parked his cruiser behind the stopped hearse, blocking traffic inches away from vehicles travelling along Canada's busiest highway.

"At that time I didn't realize there was a spare hearse following further back. But it was a ray of sunshine when he showed up, because I wasn't sure what I was going to do. It was my first time out and something like that happened."

Johnson, along with four other men — the hearse driver with the flat, the soldier accompanying the fallen, the spare hearse driver, and a Military Police officer who was also in the procession — quickly removed the flag-draped casket from one hearse and carefully placed it into the other. "We had to transfer the casket right in the middle of the highway and [then] catch up with the procession as best we could. I'll always remember that. I would think for anybody travelling along the highway it would have been something to see, because I can tell you, it was for me! It was quite a first trip."

As a veteran police officer, Johnson has dealt with the good, the bad, and the ugly during his career, but this situation caught him by surprise. "As a police officer you try to prepare for any eventuality, and I always thought we would end up either having a collision or mechanical difficulty or something. But luckily enough, in the 55 processions I was involved in, that was the only incident that ever caused us a pause."

Those who have ridden along the highway in a procession agree that it's the people on the bridges that makes one's heart swell with pride on such a sad occasion. "True Canadians," Johnson calls them. "When you see the people standing out there in the pouring rain, in minus 20 Celsius, in the cold and wind, and they are … there each and every time. It says a lot about [being] a real Canadian."

Johnson doesn't believe there is any room for politics on the bridges, and I agree. "They are there to support the families that have lost somebody. What more can you say — just good people."

Carrigan says that, during all his years as a police officer, he's never seen anything be embraced more by the people of Canada.

Johnson echoes his old partner's thoughts. "Who would have thought you'd see hundreds of people lining the bridges." Though some are covered with dozens of people waving and holding flags, on some there are only one or two people, but the message of support still comes across loud and clear. "Sometimes I'd see hundreds of people on one bridge and [think], it must have been easy to get to because it's in a town, but here's one or two guys in the middle of nowhere and it made you feel good."

During one trip, Johnson saw a man standing along the median barrier between lanes of traffic. "It was terribly unsafe. But I thought to myself, there's a guy who has his hand over his heart, and he made a point to get up there and show his respect."

He has seen farmers in the fields alongside the highway, or standing against the fence line, holding up flags. "Those are just good people who took time out of their day to come down to the highway. [T]he family may have a difficult time even seeing them because they are so far off the highway, yet there they are standing there."

Durham Regional Police Service members salute along the Highway of Heroes as the author rides in the procession for Gunner Jonathan Dion, January 2, 2008.

To the retired officers, participating in the processions along the Highway of Heroes was very important to them, and they are both proud of their service. "I'd like to think [that] in some small way I may have made things just a little easier for them," says Johnson. "There was nothing else I could do to ease their pain, but just taking part and helping is what it's all about."

Carrigan says he was honoured to have been part of the processions. "It's a great patriotic thing for me. I do have a handle on why we need to recognize these soldiers. They need to be raised on a pedestal as heroes, because they are. These are young men and women who have actually volunteered to go to a strange country and fight for freedom for all of us. For them to lose their life in fighting for freedom for us — we have to get together to recognize them. It just goes to show you how patriotic some people are. It's their way of honouring the soldiers that absolutely deserve it."

Johnson hopes that the experience of riding along the highway helps those families with the healing process, even just a little. "I hate to have to have done it, but I never wanted to miss one. I'm still proud of [being] a part of it. It's one of the best things I did in my career."

CHAPTER 9 ❧ FAMILIES OF THE FALLEN

It's something nobody wants to think about, but it's something that more than 150 families throughout Canada have had to deal with since 2002.

Their loved ones joined the military as a job, as a career, as a way to further themselves and to help others. Tragically, in war, many soldiers make the ultimate sacrifice for their country and, as an extension, for strangers in countries halfway around the world, most of whom they've never met.

Soldiers march off during the repatriation at CFB Trenton, February 15, 2010, following the repatriation of Corporal Joshua Caleb Baker.

From the moment a family is notified by the military that their loved one has been killed, it's a journey that has been described as numbing. It's a journey of pride, but also of sorrow beyond comprehension. Every soldier knows it can happen. And so does every loved one of a soldier — but they try to keep those thoughts at bay as spouses, sons, daughters, mothers, fathers, brothers, sisters, and friends are deployed, often for months at a time.

Though families deal with the pain and celebrate the lives taken from them in different ways, all those I've talked with share a common thought: they don't want their loved one to be forgotten. Here are a few of their stories.

The family of Corporal Nick Bulger acknowledges the crowds as the procession heads onto the highway from CFB Trenton, July 6, 2009.

DARLENE CUSHMAN

The following is adapted from a *Toronto Sun* article written by the author, published Friday, June 6, 2008.

It was a day of pain and pride for Darlene Cushman. On June 15, 2007, she was still in denial about the death of her son, Trooper Darryl Caswell, in Afghanistan, and she cried most of the way to CFB Trenton for her son's repatriation. "I felt that I was going to go get Darryl," Ms. Cushman told me. "A typical mom can run and get a Band-Aid; a typical mom can make things better … for some reason, I had a mixed-up denial thing that Darryl was coming home to his mom. But [this] was a different homecoming."

Ms. Cushman's 25-year-old son, who was serving with the Royal Canadian Dragoons, based at CFB Petawawa, Ontario, was killed by a roadside bomb on June 11, 2007. Remembering back to the day of repatriation, Ms. Cushman said that waiting at the base for her son was the hardest part. When the plane carrying Trooper Caswell's body touched down and taxied to the terminal, his family was escorted out onto the tarmac. When the door to the belly of the plane opened to reveal her son's casket, reality hit. "That was not a bassinet with my baby in it. It was a flag-draped casket with my son, a grown man, so close to his 26th birthday."

Ms. Cushman said her son was scheduled to fly home on his birthday and buy his first house, take his mother's dining-room furniture, and start his new life. "We had a lot of dreams that had all of a sudden just been slammed shut. Now, I had my son in a casket with all these soldiers crying, but trying to be strong."

The casket was lowered into the arms of eight soldiers, who then placed it in the hearse. Ms. Cushman and other family members walked up to the black car that sat on the tarmac while the other soldiers and dignitaries stood by. There was complete silence. "I walked out and placed a red rose on the Canadian flag … it was truly hitting me: *now he's home, but this is how he is home*." As the back door of the hearse closed, the curtains were open. Riding in the first limousine behind the hearse, she remembers seeing the rose on her son's casket the entire way to Toronto. "The red rose moved a little, but it never fell off. It stayed on top."

As the procession headed out from CFB Trenton, supporters were lined up by the roadside, where they had been watching the repatriation service from the fence line

outside the base. "Everyone was standing tall, saluting. Some were crying, some were smiling, but not that kind of smile, it was a smile of comfort." As they headed for Highway 401, she thought there would be fewer people. "But it wasn't that way. There were people all along that highway." She says she can still close her eyes and see the people standing on the bridges along the highway. "I [saw places where the people] truly, truly respected our pain, our loss, the pride they had for a Canadian soldier — and this was my son. I looked at the flag-covered casket, my rose, and back at the people." There was a delay in the repatriation, but the people waited patiently to pay their respects. "I can see everything," she says. "The support the OPP gave [us], the fire trucks, the ambulances, the people, the children, the flags. But there are some … that stand along that Highway of Heroes … that are magnified in my heart."

A brown, rusty pickup truck was pulled over near one of the bridges. No other vehicles were nearby. "There was a father and a teenage boy standing in the back of the … truck saluting as tall as a tall person could be. This man had taken the time to pull over his everyday brown pickup truck to get his teenage boy to stand. And they stood shoulder to shoulder, both arms up, in a perfect

Darlene Cushman, mother of Darryl Caswell, killed in theatre on June 11, 2007.

salute." Ms. Cushman lowered the window of the limousine enough to take her small wooden flag and salute the two men — as she had also done in Trenton to acknowledge the people there.

"The feeling, as a mother, following the casket draped with the rose, with the curtains open — look to your left, look to your right, look up at the bridges, then look back down to why you're doing this — back to reality." She knows why people lined the bridges — to pay tribute to her son — and it gave her so much comfort. "Do I get a good feeling from the Highway of Heroes? You're damn right."

As they drove by Trooper Caswell's hometown of Bowmanville, representatives from the local zoo there brought an elephant covered with a Canadian flag to the bridge. When the procession passed, the elephant stood up and saluted. Ms. Cushman remembers thinking, "Am I tired, or have I seen so many people that now I think I'm seeing elephants?"

So did Canadians disappoint her? "Not a chance." During the repatriation, she explains, families are so overwhelmed with what is happening. But the Highway of Heroes is the only form of comfort at that time. "You're still in shock. You're still in denial."

Trooper Caswell had told his mother that he wanted to be back on Canadian soil before he died. "It's no secret [that] I buried Darryl with grass in his hand. He wanted to come home and touch the grass. I buried Darryl with his little bag of marbles from when he was a little boy, our little joke was, 'Hey, Mom, I guess I didn't lose my marbles after all. I can't lose my marbles; my mom has them.' He has them," she adds softly.

As for the hundreds of people who stood along the roads and bridges that day to pay their respects to a soldier they never knew, Ms. Cushman says, "I can never thank them enough — ever." She knows that her son would be extremely proud. "He would absolutely thank everyone on those bridges, and I try very hard to do that for him, because nobody knows their son more than a mom. I know my son appreciated the small things. He loved everything. He loved adventure, but he'd give you the shirt off his back, and he was my best friend."

When the procession began at CFB Trenton, it was daylight. By the time it reached Toronto, it was dusk, but Ms. Cushman noticed a single, bright shining star in the sky. "I believe that's the beginning. Darryl was showing me light."

CAPTAIN FRED McKAY

The following was written by Toronto Fire Captain Fred McKay, whose son, Private Kevin Thomas McKay, was killed in action on May 13, 2010.

After travelling down the Highway of Heroes, Kevin's journey was over … he was finally home. Our journey, however, was just beginning. Our family had just embarked on an odyssey of sorrow that continues to this day.

How can I describe how we felt? My wife Beth and I, along with our remaining 19-year-old son, Riley, were broken-hearted. Crushed. Devastated. I never thought I could possibly be so sad. The day had gone smoothly. The limo ride from our home in Horseshoe Valley to CFB Trenton, the reception where we greeted friends and family, and meeting all the dignitaries, had gone off without a hitch. But when we were led out onto the tarmac and saw Kevin's flag-draped casket being rolled off the military transport, my dreamlike detachment was suddenly replaced by absolute despair. Our fine young son, to whom we had spoken only a week earlier, was dead.

This harsh new reality swept over me in a tidal wave of grief, and I burst into tears. As I struggled to collect myself, I was helped by

Captain Fred McKay of the Toronto Fire Department, whose son, Private Kevin MacKay, was killed on May 13, 2010.

the realization that Kevin's remains were being handled with the utmost dignity and respect. I found myself watching in wonderment and pride at the sombre and precise way the honour guard shouldered Kevin's casket and carried it slowly to the waiting hearse. I could tell that those guys were hurting, too, but they did their job and they did it very well.

They did it for Kevin and they did it for us. Many people ask themselves the question "What could I possibly do to ease the pain for the family of a fallen soldier?" I truly believe the answer can be found along the Highway of Heroes. From the moment we climbed back into the limo at CFB Trenton and started toward the coroner's office in Toronto, the fence line at the base and the road to the 401 were lined with thousands of people, waving flags and holding signs.

When I met their gaze, they all seemed to say "give me some of your pain … let me share your load … you are not alone in your grief." If you were to ask them, they would all say "It's nothing … it's the least I could do." They might think it's only a small gesture, but I can truthfully say, having been on the receiving end of these "gestures," that it helped us a lot that day. What they did lifted us from the depths of our sorrow, and replaced our grief with pride. We were so very proud of Kevin, and we were shown that they, too, were proud of Kevin and proud to be Canadian.

Canadians know how to honour their fallen soldiers better than any other country. They also know how to show their appreciation for the sacrifice made by those soldiers and their families, as well. As our motorcade made its way to Toronto, we were overwhelmed by the number of people that lined the bridges to show their respect for Kevin and their support for us. I am told that there are 55 bridges between CFB Trenton and the coroner's office in Toronto. To see every one of them jammed with firefighters, police officers, soldiers, and ordinary Canadians filled our hearts with comfort. I shouldn't call them ordinary Canadians … they were *extra*ordinary that day. We did our best to give a wave of thanks to each and every one of them as we went by. We wanted them to know how much they were helping us.

This essay would be incomplete if I didn't acknowledge the unwavering support that my family and I have received from my brother and sister firefighters in Toronto, throughout Ontario, across Canada, and even from around the world. Every bridge and overpass along the Highway of Heroes had firefighters standing at attention and snapping a salute. If that wasn't enough, the sea of firefighters that greeted the motorcade at the coroner's office demonstrated the strong bond that exists between firefighters.

A lone Canadian flag flies along the fence line of CFB Trenton, January 22, 2010, at the repatriation for RCMP members Sergeant Mark Gallager and Chief Superintendent Doug Coates.

Members of the CFB Trenton Fire Department outside the gates of the base at Trenton, March 23, 2009.

I am very aware that when many firefighters found out that the fallen soldier, Private Kevin Thomas McKay, was the son of a Toronto Fire Captain, they just had to come out and show their support. All ranks and many departments were represented at the coroner's office that day, as well as at the funeral, and again at the burial ceremony in Ottawa. To say that this turnout lifted my spirits would be a gross understatement. I will never forget what my brother and sister firefighters have done for my family and I during this ordeal. It has been said that being driven along the Highway of Heroes includes you in a very exclusive club to which nobody really wants to belong. That may be true, but I prefer to regard the Highway of Heroes as one way a nation can say thank you and show its respect for a fallen soldier who has demonstrated the true meaning of the words *Courage*, *Commitment*, and *Sacrifice*.

TARA DAWE

The following is a personal account, written by Tara Dawe, widow of Captain Matt Dawe, killed in action July 4, 2007.

On July 8, 2007, I travelled down the Highway of Heroes following my husband Matt Dawe's hearse and those of his fallen comrades. Six caskets were unloaded from the military plane that day in Trenton, Ontario. Theirs wasn't the first journey taken down the highway, nor would it be the last for Canadian troops.

Only a couple of weeks prior to my experience on the Highway of Heroes, three of Matt's men had made their journey. Matt and I spoke a number of times after he lost his men, and during one of those phone conversations I had described to him what had gone on in Trenton and en route to Toronto. Matt was comforted by the idea that the boys' final journey wasn't taken alone. The fact that it was acknowledged by so many of his fellow Canadians made Matt very proud. He was happy to hear things were being done right back home. Those boys gave everything for their country and the country said thank you; that is all any of them want, anyway.

When it was my turn to take the extremely emotional trek down the highway, I had some idea of what Matt would have thought, and that helped a great deal. I also knew our country would be watching and waving with love and support. For those reasons, I was able to place my two-year-old son, Lucas, into his car seat and climb in alongside the rest of my family for our trip down the Highway of Heroes. Our car joined … the other cars, full of grieving families; it must have been a 30-car procession.

There are a lot of raw emotions that can surface during a two-hour car ride following your husband's dead body. However, from the moment the car drives off the Trenton tarmac you are engulfed in a sea of red. The people, the flags, the motorcycles, the fire trucks and other … vehicles, are simply incredible. All those dark, emotional feelings are pushed aside, just for a short while, because of this beautiful outpouring of support.

Riding alongside Lucas and I were my mother, father, and sister, Matt's best friend, and my Assisting Officer. [W]e rolled down our windows and waved, because that is what felt right. Even Lucas waved. In the beginning, I don't think Lucas knew what to think about all the people. He was more into checking out the fire trucks with their big ladders — remember, he was a two-year-old boy. Yet, as we continued to pass under the filled overpasses he asked why everyone was waving. I told him the people were there to support and cheer on the military boys. So Lucas, with his little hand out the window, started yelling, "Go Daddy's Boys." The expression stuck, and so for the remainder of our journey down the highway, each time we passed under an overpass, draped in Canadian flags, Lucas would wave his hand out the window and shout, "Go Daddy's Boys," together with the rest of us in the car. Lucas's phrase took on such meaning for us in our car that, not long after, my father got his first tattoo: on his bicep, it will forever read "Go Daddy's Boys."

My journey down the Highway of Heroes will never be forgotten. We live in an incredible country, and it has never been more evident to me than on July 8, 2007. This was Matt's homecoming. It was not full of smiles, hugs, and kisses like it was supposed to be. It was a sombre day. My husband's body travelled from Trenton to Toronto in a coffin; but he wasn't alone, and for that I will always be grateful to all those people who came out to show their support. Thank you!

Courtesy of the Department of National Defence.

A Department of National Defence photo of Captain Matthew Dawe, killed on July 4, 2007, along with five other Canadian soldiers.

LIEUTENANT-COLONEL (RETIRED) PETER DAWE

The following heartfelt account was written by the father of Captain Matthew Dawe.

I have been asked to recount what the Highway of Heroes means to my family. Of course it means different things to all of us, but there are probably some sentiments that transcend individual reaction to events and things. Therefore, I will express my feelings in the hope I do justice to the feelings the rest of my family might be experiencing.

Of course it is somewhat trite to say that July 4, 2007, and the days that ensued in the aftermath of Matthew being killed in action as the result of an IED attack in the Panjwaii District of Afghanistan, were the worst days of my life. Our world imploded, but so also did the worlds of the other five Canadian families and the Afghan interpreter who perished with Matt that day. One finds oneself in a state of disbelief, peppered by periods of extreme anguish, in such a time. One is forced to make decisions that matter, and to generally cope, although one's basic instinct is to curl up in the fetal position and to die. I was in that state of mind when we went to Trenton to receive the body of our loved one. The presence of many people with whom I had served did little to relieve the pain but, on some level, it helped that they made the effort to travel to Trenton to show their love and support.

So we went through the agony of waiting for Matt's body to come off the aircraft and watched as the other families received their sons, fathers, and husbands. With six coffins, the ceremony was very long, and we were obliged to stand in the hot sun of early July. So when we got in the hearses, probably 15 to 20 in all, we were physically and mentally exhausted. I think I was looking forward to a quick trip to Toronto in air-conditioned comfort and a shower. But that changed in a hurry.

I must say that I noticed somewhere in the back of my mind the throng of onlookers, not gawkers, who watched the ramp ceremony from outside the fence at CFB Trenton. I probably thought that this was a respectful gesture and probably half wondered why they had to be outside the fence, having come this far. In any event, the motorcade proceeded from the airfield to the 401 for the trip to the morgue in Toronto. Immediately, we encountered the spectators at the gate, a group that included the bikers comprised of former and serving military folks, who lined the road and waved to us. It was most touching. Eventually we got to the 401, having passed a continuous line of people who had gathered along the road to simply wave and express their sorrow and support. I recall thinking that this was an unusual occurrence, given that six young Canadian soldiers had died in one incident.

Entering the on-ramp of the 401, I noticed for the first time that the overpass was packed with people and vehicles and Canadian flags. I still didn't realize what awaited me. I do remember opening the hearse window to say thanks to those who had gathered on a hot Saturday afternoon instead of going to the beach. I didn't yet understand the overpass phenomenon, however.

Of course, every overpass to Toronto and even at intersections in Toronto itself, were absolutely packed. I began to see the common theme. Near the centre of the overpasses were parked two or three fire trucks with uniformed firefighters beside and on top of the vehicles waving Canadian flags of all sizes. There were also police officers of every stripe standing rigidly at attention and saluting. And then there were the families who crowded the rails and stood on the slopes of the overpasses waving and displaying the omnipresent Canadian flag. After the third or fourth such sight, I got it; this was going to continue for a while. Whereas I think I may have been alone at first in rolling down my window to acknowledge this thoughtfulness and respect, I think that there were increasingly more windows opening as we progressed. The procession managed to somehow slow down as we passed these overpasses and that allowed us to wave back.

Some images remain with me to this day. The family units spending a beautiful summer day waiting for hours in some cases for the procession to arrive, just to show, for the brief time that it took for the motorcade to pass, their respects to the families of the fallen. Then there were the new Canadians who stood out because almost all saluted in some manner, with either hand, and certainly not in the rigid precise military salute we are used to. In general, I witnessed many forms of salutes — from the kind just noted to the hand over the heart in the America tradition. It didn't matter; it was a heartfelt tribute of respect and sympathy.

And then there were the uniforms. I suspect there was a good deal of collusion in the paramilitary community given the layout on every overpass was similar. The prominent location of the firemen and their vehicles tells me they may have been key players in providing momentum to this wonderful show of support, willingly aided and abetted by our wonderful police forces.

Not long after witnessing this, I came to realize what it meant. Canadians of all stripes and political leanings are absolutely united in wanting to show that they appreciate the sacrifice of the Canadian servicemen who have fallen in the line of duty. That the people who live in communities from Trenton to Toronto would choose to show that appreciation on a stretch of road leading to the mortuary is unusual and unique in my view. Nonetheless, it works. Other Canadians found other means to show their love and respect; from lakes in Manitoba and DND buildings being named after the fallen, to the establishment of trust funds for surviving children, and everything in between.

LIEUTENANT-COLONEL (RET'D) PETER N. DAWE

Lieutenant-Colonel Peter Dawe was born in St. John's, Newfoundland, to two war veterans who married in England in 1943. His father, Bob Dawe, was a gunner, and his mother, Pamela Novelle, from Ardingly, served with the Royal Air Force.

Peter earned a diploma in Engineering from Memorial University in 1967, a bachelor's degree in Civil Engineering from Nova Scotia Technical College (now Daltech) in 1969, and a Master of Science (Engineering) degree in 1980 from Queen's University.

During his thirty-three years of service as a Military Engineer, some of his employment included service at the Royal Military College (RMC) as a lecturer and assistant professor of Civil Engineering, 1976–80; command of 5e Régiment de Génie du Combat from 1984–86; member of the Directing Staff of the Army Staff College at Fort Frontenac, 1991–94; and the Base Technical Services Officer at Base Kingston until his retirement from the CF in 1995. He later held the position of Executive Secretary of the RMC Board of Governors, 1997–2001, after which he assumed his current position of Executive Director of the RMC Club of Canada, the alumni association for the college.

Colonel Dawe is married to the former Reine Samson from St. Prosper, Quebec. They raised four sons, who all served with the Princess Patricia's Canadian Light Infantry (PPCLI): Lieutenant-Colonel Peter Jr. is the Commanding Officer of 3 PPCLI in Edmonton; Major Philip is an MD serving in Winnipeg; Captain James is retired from the Canadian Forces and now works for CINTAS; and Captain Matthew was killed in action in Kandahar, Afghanistan, on July 4, 2007, while leading a company operation. Peter and Reine live on Buck Lake, where they entertain their six grandchildren, including Lucas, Matt's son.

I have noticed a groundswell of support for various fundraising schemes, from the huge Bay Street–directed True Patriot Love Dinner in Toronto to the Boomer's Legacy Dinner in Victoria, many supporting initiatives to care for the wounded and the families of the fallen with their special needs. All this is occurring in a tough economic climate. Given this generosity, I think Canada is a better place because of the sacrifice of our servicemen.

I think summing up the whole 401 phenomenon with the title "Highway of Heroes" is absolutely brilliant and appropriate. It is a symbol that speaks to how Canadians feel, not so much about the mission as showing support for our brave young Canadians. Not that I disagree with the notion of the most fortunate country on the planet doing its share to assist others to better their lives, not in the least. It is also an example for the rest of the world, certainly those countries that share the load in Afghanistan and elsewhere, about how best to honour the fallen, and by extension, how to care for those who survive.

IN MEMORIUM  OUR FALLEN HEROES*

*(*List is complete as of July 8, 2011)*

Captain Mark Peebles salutes during the repatriation of Sapper Mathieu Allard, 21, and Corporal Christian Bobbitt, 23, CFB Trenton, August 4, 2009.

"Lest We Forget"

Sergeant Marc D. Léger
Age: 29
Hometown: Lancaster, Ontario
Unit: 3rd Battalion, Princess Patricia's Canadian Light Infantry, Edmonton, Alberta
Deceased: April 18, 2002

Corporal Ainsworth Dyer
Age: 24
Hometown: Montreal, Quebec
Unit: 3rd Battalion, Princess Patricia's Canadian Light Infantry, Edmonton, Alberta
Deceased: April 18, 2002

Private Richard Green
Age: 21
Hometown: Mill Cove, Nova Scotia
Unit: 3rd Battalion, Princess Patricia's Canadian Light Infantry, Edmonton, Alberta
Deceased: April 18, 2002

Private Nathan Smith
Age: 26
Hometown: Tatamagouche, Nova Scotia
Unit: 3rd Battalion, Princess Patricia's Canadian Light Infantry, Edmonton, Alberta
Deceased: April 18, 2002

Sergeant Robert Alan Short
Age: 41
Hometown: Fredericton, New Brunswick
Unit: 3rd Battalion, Royal Canadian Regiment, Petawawa, Ontario
Deceased: October 2, 2003

Corporal Jamie Brendan Murphy
Age: 26
Hometown: Conception Harbour, Newfoundland and Labrador
Unit: 1st Battalion, Royal Canadian Regiment, Petawawa, Ontario
Deceased: January 27, 2004

Private Braun Scott Woodfield
Age: 24
Hometown: Eastern Passage, Nova Scotia
Unit: 2nd Battalion, Royal Canadian Regiment, Oromocto, New Brunswick
Deceased: November 24, 2005

Minister-Counsellor Glyn Berry
Age: 59
Hometown: Northhampton, U.K.
Canada's Senior Political Director at the Kandahar Provincial Reconstruction Team in Afghanistan
Deceased: January 15, 2006

Corporal Paul Davis
Age: 28
Hometown: Bridgewater, Nova Scotia
Unit: 2nd Battalion, Princess Patricia's Canadian Light Infantry, Shilo, Manitoba
Deceased: March 2, 2006

Master Corporal Timothy Wilson
Age: 30
Hometown: Grande Prairie, Alberta
Unit: 2nd Battalion, Princess Patricia's Canadian Light Infantry, Shilo, Manitoba
Deceased: March 5, 2006

Private Robert Costall
Age: 22
Hometown: Thunder Bay, Ontario
Unit: 1st Battalion, Princess Patricia's Canadian Light Infantry, Edmonton, Alberta
Deceased: March 29, 2006

Corporal Matthew David James Dinning
Age: 23
Hometown: Richmond Hill, Ontario
Unit: 2 Military Police Platoon, Petawawa, Ontario
Deceased: April 22, 2006

Lieutenant William Turner
Age: 45
Hometown: Toronto, Ontario
Unit: Land Force Western Area Headquarters, Edmonton, Alberta (20th Field Artillery Regiment)
Deceased: April 22, 2006

Corporal Randy Payne
Age: 32
Hometown: Gananoque, Ontario
Unit: 1 Garrison Military Police Company, Detachment Wainwright, Alberta
Deceased: April 22, 2006

Bombardier Myles Stanley John Mansell
Age: 25
Hometown: Victoria, British Columbia
Unit: 5th (British Columbia) Field Artillery Regiment, Victoria, British Columbia
Deceased: April 22, 2006

Captain Nichola Kathleen Sarah Goddard
Age: 26
Hometown: Calgary, Alberta
Unit: 1st Royal Canadian Horse Artillery, Shilo, Manitoba
Deceased: May 17, 2006

Corporal Anthony Joseph Boneca
Age: 21
Hometown: Thunder Bay, Ontario
Unit: Lake Superior Scottish Regiment, Thunder Bay, Ontario
Deceased: July 9, 2006

Corporal Jason Patrick Warren
Age: 29
Hometown: Quebec City, Quebec
Unit: The Black Watch (Royal Highland Regiment) of Canada, Montreal, Quebec
Deceased: July 22, 2006

Corporal Francisco Gomez
Age: 44
Hometown: Edmonton, Alberta
Unit: 1st Battalion, Princess Patricia's Canadian Light Infantry, Edmonton, Alberta
Deceased: July 22, 2006

Major Paeta Derek Hess-von Kruedener
Age: 44
Hometown: Burlington, Ontario
Unit: Princess Patricia's Canadian Light Infantry/UN Military Observer (deployed as member of UNTSO at time of death)
Deceased: July 25, 2006

Corporal Christopher Jonathan Reid
Age: 34
Hometown: Truro, Nova Scotia
Unit: 1st Battalion, Princess Patricia's Canadian Light Infantry, Edmonton, Alberta
Deceased: August 3, 2006

Corporal Bryce Jeffrey Keller
Age: 27
Hometown: Regina, Saskatchewan
Unit: 1st Battalion, Princess Patricia's Canadian Light Infantry, Edmonton, Alberta
Deceased: August 3, 2006

Sergeant Vaughan Ingram
Age: 35
Hometown: Burgeo, Newfoundland and Labrador
Unit: 1st Battalion, Princess Patricia's Canadian Light Infantry, Edmonton, Alberta
Deceased: August 3, 2006

Private Kevin Dallaire
Age: 22
Hometown: Calgary, Alberta
Unit: 1st Battalion, Princess Patricia's Canadian Light Infantry, Edmonton, Alberta
Deceased: August 3, 2006

Master Corporal Raymond Arndt
Age: 31
Hometown: Edson, Alberta
Unit: The Loyal Edmonton Regiment, Edmonton, Alberta
Deceased: August 5, 2006

Master Corporal Jeffrey Scott Walsh
Age: 33
Hometown: Regina, Saskatchewan
Unit: 2nd Battalion, Princess Patricia's Canadian Light Infantry, Shilo, Manitoba
Deceased: August 9, 2006

Corporal Andrew James Eykelenboom
Age: 23
Hometown: Comox, British Columbia
Unit: 1st Field Ambulance, Edmonton, Alberta
Deceased: August 11, 2006

Corporal David Braun
Age: 27
Hometown: Raymore, Saskatchewan
Unit: 2nd Battalion Princess Patricia's Canadian Light Infantry, Shilo, Manitoba
Deceased: August 22, 2006

Sergeant Shane Stachnik
Age: 30
Hometown: Waskatenau, Alberta
Unit: 2 Combat Engineer Regiment, Petawawa, Ontario
Deceased: September 3, 2006

Warrant Officer Richard Francis Nolan
Age: 39
Hometown: Mount Pearl, Newfoundland and Labrador
Unit: 1st Battalion, The Royal Canadian Regiment, Petawawa, Ontario
Deceased: September 3, 2006

Warrant Officer Frank Robert Mellish
Age: 38
Hometown: Truro, Nova Scotia
Unit: 1st Battalion, The Royal Canadian Regiment, Petawawa, Ontario
Deceased: September 3, 2006

Private William Jonathan James Cushley
Age: 21
Hometown: Port Lambton, Ontario
Unit: 1st Battalion, The Royal Canadian Regiment, Petawawa, Ontario
Deceased: September 3, 2006

Private Mark Anthony Graham
Age: 33
Hometown: Hamilton, Ontario
Unit: 1st Battalion, The Royal Canadian Regiment, Petawawa, Ontario
Deceased: September 4, 2006

Corporal Keith Morley
Age: 30
Hometown: Winnipeg, Manitoba
Unit: 2nd Battalion, Princess Patricia's Canadian Light Infantry, Shilo, Manitoba
Deceased: September 18, 2006

Corporal Shane Keating
Age: 30
Hometown: Dalmeny, Saskatchewan
Unit: 2nd Battalion, Princess Patricia's Canadian Light Infantry, Shilo, Manitoba
Deceased: September 18, 2006

Private David Byers
Age: 22
Hometown: Espanola, Ontario
Unit: 2nd Battalion, Princess Patricia's Canadian Light Infantry, Shilo, Manitoba
Deceased: September 18, 2006

Corporal Glen Arnold
Age: 32
Hometown: McKerrow, Ontario
Unit: 2 Field Ambulance, Petawawa, Ontario
Deceased: September 18, 2006

Private Josh Klukie
Age: 23
Hometown: Shuniah, Ontario
Unit: 1st Battalion, The Royal Canadian Regiment, Petawawa, Ontario
Deceased: September 29, 2006

Corporal Robert Thomas James Mitchell
Age: 32
Hometown: Owen Sound, Ontario
Unit: Royal Canadian Dragoons, Petawawa, Ontario
Deceased: October 3, 2006

Sergeant Craig Paul Gillam
Age: 40
Hometown: South Branch, Newfoundland and Labrador
Unit: Royal Canadian Dragoons, Petawawa, Ontario
Deceased: October 3, 2006

Trooper Mark Andrew Wilson
Age: 39
Hometown: London, Ontario
Unit: Royal Canadian Dragoons, Petawawa, Ontario
Deceased: October 7, 2006

Private Blake Neil Williamson
Age: 23
Hometown: Ottawa, Ontario.
Unit: 1st Battalion, The Royal Canadian Regiment, Petawawa, Ontario
Deceased: October 14, 2006

Sergeant Darcy Scott Tedford
Age: 32
Hometown: Calgary, Alberta
Unit: 1st Battalion, The Royal Canadian Regiment, Petawawa, Ontario
Deceased: October 14, 2006

Corporal Albert Storm
Age: 36
Hometown: Niagara Falls, Ontario
Unit: 1st Battalion, The Royal Canadian Regiment, Petawawa, Ontario
Deceased: November 27, 2006

Chief Warrant Officer Robert Girouard
Age: 46
Hometown: Bouctouche, New Brunswick
Unit: 1st Battalion, The Royal Canadian Regiment, Petawawa, Ontario
Deceased: November 27, 2006

Corporal Kevin Megeney
Age: 25
Hometown: New Glasgow, Nova Scotia
Unit: 1st Battalion, The Nova Scotia Highlanders (North), Truro, Nova Scotia
Deceased: March 6, 2007

Private Kevin Vincent Kennedy
Age: 20
Hometown: St. John's, Newfoundland and Labrador
Unit: 2nd Battalion, The Royal Canadian Regiment, Gagetown, New Brunswick
Deceased: April 8, 2007

Private David Robert Greenslade
Age: 20
Hometown: Saint John, New Brunswick
Unit: 2nd Battalion, The Royal Canadian Regiment, Gagetown, New Brunswick
Deceased: April 8, 2007

Corporal Aaron Edward Williams
Age: 23
Hometown: Perth-Andover, New Brunswick
Unit: 2nd Battalion, The Royal Canadian Regiment, Gagetown, New Brunswick
Deceased: April 8, 2007

Corporal Christopher Paul Stannix
Age: 24
Hometown: Dartmouth, Nova Scotia
Unit: Princess Louise Fusiliers, Halifax, Nova Scotia
Deceased: April 8, 2007

Corporal Brent Donald Poland
Age: 37
Hometown: Sarnia, Ontario
Unit: 2nd Battalion, The Royal Canadian Regiment, Gagetown, New Brunswick
Deceased: April 8, 2007

Sergeant Donald Lucas
Age: 31
Hometown: St. John's, Newfoundland and Labrador
Unit: 2nd Battalion, The Royal Canadian Regiment, Gagetown, New Brunswick
Deceased: April 8, 2007

Trooper Patrick James Pentland
Age: 23
Hometown: Geary, New Brunswick
Unit: The Royal Canadian Dragoons, Petawawa, Ontario
Deceased: April 11, 2007

Master Corporal Allan Stewart
Age: 31
Hometown: Newcastle, New Brunswick
Unit: The Royal Canadian Dragoons, Petawawa, Ontario
Deceased: April 11, 2007

Master Corporal Anthony Klumpenhouwer
Age: 25
Hometown: Listowel, Ontario
Unit: Canadian Special Operations Forces Command
Deceased: April 18, 2007

Corporal Matthew McCully
Age: 25
Hometown: Orangeville, Ontario
Unit: 2 Canadian Mechanized Brigade Group Headquarters and Signals Squadron, Petawawa, Ontario
Deceased: May 25, 2007

Master Corporal Darrell Jason Priede
Age: 30
Hometown: Burlington, Ontario
Unit: Army News Team, 3 Area Support Group, Canadian Forces Base Gagetown
Deceased: May 30, 2007

Trooper Darryl Caswell
Age: 25
Hometown: Bowmanville, Ontario
Unit: The Royal Canadian Dragoons, Petawawa, Ontario
Deceased: June 11, 2007

Private Joel Wiebe
Age: 22
Hometown: Edmonton, Alberta
Unit: 3rd Battalion, Princess Patricia's Canadian Light Infantry, Edmonton, Alberta
Deceased: June 20, 2007

Corporal Stephen Frederick Bouzane
Age: 26
Hometown: Springdale, Newfoundland and Labrador
Unit: 3rd Battalion, Princess Patricia's Canadian Light Infantry, Edmonton, Alberta
Deceased: June 20, 2007

Sergeant Christos Karigiannis
Age: 31
Hometown: Montreal, Quebec
Unit: 3rd Battalion, Princess Patricia's Canadian Light Infantry, Edmonton, Alberta
Deceased: June 20, 2007

Private Lane William Thomas Watkins
Age: 20
Hometown: Winnipeg, Manitoba
Unit: 3rd Battalion, Princess Patricia's Canadian Light Infantry, Edmonton, Alberta
Deceased: July 4, 2007

Corporal Cole D. Bartsch
Age: 23
Hometown: Saskatchewan
Unit: 3rd Battalion, Princess Patricia's Canadian Light Infantry, Edmonton, Alberta
Deceased: July 4, 2007

Master Corporal Colin Stuart Francis Bason
Age: 28
Hometown: Burnaby, British Columbia
Unit: The Royal Westminster Regiment, New Westminster, British Columbia
Deceased: July 4, 2007

Captain Matthew Johnathan Dawe
Age: 27
Hometown: Kingston, Ontario
Unit: 3rd Battalion, Princess Patricia's Canadian Light Infantry, Edmonton, Alberta
Deceased: July 4, 2007

Corporal Jordan Anderson
Age: 25
Hometown: Iqaluit, Nunavut
Unit: 3rd Battalion, Princess Patricia's Canadian Light Infantry, Edmonton, Alberta
Deceased: July 4, 2007

Captain Jefferson Clifford Francis
Age: 37
Hometown: New Brunswick
Unit: 1 Royal Canadian Horse Artillery, Shilo, Manitoba
Deceased: July 4, 2007

Private Simon Longtin
Age: 23
Hometown: Longueuil, Quebec
Unit: 3rd Battalion, Royal 22e Régiment, Valcartier, Quebec
Deceased: August 19, 2007

Master Warrant Officer Mario Mercier
Age: 43
Hometown: Weedon, Quebec
Unit: 2nd Battalion, Royal 22e Régiment, Valcartier, Quebec
Deceased: August 22, 2007

Master Corporal Christian Duchesne
Age: 34
Hometown: Montreal, Quebec
Unit: 5th Field Ambulance, 5 Area Support Group, Valcartier, Quebec
Deceased: August 22, 2007

Major Raymond Mark Ruckpaul
Age: 42
Hometown: Hamilton, Ontario
Unit: Armoured Corps, The Royal Canadian Dragoons
Deceased: August 29, 2007

Corporal Nathan Hornburg
Age: 24
Hometown: Calgary, Alberta
Unit: The King's Own Calgary Regiment, Alberta
Deceased: September 24, 2007

Corporal Nicolas R. Beauchamp
Age: 28
Hometown: Montreal, Quebec
Unit: 5 Field Ambulance, Valcartier, Quebec
Deceased: November 17, 2007

Private Michel Jr. Lévesque
Age: 25
Hometown: Rivière-Rouge, Quebec
Unit: 3 Battalion, Royal 22e Régiment, Valcartier, Quebec
Deceased: November 17, 2007

Gunner Jonathan Dion
Age: 27
Hometown: Gatineau, Quebec
Unit: 5e Régiment d'artillerie légère du Canada, Valcartier, Quebec
Deceased: December 30, 2007

Corporal Éric Labbé
Age : 31
Hometown: Rimouski, Quebec
Unit: 2nd Battalion, Royal 22e Régiment, Valcartier, Quebec
Deceased: January 6, 2008

Warrant Officer Hani Massouh
Age : 41
Hometown: Alexandria, Egypt
Unit: 2nd Battalion, Royal 22e Régiment, Valcartier, Quebec
Deceased: January 6, 2008

Trooper Richard Renaud
Age: 26
Hometown: Alma, Quebec
Unit: 12e Régiment blindé du Canada, Valcartier, Quebec
Deceased: January 15, 2008

Corporal Étienne Gonthier
Age: 21
Hometown: St-Georges-de-Beauce, Quebec
Unit: 5 Combat Engineer Regiment, Valcartier, Quebec
Deceased: January 23, 2008

Trooper Michael Y. Hayakaze
Age: 25
Hometown: Edmonton, Alberta
Unit: Lord Strathcona's Horse (Royal Canadians), Edmonton, Alberta
Deceased: March 2, 2008

Bombardier Jérémie Ouellet
Age: 22
Hometown: Matane, Quebec
Unit: 1st Regiment, Royal Canadian Horse Artillery, Shilo, Manitoba
Deceased: March 11, 2008

Sergeant Jason Boyes
Age: 32
Hometown: Napanee, Ontario
Unit: 2nd Battalion, Princess Patricia's Canadian Light Infantry, Shilo, Manitoba
Deceased: March 16, 2008

Private Terry John Street
Age: 24
Hometown: Surrey, British Columbia
Unit: 2nd Battalion, Princess Patricia's Canadian Light Infantry, Shilo, Manitoba
Deceased: April 4, 2008

Corporal Michael Starker
Age: 36
Hometown: Calgary, Alberta
Unit: 15 (Edmonton) Field Ambulance, Calgary, Alberta
Deceased: May 6, 2008

Captain Richard Steven Leary
Age: 32
Hometown: Brantford, Ontario
Unit: 2nd Battalion, Princess Patricia's Canadian Light Infantry, Shilo, Manitoba
Deceased: June 3, 2008

Corporal Brendan Anthony Downey
Age: 36
Hometown: Toronto, Ontario
Unit: Military Police Detachment in Dundurn, Saskatchewan
Deceased: July 4, 2008

Private Colin William Wilmot
Age: 24
Hometown: Fredericton, New Brunswick
Unit: 1 Field Ambulance, Edmonton (Alberta)
Deceased: July 5, 2008

Corporal James (Jim) Hayward Arnal
Age: 25
Hometown: Winnipeg, Manitoba
Unit: 2nd Battalion, Princess Patricia's Canadian Light Infantry, Shilo, Manitoba
Deceased: July 18, 2008

Master Corporal Joshua Brian Roberts
Age: 29
Hometown: Prince Albert, Saskatchewan
Unit: 2nd Battalion, Princess Patricia's Canadian Light Infantry, Shilo, Manitoba
Deceased: August 9, 2008

Master Corporal Erin Doyle
Age: 32
Hometown: Kamloops, British Columbia
Unit: 3rd Battalion, Princess Patricia's Canadian Light Infantry, Edmonton Alberta
Deceased: August 11, 2008

Sergeant Shawn Allen Eades
Age: 33
Hometown: Hamilton, Ontario
Unit: 1 Combat Engineer Regiment (1 CER)
Deceased: August 20, 2008

Corporal Dustin Roy Robert Joseph Wasden
Age: 25
Hometown: Spiritwood, Saskatchewan
Unit: 1 Combat Engineer Regiment (1 CER)
Deceased: August 20, 2008

Sapper Stephan John Stock
Age: 25
Hometown: Campbell River, British Columbia
Unit: 1 Combat Engineer Regiment (1 CER)
Deceased: August 20, 2008

Private Chadwick James Horn
Age: 21
Hometown: Calgary, Alberta
Unit: 2nd Battalion Princess Patricia's Canadian Light Infantry Battle Group
Deceased: September 3, 2008

Corporal Michael James Alexander Seggie
Age: 21
Hometown: Winnipeg, Manitoba
Unit: 2nd Battalion Princess Patricia's Canadian Light Infantry Battle Group
Deceased: September 3, 2008

Corporal Andrew Paul Grenon
Age: 23
Hometown: Windsor, Ontario
Unit: 2nd Battalion Princess Patricia's Canadian Light Infantry Battle Group
Deceased: September 3, 2008

Sergeant Prescott Shipway
Age: 36
Hometown: Saskatoon, Saskatchewan
Unit: 2nd Battalion Princess Patricia's Canadian Light Infantry Battle Group
Deceased: September 7, 2008

Private Demetrios Diplaros
Age: 24
Hometown: Scarborough, Ontario
Unit: 1st Battalion, The Royal Canadian Regiment
Deceased: December 5, 2008

Corporal Mark Robert McLaren
Age: 23
Hometown: Peterborough, Ontario
Unit: 1st Battalion, The Royal Canadian Regiment
Deceased: December 5, 2008

Warrant Officer Robert John Wilson
Age: 37
Hometown: Keswick, Ontario
Unit: 1st Battalion, The Royal Canadian Regiment
Deceased: December 5, 2008

Private John Michael Roy Curwin
Age: 26
Hometown: Mount Uniacke, Nova Scotia
Unit: 2nd Battalion, The Royal Canadian Regiment
Deceased: December 13, 2008

Private Justin Peter Jones
Age: 21
Hometown: Baie Verte, Newfoundland
Unit: 2nd Battalion, The Royal Canadian Regiment
Deceased: December 13, 2008

Corporal Thomas James Hamilton
Age: 26
Hometown: Truro, Nova Scotia
Unit: 2nd Battalion, The Royal Canadian Regiment
Deceased: December 13, 2008

Private Michael Freeman
Age: 28
Hometown: Peterborough, Ontario
Unit: 3rd Battalion, The Royal Canadian Regiment
Deceased: December 26, 2008

Warrant Officer Gaétan Roberge
Age: 45
Hometown: Hanmer, Ontario
Unit: 2nd Battalion, The Irish Regiment of Canada
Deceased: December 27, 2008

Sergeant Gregory John Kruse
Age: 40
Hometown: Gaspé, Quebec
Unit: 2 Combat Engineer Regiment, serving as a member of 3rd Battalion, The Royal Canadian Regiment Battle Group
Deceased: December 27, 2008

Trooper Brian Richard Good
Age: 43
Hometown: Ottawa, Ontario
Unit: 3rd Battalion, The Royal Canadian Regiment Battle Group
Deceased: January 7, 2009

Sapper Sean David Greenfield
Age: 25
Hometown: Pinawa, Manitoba
Unit: 24 Field Engineer Squadron, 2 Combat Engineer Regiment, 3rd Battalion of the Royal Canadian Regiment Battle Group
Deceased: January 31, 2009

Corporal Kenneth Chad O'Quinn
Age: 25
Hometown: Happy Valley-Goose Bay, Newfoundland
Unit: 2 Canadian Mechanized Brigade Group Headquarters and Signals Squadron
Deceased: March 3, 2009

Corporal Dany Olivier Fortin
Age: 29
Hometown: Baie-Comeau, Quebec
Unit: 425 Tactical Fighter Squadron at 3 Wing Bagotville
Deceased: March 3, 2009

Warrant Officer Dennis Raymond Brown
Age: 38
Hometown: St. Catharines, Ontario
Unit: The Lincoln and Welland Regiment
Deceased: March 3, 2009

Trooper Marc Diab
Age: 22
Hometown: Mississauga, Ontario
Unit: Royal Canadian Dragoons, 3rd Battalion the Royal Canadian Regiment Battle Group
Deceased: March 8, 2009

Trooper Corey Joseph Hayes
Age: 22
Hometown: Ripples, New Brunswick
Unit: Royal Canadian Dragoons, 3rd Battalion the Royal Canadian Regiment Battle Group
Deceased: March 20, 2009

Trooper Jack Bouthillier
Age: 20
Hometown: Hearst, Ontario
Unit: Royal Canadian Dragoons, 3rd Battalion the Royal Canadian Regiment Battle Group
Deceased: March 20, 2009

Corporal Tyler Crooks
Age: 24
Hometown: Port Colborne, Ontario
Unit: 3rd Battalion, The Royal Canadian Regiment Battle Group
Deceased: March 20, 2009

Master Corporal Scott Francis Vernelli
Age: 28
Hometown: Sault Ste. Marie, Ontario
Unit: 3rd Battalion, The Royal Canadian Regiment Battle Group
Deceased: March 20, 2009

Corporal Karine Blais
Age: 21
Hometown: Les Méchins, Quebec
Unit: 12e Régiment Blindé du Canada, 2nd Battalion, Royal 22e Régiment Battle Group
Deceased: April 13, 2009

Major Michelle Mendes
Age: 30
Hometown: Wicklow, Ontario
Unit: Chief of Defence Intelligence
Deceased: April 23, 2009

Private Alexandre Péloquin
Age: 20
Hometown: Brownsburg-Chatham, Quebec
Unit: 3rd Battalion, Royal 22nd Regiment
Deceased: June 8, 2009

Corporal Martin Dubé
Age: 35
Hometown: Quebec City, Quebec
Unit: 5 Combat Engineer Regiment
Deceased: June 14, 2009

Corporal Nicholas Bulger
Age: 30
Hometown: Peterborough, Ontario
Unit: 3rd Battalion, Princess Patricia's Canadian Light Infantry
Deceased: July 3, 2009

Master Corporal Charles-Philippe Michaud
Age: 28
Hometown: Edmundston, New Brunswick
Unit: 2nd Batallion, Royal 22e Régiment
Deceased: July 4, 2009

Corporal Martin Joannette
Age: 25
Hometown: Saint-Calixte, Quebec
Unit: 3e Bataillon, Royal 22e Régiment
Deceased: July 6, 2009

Master Corporal Patrice Audet
Age: 38
Hometown: Montreal, Quebec
Unit: 430e Escadron tactique d'hélicoptères
Deceased: July 6, 2009

Private Sébastien Courcy
Age: 26
Hometown: St-Hyacinthe, Quebec
Unit: 2nd Battalion, Royal 22e Régiment
Deceased: July 16, 2009

Corporal Christian Bobbitt
Age: 23
Hometown: Sept-Îles, Quebec
Unit: 5 Combat Engineer Regiment, 2nd Battalion, Royal 22e Régiment Battle Group
Deceased: August 1, 2009

Sapper Matthieu Allard
Age: 21
Hometown: Val d'Or, Quebec
Unit: 5 Combat Engineer Regiment, 2nd Battalion, Royal 22e Régiment Battle Group
Deceased: August 1, 2009

Major Yannick Pépin
Age: 36
Hometown: Warwick, Quebec
Unit: 5 Combat Engineer Regiment, 2nd Battalion, Royal 22e Régiment Battle Group
Deceased: September 6, 2009

Corporal Jean-François Drouin
Age: 31
Hometown: Beauport, Quebec
Unit: 5 Combat Engineer Regiment, 2nd Battalion, Royal 22e Régiment Battle Group
Deceased: September 6, 2009

Private Patrick Lormand
Age: 21
Hometown: Chute-à-Blondeau, Ontario
Unit: 2nd Battalion, Royal 22e Régiment
Deceased: September 13, 2009

Corporal Jonathan Couturier
Age: 23
Hometown: Loretteville, Quebec
Unit: 2nd Battalion, Royal 22e Régiment
Deceased: September 17, 2009

Lieutenant Justin Boyes
Age: 26
Hometown: Saskatoon, Saskatchewan
Unit: 3rd Battalion Princess Patricia's Canadian Light Infantry
Deceased: October 28, 2009

Sapper Steven Marshall
Age: 24
Hometown: Calgary, Alberta
Unit: 1 Combat Engineer Regiment
Deceased: October 30, 2009

Lieutenant Andrew Richard Nuttall
Age: 30
Hometown: Prince Rupert, British Columbia
Unit: 1st Battalion Princess Patricia's Canadian Light Infantry
Deceased: December 23, 2009

Michelle Lang
Age: 34
Hometown: Vancouver, British Columbia
Calgary Herald reporter
Deceased: December 30, 2009

Sergeant George Miok
Age: 28
Hometown: Edmonton, Alberta
Unit: 41 Combat Engineer Regiment
Deceased: December 30, 2009

Sergeant Kirk Taylor
Age: 28
Hometown: Yarmouth, Nova Scotia
Unit: 84 Independent Field Battery, Royal Canadian Artillery
Deceased: December 30, 2009

Corporal Zachery McCormack
Age: 21
Hometown: Edmonton, Alberta
Unit: Loyal Edmonton Regiment, 4th Battalion Princess Patricia's Canadian Light Infantry
Deceased: December 30, 2009

Private Garrett William Chidley
Age: 21
Hometown: Cambridge, Ontario
Unit: 2nd Battalion Princess Patricia's Canadian Light Infantry
Deceased: December 30, 2009

Sergeant John Faught
Age: 44
Hometown: Sault Ste. Marie, Ontario
Unit: 1st Battalion Princess Patricia's Canadian Light Infantry
Deceased: January 16, 2010

Sergeant Mark Gallagher, RCMP
Age: 50
Hometown: Woodstock, New Brunswick
Deceased: January 12, 2010

Chief Superintendant Doug Coates, RCMP
Age: 57
Hometown: Gatineau, Quebec
Acting Commissioner of Operations for MINUSTAH (United Nations Stabilization Mission in Haiti)
Deceased: January 12, 2010

Captain Frank Paul
Age: 53
Hometown: Badger, Newfoundland
Unit: 28 Field Ambulance, Ottawa
Deceased: February 10, 2010

Corporal Joshua Caleb Baker
Age: 24
Hometown: Edmonton, Alberta
Unit: Loyal Edmonton Regiment 4th Battalion Princess Patricia's Canadian Light Infantry
Deceased: February 12, 2010

Corporal Darren James Fitzpatrick
Age: 21
Hometown: Prince George, British Columbia
Unit: 3rd Battalion Princess Patricia's Canadian Light Infantry
Deceased: March 20, 2010

Private Tyler William Todd
Age: 26
Hometown: Bright, Ontario
Unit: 1st Battalion Princess Patricia's Canadian Light Infantry
Deceased: April 11, 2010

Petty Officer Second Class Craig Blake
Age: 37
Hometown: Simcoe, Ontario
Unit: Fleet Diving Unit (Atlantic)
Deceased: May 3, 2010

Private Kevin Thomas McKay
Age: 24
Hometown: Richmond Hill, Ontario
Unit: 1st Battalion Princess Patricia's Canadian Light Infantry
Deceased: May 13, 2010

Colonel Geoff Parker
Age: 42
Hometown: Oakville, Ontario
Unit: Land Forces Central Area Headquarters
Deceased: May 18, 2010

Trooper Larry Rudd
Age: 26
Hometown: Brantford, Ontario
Unit: Royal Canadian Dragoons
Deceased: May 24, 2010

Sergeant Martin Goudreault
Age: 35
Hometown: Sudbury, Ontario
Unit: 1 Combat Engineer Regiment
Deceased: June 6, 2010

Sergeant James Patrick MacNeil
Age: 28
Hometown: Glace Bay, Nova Scotia
Unit: 2 Combat Engineer Regiment
Deceased: June 21, 2010

Private Andrew Miller
Age: 21
Hometown: Sudbury, Ontario
Unit: 2 Field Ambulance
Deceased: June 26, 2010

Master Corporal Kristal Giesebrecht
Age: 34
Hometown: Wallaceburg, Ontario
Unit: 1 Canadian Field Hospital
Deceased: June 26, 2010

Sapper Brian Collier
Age: 24
Hometown: Bradford, Ontario
Unit: 1 Combat Engineer Regiment
Deceased: July 20, 2010

Corporal Brian Pinksen
Age: 20
Hometown: Corner Brook, Newfoundland and Labrador
Unit: 2nd Battalion, Royal Newfoundland Regiment
Deceased: August 30, 2010

Corporal Steve Martin
Age: 24
Hometown: St-Cyrille-de-Wendover, Quebec
Unit: 3e Bataillon, Royal 22e Régiment
Deceased: December 18, 2010

Corporal Yannick Scherrer
Age: 24
Hometown: Montreal, Quebec
Unit: 22nd Royal Infantry Regiment
Deceased: March 27, 2011

Bombardier Karl Manning
Age: 31
Hometown: Chicoutimi, Quebec
Unit: 5e Régiment d'artillerie légère du Canada
Deceased: May 27, 2011

Master Corporal Francis Roy
Age: 32
Hometown: Rimouski, Quebec
Unit: Canadian Special Operations Regiment
Deceased: June 25, 2011

WOUNDED WARRIORS.CA 

Wounded Warriors.ca is an independent not-for-profit charity that supports Canadian soldiers wounded overseas. It is primarily a fundraising mechanism that supports existing programs that tend to injured soldiers.

In four years, Wounded Warriors.ca has raised more than $1,500,000 and, as a largely volunteer organization, is able to keep its administration costs well below 5 percent. The health of this fund is a credit to the benevolence of Canadian corporations and citizens alike. Wounded Warriors.ca recognizes the priority to treat visible and non-visible injuries, like that of Post-Traumatic Stress Disorder.

Wounded Warriors.ca helps in five streams of support:

- Program Support — funding existing credible support programs;
- Individual Support — assisting wounded members directly;
- New Programs — funding support for pilot and forward thinking programs;
- Awareness — contributing a voice for issues about the wounded; and
- Partnerships — with agencies that tend to injured members and veterans.

Wounded Warriors.ca was started by Captain Wayne Johnston when he was a military Assisting Officer for a severely wounded 20-year-old soldier injured on September 18, 2006, in a suicide bombing near Kandahar City in Afghanistan. While he was at the hospital in Germany, he was touched by the generosity of medical staff who dipped into their own pockets to provide quality-of-life needs for wounded soldiers. He started the charity immediately upon his return, and it has grown steadily. It is now the military charity of choice, from corporations seeking an official charity to citizens holding local fundraising events.

Please consider supporting this most worthy cause with a tax-deductible donation. Please visit *www.woundedwarriors.ca* for details.

TRUE PATRIOT LOVE FOUNDATION 

True Patriot Love is a national foundation that supports and honours members of the Canadian military and their families. It was founded by a group of citizens dedicated to building bridges between Canadian civilians and their military, in order to better understand and appreciate the sacrifices of soldiers and their families. In celebrating the patriotism of our military families, our foundation also strives to inspire Canadians to serve their country, whether it's in or out of uniform.

True Patriot Love's Highway of Heroes program honours those who have lost their lives serving our country. In partnership with the Government of Ontario, True Patriot Love has commissioned a memorial plaque to display on a select number of bridges.

To improve the morale and well-being of those who serve on our behalf and to learn more about True Patriot Love's Highway of Heroes program, please visit *www.truepatriotlove.com.*

ABOUT THE AUTHOR 

Photo by Gerri Photography.

Pete Fisher is a photojournalist with over twenty years of experience tracking down news stories. He has won a number of provincial and national awards for his work and was one of the driving forces behind getting the stretch of the 401 officially named the "Highway of Heroes" and to have an official coin minted to memorialize the route. Pete was recently made an honorary associate member of 401 (R.L. Edwards) Wing, Air Force Association of Canada. He was born and raised in Cobourg, Ontario, and he currently lives there with his two children. He can be reached at *pfisher@eagle.ca*.